A Twist
of
Fortune

Mike Martin

A TWIST OF FORTUNE

© Mike Martin – 2015

ISBN 978-1-77216-029-1

ALSO BY MIKE MARTIN

The Walker on the Cape

The Body on the T

Beneath the Surface

PRINTED BY DOCUMENTS MAJEMTA INC.

PUBLISHED BY:
BAICO PUBLISHING INC.
E-mail: info@baico.ca
Web site: www.baico.ca

DEDICATION

To Joan:
I am grateful that we share
this journey together.
Thank you for being
my light in the darkness.

Acknowledgements

I would like to thank a number of people for helping me on this journey. It takes a village to write a book. My village includes beta readers and advisers: Mike MacDonald, Andy Redmond, Barb Stewart, Robert Way, Lynne Tyler, Karen Nortman and Denise Zendel. And to T.R. Perri for his editing advice and guidance and Elliott Youden for final proofreading.

Chapter One

S ergeant Winston Windflower blinked twice. He was sure his eyes were deceiving him. He doubted it was Sheila, his girlfriend and the love of his life, being led away in handcuffs. But when he saw her distinctive loving smile as she stepped into the RCMP van, he knew it was her.

"I can follow them over to Marystown to make sure she gets a ride back," said Corporal Eddie Tizzard, Windflower's second-in-command.

"No, I think she's on her own on this one," said Windflower as he scowled and walked away.

Windflower decided he needed to regroup because his spirit was as gray as the early December sky. He headed for the local café, the Mug-Up, for a cup of coffee and a reprieve from the gently falling snow. When he got there, he took a seat by himself but found the only warmth that greeted him was the steam from the coffee.

The reasons for both the dearth of goodwill and Sheila's arrest were likely the same. For the past few weeks the small community of Grand Bank had been aboil, first with rumours that the fish plant had been sold to new owners from Nova Scotia, and now that they would be dismantling the refrigeration equipment and shipping it to other plants they owned around the Maritimes. People knew what this meant: their fish plant was gone, and that part of their life in Grand Bank was over. It was never coming back.

This had led to escalating emotions and reactions from the locals who started with a community meeting that developed into a committee to try and save the fish plant. It continued with daily protests and then a call for what community activists were calling 'direct action' to block the fish plant gates to prevent New Wave Fisheries from moving the equipment to Lunenburg. That call had been answered swiftly, loudly, and in great numbers by local citizens who were gathering each morning at the entrance to stop any trucks with the equipment on board from leaving the fish plant.

Windflower had been away for the past few days when this 'direct action' had begun. He was working on a special assignment with Acting Inspector Bill Ford in Marystown but got regular updates from Eddie Tizzard. At first, the RCMP allowed the protesters to assemble and delay the trucks from leaving, but when they started blocking access to the fish plant, the RCMP stepped in and started arresting people. About 40 locals had already been arrested and released on bond with conditions to stay away from the fish plant.

And now 44. Windflower sipped his coffee in the corner.

Finally one person emerged from the coffee klatch on the other side of the café. It was the Mayor of Grand Bank, Bill Sinnott. Windflower wondered what he wanted, but the Mayor's open smile disarmed him, and he quickly smiled back.

"Mornin', Sergeant," said Mayor Sinnott. "Looks like we're in for a bit of snow. Forecast says we're getting a little, ten centimetres I think they said. But my old bones tell me there's more blowin' in from offshore than dat."

"Good morning, Mr. Mayor," said Windflower. "You may be right about the weather. I never know what to expect anymore, except that we will get snow, and sometimes a lot of it. And a big snowstorm that keeps everybody at home for a few days might help defuse the situation around here."

"It might," said the Mayor. "But you know tings have a way of working themselves out. Sometimes we have to sit back and let nature run its course."

Windflower just sat quietly again with his coffee as he pondered the Mayor's quirky, but often correct philosophy on life.

"And sometimes we have to let the people we love make their own way in life," Mayor Sinnott continued. Before Windflower could respond to this bon mot, Sinnott lumbered his way back to his constituents to continue his informal consultations.

Windflower suspected that he'd heard about Sheila. He was still in a state of melancholy and amazement that the woman he loved was now in the back of an RCMP paddy wagon, on her way to being booked for trespassing and public nuisance.

CHAPTER TWO

As she was sitting in that RCMP vehicle, Sheila was also wondering about Windflower, and what he must have thought when he saw her being arrested. She was sure he wouldn't be pleased. But she had no choice. The fish plant was the last connection Grand Bank had to the fishery and in some ways its last link to its schooner and the fabulous Banks Fishery. As she sat there, Sheila thought about how the fishery was so tied to both the history and future of Grand Bank.

There had been fishing off the Grand Banks of Newfoundland for hundreds of years, maybe even before the arrival of Columbus. By the 16th century there were hundreds of ships from England, Spain, France and Portugal plying the waters off the coast and carrying home boatloads of codfish to help feed Europe. The first reports from the 'New Lande' from people like John Cabot were that you could lower baskets from the side of your boat and raise them full of cod.

For many years the European fishermen would visit for the summer and return home for the winter, but by the middle 1800's there was a thriving 'livyer' community of year-round settlers and fisherman. They fished the inshore harbours but also developed schooners which became known as Grand Bank schooners which allowed them to venture further afield. These ships were built in Grand Bank and at its peak there may have been six or seven schooners being built at the same time.

The schooners made the Banks Fishery possible and created one of the most remarkable and profitable fisheries ever seen in the world. For nearly a hundred years crews would venture out for three or four trips from May to October. Then they'd bring their fish back to Grand Bank for onshore salting and drying. People thought both the cod and the Banks Fishery would last forever but technological changes and greed would alter that projection.

By the mid 1900's, there had been a shift from the sailing schooners to more mechanized vessels and more effective methods for catching codfish. The vessels used enormous nets that hauled in large numbers of fish but devastated the cod population. Then the fish companies developed trawlers that swept up everything in their path and dragged the bottom of the ocean. By the 1980's they were dredging the waters, scooping up everything. Soon they were joined by floating factory ships that caught and processed the fish right on the water.

The decline of King Cod was steep and dramatic. In 1968 the cod catch from the Grand Banks was 810,000 tons; in 1974 it was 34,000 tons. By the 1990's the cod fishery was thought to be over and had only returned in a very limited capacity. Scientists feared it would never return to a viable industry. The depletion of the cod stocks had destroyed many communities on the coast of the island of Newfoundland and threatened many more, including Grand Bank.

It was a grand and glorious history that Sheila was reflecting on as their vehicle pulled into Marystown. But it was the future of Grand Bank that preoccupied her, and as she gazed out through the back window she wondered what she could do to both preserve the past and protect the future.

The loud banging noises that accompanied the RCMP van's arrival at the Marystown jail brought Sheila back to reality. She was nervous, but knew enough about the procedures that would follow from her time with Windflower, that she could help the other three protestors who were sitting beside her in the vehicle. There were two older ladies who had worked in the Grand Bank fish plant when it was processing cod and operating around the clock. The other person was young Ches Hillier who was barely old enough to be arrested, but was as passionate as any of them.

Sheila spoke quietly to them to run through what she thought would happen next, telling them to relax and not worry. Having been around Windflower for so long, she relayed to them how the process would likely be smooth and professional. That's what she had learned to expect from the RCMP.

Nonetheless, Sheila and her fellow protesters were soon to be processed and fingerprinted and charged with a crime.

Chapter Three

B ack in Grand Bank, Windflower was still worried about Sheila. But he had more to deal with right now. When he came out of the café, the tiny flakes were growing larger and more plentiful by the minute. In the short distance from the Mug-Up to the Grand Bank detachment, his Jeep collected a full coating of the white stuff. He pulled into the parking lot just before his younger Corporal slid and swerved his own vehicle into the parking space next to him.

"Hey, Sarge," said Tizzard as both men brushed off their hats and coats in the small detachment vestibule. "It looks like we're in for a big one. Forecast has been revised to twenty-five centimetres." The duo waved good morning to Betsy Molloy, the administrative assistant who was fully engaged with someone at the other end of her telephone headset.

"You could be right," said Windflower. "Mayor Sinnott is making the same prediction. I guess we should call everybody in for the night shift. Who's on days?"

"Evanchuk and Fortier are on now and MacDonald is due for the overnighter," said Tizzard. "I'll get Fortier to go home now so he can come back this evening and relieve Evanchuk."

"Can you also find out what's happening in Marystown?" asked Windflower.

"Sure thing, boss," said Tizzard as he left his Sergeant at the entrance to his office.

Chapter Four

Windflower shuffled the papers on his desk and pretended to work while he waited for his update from Tizzard. His phone rang and Betsy's chipper voice said, "Inspector Ford on line 1, sir."

"Thanks, Betsy," said Windflower as he punched the number 1 button on his phone and greeted the inspector.

"Mornin', Sergeant," said Acting Inspector Bill Ford. Ford had taken over responsibilities for the area that included Grand Bank, after the spectacular crash of the former Inspector in a sex and human trafficking scandal a few months ago. That case was still winding its way through the justice system, and Ford relied heavily on Windflower's expertise to help guide him in this interim period. Windflower expected Ford to ask him about any one of a half a dozen files he was working on, but instead Ford asked him about Sheila.

At first Windflower was just stunned and didn't speak, so Ford continued, "I saw her today in the holding area waiting to be processed. She was clearly uncomfortable seeing me so I just nodded and went on."

"Is she okay?" asked Windflower, finally recovering his lost voice.

"She seemed fine," said Ford. "In fact she looked like she was mothering the others that were brought in with her. But you know this is not a good thing for the Force, and not a good thing for you, Winston, to have her brought in like this. It sends all the wrong signals to the community when one of our officers is involved."

"I'm not involved," Windflower started, but then he realized that in fact he was involved, at least by association. "Sheila is her own person, Bill. I don't control her activities, and I wouldn't even try to. I did talk to her about getting involved in this protest but she simply said it was something she had to do for her community. I didn't think it would come this far."

"Well it has," said Ford. "Now we all have to deal with the consequences. Let's just hope this is the end of this situation. What's the status on the equipment removal?"

"I believe this morning was the last truckload," said Windflower.

"Good," said Ford. "Maybe now we can get back to normal over there."

"Yes, sir," said Windflower as he hung up the phone. He hoped so too.

When he looked up Tizzard was standing in front of him.

"I've got everybody lined up for tonight," said Tizzard.

"Any word from Marystown?" asked Windflower.

"They have all been processed and are sitting in a holding cell waiting for the judge to release them," said Tizzard. Since the protests and arrests had begun, the procedure had been to have a judge or justice of the peace formally charge the protesters and then release them with the conditions of staying away from the protest site, and agreeing to reappear in court at a later date. "The boys said that Sheila was calm and helped the older ladies who were with her. You should take a break yourself, you know. It could be a long night."

"I think I will," said Windflower. He packed up his briefcase and headed out the door, waving goodbye to Betsy on the way out.

A few minutes and a lot of snow later he was sitting at his kitchen table eating lunch and mindlessly flipping through some old magazines that Sheila had left behind. He wondered what she'd gotten them into. But before he could think anymore his cell phone rang.

It was Sheila.

"Hi, Winston. I think we are going to stay in Marystown tonight. It looks too stormy to head back and the forecast is calling for even more snow this afternoon."

"Will you get a room at the hotel?" asked Windflower, trying to hold an even tone in his voice.

"We will," said Sheila. "Kind of like a camping trip, with a kid and two old aunts," she added.

"That's good. Are you okay, Sheila?" he asked, finally getting a handle on his emotions and asking the right question.

"I will be. I'll call you tonight, okay?"

"Okay, I'll talk to you then," said Windflower.

After he hung up, Windflower spent a long time staring out his kitchen window, watching as the snowflakes got fatter and thicker. There were a lot of conflicting feelings circulating inside of him. But at least the falling snow calmed him down until he finally relaxed enough to realize he was tired. That was something he knew how to handle. Ten minutes later with a heavy quilt over his shoulders he was fast asleep.

CHAPTER FIVE

Windflower woke a little foggy from his nap but could tell by the growing darkness he had been asleep for much longer than he wanted. He jumped out of bed and was quickly in the shower and out again. As he dressed he glanced out the bedroom window. The drifting snow was being piled up against his back fence; looks like the wind has picked up too.

When he got outside that theory was confirmed by biting winds that accompanied the steady snowfall. That likely meant it wouldn't be long before the call would come to close the highway outside of Grand Bank. Half a dozen times a year, more in a bad one, the snow and gale force winds united in an unholy marriage that drove all sensible people back into their cozy homes. It also made it both unsafe and unwise to venture out again until the storm had done its worst.

Long before the storm hit its peak, the RCMP would be asked to consider closing parts of the Southern Peninsula highway, which almost always included the portions outside Marystown, the central hub of the area, up near the town limits of Grand Bank. This zone was sparsely populated and consisted of mostly what the locals called 'the barrens'. It was bare, with a few small stumps of trees, many rocks and little else. In the summer it looked more interesting, and some would say 'magical'. But in a storm it became nearly impossible to traverse, especially in a motor vehicle.

Despite this, every year at least one person would try, fail, and then there would be a call to the RCMP to come and get them out. That meant Windflower and his team had to be on call during every storm, just in case. They had to help monitor the telephone and now computer lines for emergency calls, as well as continuing to patrol the parts of the highway the Highways people would try to keep open, which was usually the stretch between Grand Bank south and Fortune. Needless to say, there was always a lot to do on a storm night which was why Windflower was heading back to work, along with all other available RCMP officers.

Since Windflower knew it would be a long night, he stopped in to the Mug-Up along the way. He brought his Thermos to fill with Moira Stoodley's new Jumping Bean coffee. He parked in front of the café and ran the few steps to the entrance. The wind pulled mightily against him as he opened the door, which banged loudly behind him when he pulled it closed.

"Come in out of the snow, Sergeant," said Moira Stoodley, the proprietor of the Mug-Up and partner of Windflower's best friend in the community, retired Crown Attorney, Herb Stoodley. "It's not a fit night for man or beast out there. I thought you might be coming by. I've got a tray of sandwiches in the back if you needs 'em."

"You are a sweetheart, Moira. That would be great. Just put them on my tab and I'd love a few cups of java in my Thermos if you've got any left."

"Absolutely," she said as she took the Thermos with her to the back. "You can sit anywhere you'd like," she said with a laugh, pointing to the empty café.

Windflower sat in his usual corner seat while Moira got his order together. When she came out a few minutes later with his coffee and sandwiches he gave her a hug along with his thanks.

"Sheila called me," said Moira after Windflower released her from his grasp. "It wasn't as bad as she thought and they're now at the hotel in Marystown."

"I talked to her too."

"She had to do it, you know."

Windflower smiled weakly and tipped his hat goodnight.

"Close her up, Moira. This is going to be a big one."

With that, he was soon back in his car and shortly afterwards offering the tray of sandwiches around the detachment lunchroom. It looked like Tizzard was planning to eat the whole kit and caboodle so Windflower packaged up the remnants and put them in the fridge for later.

Constable Carrie Evanchuk was just coming back in from her highway tour so everybody sat around to hear her report on the highway conditions. It was very predictable: snow, blowing snow, drifting snow, and more drifting snow. And of course the wind had picked up. They decided to have a friendly pool on when the highway would be officially closed.

Windflower had guessed 7:30 but they didn't get that far. It was just past 7 when the call was made to close the highway from outside Marystown to Grand Bank.

Tizzard and Fortier left in one vehicle to head towards Marystown. They would meet up with the Marystown patrol near Creston and work backwards towards Garnish. Their job was to secure the highway and ensure nobody had been stranded on that stretch. At Garnish they would travel the loop down through that small community and Frenchman's Cove with their lights flashing as a signal to everyone that the highway behind them was now closed.

They made a point of stopping in at Skipper Handrigan's house to check in with the Skipper and to give him the news. Skipper Handrigan, or more specifically his wife, would then pass the word to everybody else. It was an old-fashioned but highly effective method of getting the word out. When they returned from the Garnish loop, the two officers slid the wooden barriers across the highway behind them and turned on the flashing red lights on top of them.

While they were doing this, Evanchuk took over the radio chair, which became the emergency central point for the evening. She notified the highway department of their activities, and sent notices to both local and regional media. She also turned on the emergency beacons, a set of strategically placed lights that would blink red all along the portions of the highway that were closed. Finally, she advised Marystown and RCMP NHQ that the Grand Bank RCMP detachment was now operating on an emergency basis. That would allow them to easily access additional resources, such as Medivac, if the need arose.

Windflower took the job of patrolling the still open parts of the highway. He left Grand Bank and drove slowly southwest towards Fortune. The highway had just been cleared and despite the poor visibility he didn't have any trouble travelling along this portion of the route. He passed the snowplow operator just before Fortune and waved him goodnight. That was one job he didn't want, that's for sure. When he reached the wharf in Fortune he turned around and headed back up the highway until he met Tizzard and Fortier near Grand Beach where they were erecting the last of their wooden barriers. He flashed his lights as acknowledgement and turned back towards the detachment.

So far so good. But it was still early and a lot could happen between now and whenever the storm decided to move on.

CHAPTER SIX

Back at the RCMP offices Windflower felt relieved Constable Evanchuk had everything under control. The diminutive self-proclaimed 'prairie girl' from Estevan, Saskatchewan relished the opportunity to show her ability to perform under pressure. Windflower often thought of her as the tiny, perfect cop, always prepared and always ready to volunteer for a difficult assignment. In contrast was Constable Anne MacDonald, who would be relieving Evanchuk for the evening.

MacDonald was tall and gangly, like a teenager who hadn't fully grown up yet. And she may not have at 22, even though she was already almost 6 feet tall. She had the wide-open smile that was a trademark of her hometown in Summerside, Prince Edward Island, and long red hair and freckles to indicate her relation to the more famous redheaded Anne from the Gentle Island. MacDonald was full of life and as eager as

Evanchuk but in a certainly more relaxed and less-organized fashion than her fellow female Constable.

The latter aspect of her character concerned Windflower and he had made a mental note to talk to Tizzard later about that. Evanchuk and MacDonald, along with Tizzard and Constable Mario Fortier, who had just returned, made up the current RCMP contingent at Grand Bank. It wasn't often that Windflower had the whole team together at once, so he made a point of gathering everyone around the few remaining sandwiches in the lunchroom before Evanchuk took off for the night.

"I just want to thank you all for the hard work you've been doing over the past few months while I was away. We've been lucky so far this winter with the snow, but it looks like that might change, starting tonight. Be careful out there. And don't forget it's Mario's party on Saturday night. We're going to miss you Mario," said Windflower. "You've been here almost as long as me."

"I'm going to miss you guys too," said Fortier. "I have really enjoyed my time here in Grand Bank but this gives me a chance to get back to New Brunswick. My daughters are doing okay in school here too, but I want them to experience growing up in a Francophone community like Shediac."

"It must be good to get close to home," said Tizzard. "How far is it from Moncton to Shediac?"

"Less than from here to Marystown," said Fortier, "and the roads are a hell of a lot better, especially in the winter. Maudit!"

Everyone laughed at Fortier's mild lapse into French slang and the group broke up in good spirits. Tizzard and MacDonald cleaned up the lunchroom and Fortier took over the radio chair. The snow was still falling outside but it was warm and comfortable inside the detachment. Windflower helped Fortier by monitoring the weather reports and even took a stab at cleaning up a bit of the filing backlog that had accumulated in his absence.

The next couple of hours passed quickly and quietly as the snow continued to build outside. Windflower started to feel a little drowsy and went to the back to make a fresh batch of coffee to wake himself and everybody else up. But they wouldn't need that pot of coffee right away.

Windflower could hear the commotion from the lunchroom at the back of the building and raced to the front. Fortier was relaying information to both Emergency Services at the clinic and the Volunteer Fire Department. "Car in the ditch on Highway 210 just outside Fortune... requesting paramedics and fire department to the scene... at least one injury reported... RCMP en route."

Windflower grabbed his coat and hurried to catch up with Tizzard and MacDonald who were already in their vehicle outside the building. He waved them on and jumped into his Jeep. As he drove past the Grand Bank clinic he could see the ambulance with its lights flashing. That vehicle was soon behind him. When Windflower arrived at the accident scene, Tizzard was already peering into the windows of an SUV that had jumped the snowbank and was now fully embedded in the ditch on the side of the highway. Windflower ran over to join him.

"There's only one person," Tizzard yelled over the wind. "Lot of blood, and he's not moving." He struggled to pull open the driver's side door. "Can't open it."

"Smash the window," Windflower shouted back. "Paras are behind me."

Tizzard used the barrel of his industrial sized flashlight to break the driver's side window, and then stepped back to allow the paramedic to reach in and check the pulse of the driver. The paramedic looked back at Windflower and shook his head. "No pulse, Sergeant."

"Fire department," said Tizzard, as the next siren and set of flashing lights came over the horizon.

"You look after them," said Windflower. "Me and MacDonald will close the road." He motioned to the female Constable to follow him. He handed her a package of road flares and pointed down the highway towards Fortune.

She went to set hers up while he placed another set on the highway closer to the Grand Bank side.

By the time Windflower got back, the firemen had pulled the driver's door back and cut off the hinges, allowing the paramedics to reach into the vehicle and release the person trapped inside. Even though there was no sign of life from the driver, the paramedics would continue their efforts until they got back to the clinic where a doctor could make the formal declaration. The paramedics sped down the road to the Grand Bank clinic with full lights and sirens.

Windflower hadn't noticed during the adrenaline rush of the past few minutes that the snow had indeed stopped falling. Maybe the worst of the storm was over. That would be a break. He walked back over to where Tizzard was holding court with the remainder of the fire crew and pulled him out of the crowd. "You complete the report," said Windflower. "When you're finished, get MacDonald to search the vehicle and get it towed to the Customs pound in Fortune.

"The snow may be done," said Tizzard.

"Maybe," said Windflower. "I'll check the weather office and Marystown. We may be able to move back to regular operations later on. Check in when you're done here. I'm going to the clinic to get an update."

Tizzard nodded and went off to talk to MacDonald. Windflower drove back along the now quieter highway towards the clinic. When he arrived at the emergency entrance the ambulance was still running with its lights on. Inside, a team of orderlies, paramedics, nurses and the duty doctor were hovering over the body just pulled from the accident scene. As Windflower approached they stepped back from the body and the doctor said "Time of death is 11:43 p.m."

The orderlies covered the body with a sheet and wheeled it quietly to the back of the clinic where Windflower knew the coroner's small office was located. It would be placed in a refrigerated area overnight awaiting the morning examination by Doctor Vijay Sanjay, the Coroner for the District of Grand Bank.

"Isn't that the pharmacist from Fortune?" Windflower asked the doctor once the body had been removed. Windflower didn't know him but his badge read 'Dr. J. Redfern'.

"Yes," Doctor Redfern said. "His name is Michael Ridgeway. I've met him a few times around the hospital. I don't know him personally. You?"

"Just to say hello. I'll send someone over to collect his personal effects later," said Windflower.

The young doctor just nodded and walked back to his desk in the Emergency section. Windflower spent a few moments saying hello to the paramedics and the other medical personnel and then slipped out the way he came in to head back towards the RCMP detachment.

Chapter Seven

Fortier was valiantly trying to keep up with the ringing telephones but quickly losing the battle. Windflower signalled to hang up the receiver and join him for a coffee in the back room. A very relieved and tired Fortier followed Windflower and sat down with his Sergeant who got them both a hot drink.

"It's crazy out there," said Fortier after he had a few sips of coffee and was back to breathing normally again.

"Yeah, it's not a job for everybody," said Windflower sympathetically. "Why don't you go into my office and call for an update on road conditions, and when they think we might re-open the highway? I'll check in with the weather office and give Public Relations in Marystown a quick report. Once you're done will you swing by the clinic and pick up the victim's personal belongings? We'll need to have a look at them before they're released to his next of kin."

Fortier stayed behind to nurse his coffee while Windflower took over the radio chair. He ignored the ringing phones and put all of the in-coming lines on hold. Then he phoned the Marystown RCMP HQ to give his interim report: "Single vehicle accident on Route 210 just outside Fortune. One male deceased. Investigation underway by Grand Bank detachment. No further details until next of kin are notified."

It sounded so cold and harsh, but so was accidental death. Windflower had seen more than his share of highway carnage during his time on highway patrol in British Columbia. It always shook him up, though, because the sudden and violent nature of someone passing in this way felt surreal and even unreal. Yet, there was a very real dead person lying in the clinic half a mile away. As usual, the RCMP was left to pick up the pieces and inform the surviving relatives.

But first, the highway had to be re-opened after the storm. The latest information from the weather office reported a chance of flurries and the possibility of drifting snow from the persisting winds, but that the worst of the storm had passed over the Burin Peninsula and was now heading out to sea. That meant they could start re-opening the highway as soon as the snow clearing crews were ready to roll.

Windflower's reverie was broken by Fortier who came in with some news.

"I just got a call from Highways, boss," said Fortier. "They think they should be back on the roads by 2. I'm just going up to the clinic to pick up Ridgeway's belongings."

"Okay," said Windflower. "I'll see you when you get back."

In the quiet of the detachment with just the blinking lights on the phone for company, Windflower said a silent prayer for the late Mr. Ridgeway and for any family and friends he left behind. Windflower hadn't really known him in life, but he was going to find out all he could about Ridgeway now that he was dead.

The next couple of hours passed quickly for Windflower. He covered the phones and kept the information lines open to and from Marystown and the public relations section. Fortier came back with Mr. Ridgeway's personal effects from the clinic. They included a cell phone, car and house keys, and what looked like the keys to the Fortune Pharmacy. There was also a wallet with bank and credit cards, just over two hundred dollars in cash and a business card for Michael Ridgeway B.Sc. Pharm., Fortune Pharmacy. His driver's licence had a date of birth 04-14-79. According to Windflower's quick math that made him 35.

Windflower turned the card over and on the back saw a handwritten note 'In case of emergency please notify Mrs. Murial Ridgeway, Rexdale, Ontario' with a 416 area code underneath. At least they know who to call. That would be Windflower's job, although it could probably wait until the morning. Nothing would change between now and then.

"Was there a wedding ring?" Windflower yelled to Fortier, who had gone to the back to freshen up his coffee.

"I didn't see one," said Fortier who was now walking back into Windflower's area with a new cup of coffee for himself and one for Windflower. "I don't think he was married."

"Did you know him?" asked Windflower.

"Not really," said Fortier. "My daughters had a few prescriptions that I got filled over there. We had an account at the pharmacy. I know he had a dog, a collie. I used to see him walking along the path down below Fortune. You know, the one that comes back in over the top of Grand Bank."

"Yeah, I've taken that a few times," said Windflower. "It's a nice walk over the Cape when the weather is fine."

As they were sipping their coffee, Tizzard came in from the accident scene. "I left MacDonald with the tow truck. She should be back soon. Is that fresh coffee? And I'm starved."

"Go get yourself warmed up," said Windflower. "I'll take Fortier with me and we'll go open the highway. You and MacDonald hold the fort till I get back."

"Okay, boss," said Tizzard who had already managed to stuff one buttered Purity Cream Cracker in his mouth and held another four in his fist. "I'll be here."

CHAPTER EIGHT

Windflower and Fortier laughed at Tizzard's food antics and went out to Windflower's Jeep in the parking lot. A few minutes later they were cruising along the empty highway towards Marystown. Windflower asked Fortier about his daughters. Fortier was happy to talk about what was clearly a big and important part of his life.

"They have made some good friends here," said Fortier. "If it was up to them they'd be happy to stay, but Jocelyne and I feel it would be nice for them to have some French friends as well. Plus, my parents are getting older and I can help them out a bit more."

"I understand," said Windflower. "Family is very important. I sometimes think it would be nicer to be closer to home myself."

"Why don't you transfer out West?" asked Fortier.

"Maybe one day," said Windflower. "But you know I kind of like Grand Bank. It's so different from where I come from and yet I feel a strong connection to both the land and the people."

"I know what you mean," said Fortier.

The two men pondered those thoughts together for the rest of the ride to Marystown. When they arrived at Creston about half an hour later they removed the first set of wooden barriers. Fifteen minutes afterwards they were doing the same at Garnish. There was still little traffic on the highway which was good since there was really only one lane opened in both directions and nowhere to pass. When they got to Grand Beach Windflower called back to the RCMP detachment in Grand Bank.

"Route 210 is fully open and operational, from Marystown to Grand Bank, over," said Windflower.

"Copy that," said Tizzard over the crackling radio. "See you soon, over and out."

When they got back to Grand Bank, Windflower sent Fortier home and went in to get his debrief from Tizzard and MacDonald.

"Did either of you know the deceased?" Windflower asked.

MacDonald just shook her head; she looked a little in shock. Windflower knew that accident scenes, especially ones with fatalities, were always upsetting.

Tizzard said, "I saw him at the lounge a few times. Quiet fellow, drank alone at the bar. He seemed pleasant enough, but not the talkative type."

"It looks like he was single. Ever see him with a date?" asked Windflower. Both officers shook their heads.

"Okay," said Windflower. "Michael Ridgeway, pharmacist, age 35. Is that really all we've got so far? What's the update from the scene?"

"It's hard to know exactly what happened but it looks like he lost control of the vehicle as he started down the hill. Visibility was poor and the surface was snow-covered. The plow operator was just coming back to clear it again when he saw the car in the ditch. He was the one who called it in," said Tizzard.

"What about inside the car?" asked Windflower.

"Lots of blood," said Tizzard. "But that could be just from the broken nose. The windshield was broken from the impact and the vehicle is probably a write-off. Based on my visual inspection it's hard to say what killed him. He was wearing a seat belt but we have no way of knowing about internal injuries."

"We'll find that out tomorrow after Doctor Sanjay has a look at the body," said Windflower.

"There wasn't much inside the car," said MacDonald. "The usual glove compartment stuff, maps and a flashlight. There was a dog blanket in the back seat."

"That makes sense," said Windflower. "Apparently he had a collie. Someone will have to take a run over to his house later to check on the dog."

"Okay you guys, good job," Windflower continued. "Go home and get some sleep. I'll stay until Evanchuk comes in the morning."

Tizzard started to protest but Windflower simply held up his hand. "Go, and we'll see you tomorrow."

After Tizzard and MacDonald had left, Windflower enjoyed a few minutes of relative calm. It had been a difficult and traumatic evening so he just let all his pent-up feelings dissipate for a little while. There was the shock of seeing the accident and the dead body. Windflower knew from experience that the shock following such a trauma was inevitable. Plus, there was a sadness beneath it one felt as they tried to make sense out of what looked like a senseless death. He also knew that in order to let the uncomfortable sensations go, he had to feel them first. So that once he did that, he knew he'd be able to carry on with his job.

The rest of the night was smooth and even, like the piled up snow outside his window.

Just before dawn he took one more run up the highway to check on the road conditions and to make sure no one else had driven into a ditch along the way. He paid particular attention to the area outside of town that had recently been repaved and for some reason the Highways people had made the ditches on the side of the road at least 10 feet deep. Maybe it was to keep the moose off the highway, but right now it was posing a severe winter hazard for anyone passing through.

Everything on the highway was clear and as he was pulling back into the detachment parking lot he saw Evanchuk jogging up the road. Yes, even in the middle of winter she kept up her daily running regime. Windflower thought it to be admirable, maybe a little foolhardy, but admirable none the less. He pulled over and spent a few minutes giving her as much information from the past evening he could remember, then wearily headed home for some rest.

Just as he was falling asleep he remembered he was supposed to call Sheila and roused himself with a start. He looked down at his phone and saw three missed calls, all from Sheila. Right now his tired body just needed a little sleep, so he made plans to call and check in with her later. He didn't stir again until his cell phone rang at 10:45.

It was Tizzard.

"Mornin', boss. I'm over with Doc Sanjay. I think you're going to want to hear what he has to say."

"Put him on," said Windflower.

"Good morning, Winston. I hope we are not disturbing your beauty sleep," said Doctor Vijay Sanjay, Coroner and retired Chief Medical Officer of Health.

"Good morning, Doc," said Windflower. "So why are you bothering a hard-working officer of the Royal Canadian Mounted Police?"

"I thought you'd like to know that your accident victim suffered a broken nose, two fractured ribs and several cuts, bruises and abrasions," said Dr. Sanjay.

"And?" asked Windflower.

"He did not die as a result of these injuries."

"So what did he die of?" asked Windflower.

"He died of a coronary failure," said Dr. Sanjay.

"A heart attack?" asked Windflower.

"There may be contributing factors, but yes, a heart attack. You'll have to come by so I can show you what I have found so far."

"I'll be over in an hour or so," said Windflower. "Can I speak with Corporal Tizzard please?"

"Certainly," said Dr.Sanjay and he passed the phone back to Tizzard.

"Has anybody been by Ridgeway's house in Fortune to check on his dog?" asked Windflower.

"I don't think so, but I can do that," said Tizzard.

"Good. The address and keys are in his effects envelope on my desk. I have to phone his next of kin to inform them of the death. I'll do that and then I'll be over at the office. Is everything okay there?"

"Everything is back to normal, Sarge. The media relations people are bugging us but I told them you'd get back to them with a full statement later. Other than that everything is good. What should I do with the dog?" asked Tizzard.

"Make sure it has some food and water and take it for a walk. Haven't you ever had a dog?"

"There weren't many dogs on Ramea when I was growing up," said Tizzard. "I haven't got much experience in that regard."

"Delegate it to someone who has," said Windflower. "But make sure the dog is looked after. It's probably out of its mind after being alone for so long. See you soon."

Windflower smiled at the sight of Tizzard trying to determine whether or not the lonely dog would bite him when he went to visit. Never had a dog, now that's a weird one. In his home community of Pink Lake there were almost as many dogs as children. Everybody had a pet from a young age and Windflower could remember his childhood dogs better than any of his friends. There was always more than one following him around as he explored the rivers and valleys of his Northern Alberta homeland. It was hard to imagine that someone could grow up without a dog to help them along the way.

Now Windflower was wide-awake. He put on the coffee and decided to make his next-of-kin phone call first. He pulled the number out of his notebook and listened to it ring at the other end. It was still early in Ontario so maybe they weren't up yet. But just as he was about to leave a message he heard a click and a woman's soft voice say hello.

"Is this Mrs. Ridgeway, Mrs. Murial Ridgeway?" he asked.

"Yes, this is her," the woman answered back. "Who is calling please?"

"Mrs. Ridgeway, it's Sergeant Winston Windflower from the RCMP in Grand Bank. I am calling about Michael Ridgeway. Is he your son?"

"Yes, Michael is my son. Has something happened? Is Michael okay?"

"Mrs. Ridgeway, I am very sorry to tell you there's been an accident," said Windflower. He could hear a gasp at the other end of the line but knew from experience it was better, for them and for him, to just keep going. "Michael was involved in a car accident last night during a snow storm and he died. I am very sorry for your loss."

"An accident, no it can't be. I just talked to Michael on the weekend. He was going to come home for Christmas. Oh my God, poor Michael."

"We are still conducting our investigation and we will be able to provide more information later but for now I just wanted to let you know about his passing. Are you alone? Do you have someone you can talk with, someone who can be near you?"

"Oh my God, I'll have to tell Brenda. That's Michael's sister. She lives in Toronto. She will come over if I ask her."

"We will not publicize Michael's name until tomorrow, Ma'am," said Windflower. "That will give you time to let the rest of your family know first about his passing."

"I can't believe it. Tell me it's not true," said Mrs. Ridgeway. "Oh my God, I can't take another death." Then she burst into sobs and sounded like she might be hyperventilating.

Windflower tried to calm her down. "Just try and breathe Mrs. Ridgeway. I know this must come as a terrible shock to you."

"It is," she said between sobs. "First his father, Thomas, died last year, and now Michael. It's just too much," she said.

"It is too much. I am so sorry for your loss, Ma'am. Can I give you my number? If you'd like, you can get your daughter to call me to discuss all the other details," said Windflower gently.

"Yes, yes I'll get a pen," said the woman, her breathing sounding to return to normal. "That will be good. I'll get Brenda to call you back. Thank you."

After ensuring Mrs. Ridgeway had the phone number written down correctly, Windflower said goodbye and hung up the phone.

That part of the job sucked because both giving and receiving that information were awful—though for different reasons—and that would never change. It's not easy to hear that a person you loved is no longer with you especially when it happens with absolutely no notice. And it sure sucked to be the bearer of the bad news.

CHAPTER NINE

Windflower had one more phone call to make. He called Sheila's cell phone but it must have been turned off. Or she might be on her way back.

"Hi Sheila, it's me. I'm sorry I missed your calls last night. We had a situation here I had to deal with. I hope you're okay. Give me a call when you get a chance. Talk soon."

He closed his phone and put an egg on to boil. After a quick shower he ate his boiled egg with a piece of toast and a somewhat overripe banana, and then headed to work. When he arrived at the detachment office he was greeted by Betsy with a stack of messages and even more questions for him. Most were from the media who wanted information about last night's accident, but there were also two that needed his immediate attention.

The first was from Mayor Sinnott who wanted to come over and see him. Windflower asked Betsy to call him back and set up an afternoon meeting. The second was from Inspector Ford in Marystown. That couldn't wait, so Windflower called in to Bill Ford's direct line.

"Good morning Inspector," said Windflower when he heard the familiar voice answer.

"Good day, Winston," said Bill Ford. "Having a little lie-in this morning?"

"It was pretty late when we shut it down here last night. It was more like this morning when I got out."

"What's the update on the accident?" asked Ford.

"We're still going through some details. I'm going over to see Sanjay right after we're done. He seems to think there might be a heart attack or other contributing factors."

"Heart attack?" asked Ford. "I thought the guy was in his 30's."

"Thirty-five. But I guess it can happen anytime. Sanjay said he had something to show me. I'll have more to tell you later. I also talked to the mother. She's pretty shook up. I told her we'd wait until the end of the day before releasing his name, but I suspect the media already has it and it may come out anyway."

"Okay, keep me in the loop on this one," said Ford. "Have you talked to Sheila yet?"

"Just briefly yesterday, but hopefully I'll see her today," said Windflower.

"I don't want a recurrence of what happened yesterday. It is not good for you or me."

"I share the sentiment, but I'm not the only one involved here."

"You are the only RCMP Officer involved," said Ford. "I expect you to use whatever influence you have to get this situation under control."

Windflower started to think about how to respond when he realized the Inspector was no longer on the line. Great, more pressure.

He was about to leave his office when Tizzard and a very happy collie came bouncing in. He started to say they couldn't have a dog in here when the dog came right up to him and presented her rump for a little massage.

"Her name is Lady. That's what her tag says," said Tizzard. "I found her food and water bowl, but I couldn't find her leash. She was happy to see me but she kept looking around. I think she was looking for her master."

"Hello, Lady," said Windflower as he stroked her rump and rubbed her back legs. "I had a collie when I was a kid. They are the kindest, most gentle dogs ever."

"So what are we going to do with her?" asked Tizzard.

"For now, let's put her in the kennel down near Molliers. It will be another matter to talk to the relatives about. I'm surprised there wasn't a leash though. There has to be one. Maybe it was in the SUV. Can you check with MacDonald to see if she saw one?"

"She'll be in later today. I'll check then. Are you going over to see the Doc?"

"I'm just on my way. Let's put Lady in the back cell for now and you can drop her off later. You coming?"

Both men got into Tizzard's Jeep and despite the thin layer of snow on the detachment parking lot Tizzard still managed to get a full head of speed by the time he hit the main road. Windflower thought about asking him to slow down but simply sighed and accepted his fate as the sideman of a speed demon.

Dr. Sanjay's office doubled as his examination room and was located at the rear of the clinic. Windflower and Tizzard waved good morning to the hospital personnel as they walked through the building. Windflower knocked on the office door that read 'Dr. V. Sanjay, Coroner', and called out his greeting.

"Come in, come in," said Dr. Sanjay, a diminutive but spry and seemingly ageless East Indian. "Sergeant Windflower, me son, care for a cuppa? I see you've got Boy Wonder with you as well."

"Good morning, again," said Tizzard. "I can go down to the lunch counter and get the tea, if you'd like."

"No, no," the doctor responded. "I've got the best Earl Grey leaves steeping in that pot over there. My sister sends it over from the U.K. every couple of months. Thinks we can't get a decent cuppa over here. She used to be right. Get us each a cup from the cupboard and we'll go see the late Mr. Ridgeway."

Sanjay turned to Windflower.

"Come on, Winston. How have you been by the way? It must soon be time for another scotch tasting event. I just got an 18-year-old Highland Park that is begging for a sip."

"I am well, and I'd love that," said Windflower. "You look like you haven't aged a day since I last saw you. What's your secret?"

"You are a charmer Sergeant Windflower. That must make you very popular with the ladies. How is your lady friend, Mrs. Hillier?"

"Sheila is living an interesting life. I'll tell her you asked about her. Now, what were you going to show me?" Dr. Sanjay pulled the white sheet up and turned the now stiff body onto one side to show Windflower the backs of the dead man's legs. "As you can see, these are needle marks, indicating intravenous drug injection." He let the body slide back down on the table.

"Diabetic?" asked Windflower.

"No sign of a diabetic condition. If anything, his body is emaciated as if something was eating it from the inside out."

"Opiates or heroin are more likely," said Tizzard, carrying in three cups of tea.

"What do you think, Doctor?" asked Windflower.

"We won't know for sure until we get the tox reports but I can do a blood sample here at the clinic for the most common opiates. But the fact that there are no marks on his arms is indicative of the fact that he wanted to keep his injections a secret. Diabetics don't often do that."

"Could that have caused his heart attack?" asked Windflower.

"It's possible. Intravenous drug users can develop any number of conditions including infections of the heart lining and valves. There are also cases where prolonged use of opiates dilutes the blood and results in the dilation of blood vessels. So, the answer is a qualified yes, but until we know if there was indeed opiate use, it is all speculation," said the doctor.

"If he was a drug addict, then wouldn't there be syringes and drug paraphernalia around? I didn't see anything when I went to his house this morning," said Tizzard.

"You may not have been looking for it. If he was covering up his needle marks he probably had a good plan for hiding everything else. He was a pharmacist. Maybe he kept his stuff at work," said Windflower.

"Or maybe in the car," said Tizzard. "That's something else for MacDonald to look for when she goes over to the pound."

"Mr. Ridgeway has left us with more questions than answers," said Dr. Sanjay.

"I guess so," said Windflower. "Thanks for your help, Doctor, and the tea. I'll be in touch about our social engagement."

"You do that, Sergeant. I will look forward to it."

Both men shook hands with the doctor and walked in silence to their car. "We should go over to the pharmacy. Do they know what's happened yet?" asked Windflower.

"I don't think they've been told formally, but everybody at the Mug-Up knew more about it than I did this morning. Could have been the plow operator or the snow clearing guys or the paramedics. It's a small town, Boss."

Windflower nodded and Tizzard continued to drive the short distance down the highway to Fortune.

Chapter Ten

"You know, I don't think MacDonald searched the car properly," said Windflower as they drove into the small community of Fortune. "There was no dog leash, and if you have a dog you almost always have a leash in the car and probably some water. Now that we suspect Mr. Ridgeway was using drugs, wouldn't there be some sign of that in his car? I know he was probably careful, but I'd very surprised if he didn't have something stashed in there."

"You may be right," said Tizzard. "MacDonald is a very nice person and wants to help. But she isn't always that thorough."

"Have there been problems you haven't been telling me about, Corporal?" asked Windflower as Tizzard parked his vehicle in front of the low red brick building with the Fortune Pharmacy sign across the front.

"A few minor things. I've spoken to her about it, and have made a note of them for her evaluation. Things like not locking up the detachment when she's out on night patrol and missing information on reports."

"And you didn't think to tell me about this?"

"Well, I'm supposed to be in charge of supervision, and you were busy..." Tizzard said, his voice trailing off.

"Let me be real clear. I want to know about any or all problems with personnel at the Grand Bank detachment.

Got it?" asked Windflower. He moved off and left a speechless Tizzard struggling to catch up.

Windflower walked up to the girl at the cash register and asked to speak to the manager on duty. The pretty young woman smiled at Windflower but beamed at Tizzard. "Laura, come to the front, Laura to the front," she said into the microphone that blared all over the store. The few shoppers in the pharmacy perked up their ears and watched for Laura's arrival at the checkout.

A woman in her mid-forties wearing a long white frock over a pantsuit came strolling down one of the aisles from the back of the store. When she saw Windflower and Tizzard she visibly tightened, but kept up her professional pace towards them.

"Laura Emberley," she said with a hand outstretched to the RCMP officers.

"Good morning Ms. Emberley. I'm Sergeant Winston Windflower and this is Corporal Tizzard. Is there somewhere we can talk for a few minutes?"

"Surely," she said, leading them to a small office behind the dispensing area.

"I wish I could say I'm surprised to see you, but I'm not," Emberley said when they had sat down in the small cramped office. "Bad news travels fast. I assume you're here about Michael."

"Are you the manager of the pharmacy?" asked Windflower.

"I am the owner-operator. I bought the place from the Blake family when they got tired of running everything else in Fortune. My family is from around here, but I was living in Nova Scotia when I learned of the opportunity. It was perfect. I have been back here for about two years. I'm sorry, I have a tendency to go on when I'm nervous.

Anyway, I am the owner and Michael was the other pharmacist."

"That's okay," said Windflower. "So you know about Michael's accident last night. How did you hear about it?"

"Marina, the girl at the cash, her father is a snowplow operator. As I said, bad news travels fast."

"What was Michael like?" asked Windflower, trying to ease his way into a more difficult line of questioning.

"He was a good pharmacist. He was helpful and kind and although he was shy, he was great with customers, especially the older ones; called them his old friends. He was having some health problems of his own lately, though. He started missing time because of it."

"Any idea what that was about?" asked Windflower.

"I didn't really pry too much. He was a private person and I respected that."

"Were there any problems with his work, other than the absences?" asked Windflower, starting to dip into deeper waters.

"No, he was a good worker whenever he was here. We did have an inventory shortfall, a few months back though, but I suspected that was part of the break-in."

"Break-in?" asked Tizzard. "When was this?"

"It was back in September. You didn't know about it? There was a female police officer, MacDonald, who came over and took a statement."

This news brought a short and fierce scowl from Windflower towards Tizzard who slumped well back into his incommunicative stance.

"I'm sorry but I wasn't around much at that time," said Windflower. "I didn't see that report. What was taken?"

"All of our opiates and narcotic supply along with a couple of cases of needles. Pain killers mostly, including Fentanyl and Percocet. We were lucky because there was no one here at the time. It was only a break-in; many other stores have been robbed at gunpoint."

"Thank you, Ms. Emberley, you've been helpful. Corporal Tizzard will be back to talk with you further once he has reviewed the report," said Windflower.

"You haven't told me but I am assuming that Michael is indeed dead," said the pharmacist.

"We won't publicly release that information until his next of kin are notified, but I can tell you in confidence that Michael Ridgeway is dead. Please do not share this information with anyone else."

"No, certainly not."

"Thank you again for your time," said Windflower.

He and Tizzard once again faced the stares and whispered comments of the store's customers as they walked back through the pharmacy.

"I'll get right on the report when I get back," said Tizzard in the parking lot.

"You know what?" asked Windflower. "I can't even talk to you about any of this yet. I'm afraid what I might do. I'm going across the street to get a bowl of soup at the diner and you go back and find out what's going on with MacDonald. Then send somebody back to pick me up in an hour. Got it?"

With that he left Tizzard by his Jeep and walked across the street to the Wharfside Diner and Lounge. He had just found a windowside table when his cell phone rang.

"Windflower," he answered as he watched Tizzard move slowly out of his parking place and creep onto the main road. That was a first.

"Hello, Winston," Sheila said on the other end of the line.

"Sheila, how are you? Are you back in Grand Bank?"

"We're on our way, stopping in Goobies."

"I'm sorry I didn't get a chance to talk to you last night," Windflower said.

"Me too. I hear there was an accident."

"Bad news does travel fast. That kept us pretty busy, especially on the tail end of the snowstorm."

"I understand. I guess we need to talk about a few things, Winston. Why don't you come over for supper? I'll make spaghetti or something easy."

"That would be great, Sheila. I'll come over after work."

After they had hung up Windflower spent a few moments thinking about Sheila and how they were going to walk through the minefield in front of them. Like many other parts of his life, he had many more questions than answers.

CHAPTER ELEVEN

The "Wharf" was the only real restaurant in Fortune, located right next to the ticket office for the ferry to the French islands of St. Pierre and Miquelon. It was a diner during the day and a pub at night. It also had a tourist trap gift shop with some homemade Newfoundland items like woolen mittens and scarves, but mostly what Sheila would have called 'Precious Moments' trinkets.

Regardless, they had good soup and that's what Windflower came for. He ordered the pea soup and it came as advertised, thick and creamy, with small pieces of salt beef tucked into the broth for flavour. Along with a fresh Parker House roll and a hot cup of tea, it hit the spot. Windflower was thinking about ordering the ice cream cheesecake he saw on the menu, but he noticed an RCMP cruiser pull up in front.

He waved to Evanchuk to come in and join him. He ordered the dessert while Evanchuk asked for a cup of hot tea.

"No dessert?" asked Windflower.

"No thanks, sir. I've found it's easier to keep it off than to try and take it off later."

"You don't have to worry about your weight, especially at your age," said Windflower.

"One of the reasons I run is that I used to be 'that short fat kid'," said Evanchuk.

Windflower raised an eyebrow in surprise as his ice cream cheesecake arrived. "I'm going to get back to running in the new year. For now, I'm going to enjoy myself."

Evanchuk just smiled and sipped her tea as Windflower thoroughly enjoyed his dessert. When he was finished he went to the cash to pay his bill, and then met Evanchuk outside.

"Thanks for picking me up," said Windflower as he got into the car.

"No problem, boss. I'm glad to be out of the office. Tizzard was having a pretty good go at MacDonald."

"I don't think he's too happy with her, right now. Are you two close?"

"We talk," said Evanchuk. "But we're very different."

"She doesn't seem as focused as you. Is there something going on with her?"

"That's not my place to say. I guess you would need to ask her yourself, sir."

"Right," said Windflower. "Let's go back to Grand Bank."

As he and Evanchuk were pulling into the detachment, Windflower could see Tizzard and MacDonald getting into Tizzard's Jeep. They were still having a discussion but it looked to Windflower like Tizzard was doing all the talking. And MacDonald didn't look like she was enjoying whatever was being said. In fact, Windflower thought he saw her rub her eyes as if she had been crying.

Windflower said hi to Betsy who although she was on the phone, pointed to his office, meaning that somebody was waiting for him. He picked up his messages from his slot and quickly scanned them: three media calls which he simply handed back to Betsy, one from Inspector Ford, and one from Laura Emberley. He wondered what the pharmacist wanted; he'd just spoken to her.

He walked back to his office where Mayor Bill Sinnott was occupying most of it. Sinnott was big, tall, wide, and large. He struggled to fit into the regularly-sized spaces, especially chairs that accommodated most people. The Mayor had been working with Tizzard on implementing what Sinnott referred to as a 'community policin' program formally named Coastal Watch. It was like Neighbourhood Watch for people who lived in small communities all along the southeast coast of Newfoundland.

"I hear the Coastal Watch program is going really well," said Windflower as he shook Sinnott's hand. "You must be pleased and proud of that."

"I'm happy to be doin' my part for 'community policin'. But I didn't come to talk to you about that. I am wondering if there's anything we can do about those ditches on the side of the highway. If you were to sign a letter indicatin' you thought they be a danger to the travellin' public I might be able to get something movin' on my end."

"I'll have a look at a draft letter if you want to send it over," said Windflower. Then he saw Sinnott's slight smile and added, "I assume that Betsy probably has the letter already. I'll have a look at it and get back to you by the end of the week. I have to run it by my boss in Marystown."

"That would be great," said the Mayor as he struggled to get out of his chair to leave. "Sad news about the young man in the accident. So young. It's tragic really. You never know when your heart will give out though, I guess."

Windflower appreciated the Mayor's wisdom, but didn't take the bait about the heart attack. Instead he tried a different approach. "Did you know Mr. Ridgeway?" he asked.

"Not very well," said Mayor Sinnott. "I think he kept to himself. Anyway, it's a sad day for the community," he concluded as he lumbered out of Windflower's office. "I'll be seein' ya, Sergeant."

"One more thing before you go, if you have a minute," said Windflower.

"Always time for the RCMP."

"Do you think the disturbances at the fish plant are over now? I know it hasn't been easy on anybody."

"No, it hasn't been easy. The fish plant is one last piece of history that people have been hangin' on to. That kinda died once the new owners started gutting the place. Is it over? I dunno. The 'frigeration equipment has all been removed so there's nuttin' left to protest about. Except I heard that they might want to start strippin' the metal out of the place and shippin' it off to the mainland for salvage. If that happens then tings could break out again."

"I sure hope that doesn't happen. It's causing problems between us and the residents, just when I thought we were making progress," said Windflower.

"A few might be upset but nobody really blames you guys," said the Mayor. "We all know that it's not you causing problems. This is a hard time for a lot of people, a lot to accept. But it too will pass. The storms of yesterday are easily forgotten when the sun shines in the morning. We just need to learn to forgive each other faster."

With that, Mayor Sinnott was gone and Windflower was left once again puzzling over his words, wondering if he was talking about his relationship with Sheila or life in general. Windflower liked this philosopher-Mayor a lot.

Next up was to return his phone calls. First, Laura Emberley, the pharmacist. He dialed the number on the message slip and was ready to leave a message when she answered the phone.

"Laura Emberley," she answered.

"Ms. Emberley, it's Sergeant Windflower returning your call."

"Thank you, Sergeant. I was wondering if I could come and see you, privately. Alone, I mean. There's a few things I want to tell you but I would prefer to do it with just us present, if that's okay."

"Sure," said Windflower. "You can come here tomorrow morning or I could meet you somewhere."

"I can come there. Could we do it early, though? I have to open up now with Michael gone, at least till I find somebody else."

"I'm usually here by 8:00. You can come by shortly after that if you'd like," said Windflower.

"Thank you, Sergeant. I'll see you then."

The phone clicked, and Windflower was left wondering again what that was all about. Oh well, he'd find out soon enough. Just another opportunity to practice patience. He also thought about what his Uncle Frank used to say: 'You can chase a butterfly all over the field and never catch it. But if you sit quietly in the grass it will come and sit on your shoulder.'

He was about to make another call when Tizzard burst into his office.

"You'll never guess what we found in the car!"

"What?"

"We found a body in the trunk. A dead body wrapped up in an old carpet. It's Frankie Fallon."

CHAPTER TWELVE

Frankie Fallon was well known to both RCMP officers, and indeed to most police departments from Grand Bank to the Manitoba border. Fallon was as close as one could get in these parts to an outlaw biker and had taken advantage of the hospitality of the available penal institutions at one time or another. He was currently out, on parole, after having once again fallen afoul of the normal rules and regulations governing a civil society. Fallon's latest case, as Windflower recalled, was when he had bit off a piece of another man's ear in a bar brawl and lost his liberty for yet another year. This time at Her Majesty's Penitentiary in St. John's.

"Wow," said Windflower. "Where's the body now?"

"Still in the trunk of the car," said Tizzard. "I didn't want to disturb the scene so I just closed it up and called Forensics in St. John's to come check it out. The body's frozen solid and it's secure in the pound. I taped the scene and left MacDonald there until I talked to you."

"I'll call Forensics again and make sure they're coming. We can't really leave the body there for too long," said Windflower. He opened his cell phone and found the contact number for Corporal Ted Brown in Forensics.

"Brownie, how are you?" he said when Brown answered. "Did you see the request from Tizzard?"

"You guys got a body in a trunk over there? I've got a team finishing up a piece in Whitbourne. They'll drive down first thing in the morning. I'll meet them in Fortune."

"Perfect," said Windflower. "See you tomorrow."

"Right," said Brown.

"So do we need a watch on the body overnight? I don't mind making MacDonald work the shift, since she's not exactly at the top of my hit parade today. But I hate having to spend more money on overtime for Frankie Fallon," said Tizzard.

"I hear ya. But one citizen—even dead—deserves respect, even one as bad as Frankie. So let's keep a watch on till the morning. And what the heck is going on with MacDonald anyway? She didn't search the trunk? That's basic, one of the first things you learn in training."

"I'm not really sure. I gave her the gears and was expecting some excuse but she really didn't have anything. She just broke down crying and wouldn't stop."

"There must be something going on. I'll talk to her tomorrow and see if we can't find out. But we can't afford to have any screw-ups around here. It's too small an operation."

"Yeah," said Tizzard. "We also found a doctor's bag in the trunk. It looks like some form of medication, but I don't know enough about that stuff. There are also a couple of boxes of syringes in the back. I left all of that in the trunk for Forensics to have a look at. And oh yeah, I found this," and he held up a blue and white Toronto Maple Leafs dog leash.

"Well, we can't hold that against the dog. Will you call that kennel and see if they'll keep her, at least till we sort things out? I'll phone Marystown and give them an update."

"Will do," said Tizzard and he trundled off to make his phone call, swinging the leash as he went along.

"Inspector Ford, please," said Windflower into the receiver, since Ford's administrative assistant, Louise, answered the call. Ford came on after a short delay.

"I'm glad you called. I need you in Marystown on Friday. An old friend of yours will be in town. Ron Quigley has been working in St. John's with the Constabulary on an opiates strategy. He wants to give us an update. I've got everybody else lined up. Can you be here?"

"Sure. It'll be good to see Quigley again. On another matter, I'm calling about the Michael Ridgeway case. We can let his name be released publicly. I talked to the mother this morning. Will you let the media relations guys know? It's better if they deal with the press," Windflower said

"No problem," said Ford. "Anything else?"

"Yes. Looks like Ridgeway died of a heart attack, and he was an intravenous drug user."

"Are those connected?" asked Ford.

"According to Doc Sanjay, they might be. And we discovered a body in the trunk of his car," said Windflower.

"A body? Do we have an ID?"

"It's Frankie Fallon," said Windflower.

"Fallon?" asked Ford. "I thought he was in the pen in Saint John's."

"Nope," said Windflower. "Tizzard made the ID. He found the body this afternoon."

"Why didn't you guys find the body last night?" asked Ford.

"I'm still trying to figure that out. When I do I'll let you know. Brown and the Forensics team are coming tomorrow. I'll keep you in the loop."

"Do that. Especially if you find any more bodies. It sounds to me like there's been some slacking going on over there. I want a full report on Friday," said Ford.

With that, Ford was gone and Tizzard was back, this time with a very happy collie on the end of her leash. She made a move toward Windflower and once again pressed her rump against him for a rub.

"I think she likes you," said Tizzard.

"I think she likes getting rubbed," said Windflower with a smile as he gently stroked the dog's rump and rubbed her legs. "As collies get older they often get arthritis. That's why they like getting rubbed so much."

"Anyway, she'll have to stay here tonight," said Tizzard. "The kennel is full. I'll put a blanket down in the cell out back. But now I'm going to take her out. I think she has to go."

Windflower sat back in his chair, a little dazed from all the input he had received: one fatality thought to be accidental, but now looked like much more; another dead body, usually a villain but this time a victim, stuffed in the trunk of a car. That was not to mention the fact that the whole community was still reeling over the loss of its main industry and major employer.

And on top of that, he and Sheila weren't exactly seeing eye-to-eye.

There was lots to ponder and worry about but there wasn't much more that Windflower could do today. He waited for Tizzard to come back with the dog to say goodnight. She was once again happy to see Windflower when she came back in, full of snow and high spirits.

"Ever think about getting a dog?" Windflower asked.

"Not for me. I got enough trouble looking after myself. You on the other hand, would make a great dog owner."

Windflower smiled. "I've got a few things of my own to look after these days."

"Have you talked to Sheila?"

"I'm on my way over there right now."

"She has to do what she's doing, you know."

"Everybody keeps telling me that," said Windflower. "Except for Inspector Ford, of course."

"Your family and community are the most important things in your life," said Tizzard.

"Thank you, Corporal. I'll put that on my resume when I'm looking for a new job. Have a good night. See you tomorrow."

"See you tomorrow, Boss. I'll stay until Fortier comes and then relieve MacDonald at the pound."

Chapter Thirteen

Windflower could smell dinner as soon as he opened the door to Sheila's house. Her homemade spaghetti sauce was rich, thick and garlicky. Sheila lived in her original family home in Grand Bank. It was an old two-story saltbox house that had been painstakingly restored as part of her healing journey after her husband had been killed in an industrial accident in Alberta. Around that time she also operated the local café, the Mug-Up, so she had been a very busy woman in recent years.

The Mug-Up had been a labour of love for Sheila. Like her old house it took up a lot of her time and energy, and became a thriving business that catered to weddings and other social functions. Then came the accident on the highway almost two years ago when Sheila suffered a traumatic brain injury. She required multiple operations to mend her broken body and spent almost a year in one form of rehabilitation or another, including months in a special facility in St. John's. Her body was almost as good as new and except for a slight limp and a scar that was buried under her thick reddish-brown hair, she was back to normal.

Although as everybody knows, there's no normal after a near-death experience. Sheila certainly felt that way and decided to make a number of significant changes in her life. First of all, she sold the Mug-Up to Moira Stoodley. Moira had been in that business before and jumped at the opportunity to get back in, first as the temporary manager while Sheila recovered, and then as the new owner. She recruited her husband, Herb Stoodley, to serve as her backup. He too relished the idea of being busy again after his retirement as a long-serving Crown Attorney.

Sheila had also decided to go back to school, which was also an easy decision to make. Sheila had started out in nursing years ago but left university when first her father, and then her mother, grew ill. Within a year they were gone. Sheila never regretted the decision to come home. Soon afterwards she had met Bart and they started out their life together. So nursing school was again diverted and soon Sheila was fully engaged in running the Mug-Up and enjoying her time with Bart as he tried to save up enough money to start his own construction business.

His death had ended that dream and that life for Sheila. She never thought that she would be able to love again or to have dreams of her own come true. But now she was back in school and trying to complete at least that piece of unfinished business. And she had this amazing relationship with her RCMP man that had the potential to be something great, as long as they didn't screw it up.

How were they going to be able to reconcile their opposing points of view around what was happening in their community? It was Sheila's home, but it was also Windflower's workplace. From Sheila's perspective; family and community would always come first. That was both her history and her destiny. Her accident and almost rebirth had confirmed that. So too had her commitment to protecting what she could of her home and her heritage. And if that meant going to jail for her beliefs, that was okay too. But how could the girlfriend, partner, and maybe even the wife of an RCMP officer be herself too? That was the question that she and Windflower had to sort out.

Windflower came slowly into the kitchen. "That smells so good. I can almost taste the garlic," he said.

"I'm glad you're hungry. As usual I made enough for a family of six. Why don't you open that bottle of Chianti on the counter and pour us each a glass?"

Windflower poured them both a glass of wine and soaked in the aroma of the spaghetti and Sheila's fantastic sauce. "Thank you, Sheila. This is the first real meal I've had since, well, since the last meal you cooked."

"Bon appetit!" said Sheila as they sat at table and she placed a heaping plate of spaghetti in front of Windflower.

"Enjoy," said Sheila as she scooped up a serving of salad to go along with her half-plate of spaghetti.

Windflower ate slowly and savoured the chunks of onion and tomato, and the basil and oregano in the sauce. The garlic was ever-present and it opened his scent buds and his palate. He sipped his Chianti and dipped another piece of baguette into the delicious sauce. Sheila ate much less and much more slowly, and despite the weight of the topic awaiting them, she relaxed as she watched Windflower's devotion and attention to his food.

After dinner they shared the cleaning up. Sheila then made tea and got a small tray of cookies from the fridge for dessert and led them into the living room. Sheila called it the parlor though, just like her parents had done for so many years, and probably their parents before them.

"So I guess we should talk," said Sheila. "I can go first if you'd like."

"Sure," said Windflower as he poured them each a cup of tea and selected a chocolate rum ball for his first treat.

"I know that things have not been easy for you in your position. But they have not been easy for me either."

Windflower nodded and she went on. "Since my accident, or maybe since my recovery, my whole outlook on life has changed. Inside I have always been a strong person, but I let other people speak on my behalf. That time is over." She certainly had Windflower's attention now.

She continued.

"This is my home and my community, and I will fight with every breath in my body to keep it alive and thriving. What is happening at the fish plant isn't right, and everybody knows that. We're allowing some corporation to come in and tear us apart and then leave us with a shell of what we used to be. I'm not going to let that happen. We have to fight to preserve our past and our history if we want a future."

"I understand all of that," said Windflower. "But you can't stop this from happening. In fact it's already over."

"We may have lost this battle, but it's the first time in a long time that this community has stood together as one. That means we will fight together for the future as well," said Sheila.

"I support fighting for the future, too," said Windflower. "But did you have to break the law and get arrested? You can see where I might have a problem with that. I am charged with upholding the law and you are out there breaking it."

"I had to do it. There were about 50 of us on the committee to save the plant. I was the coordinator. While I was hoping my turn wouldn't come, when it did, I had to do it. How could I stand on the sideline while those two little old ladies and a kid stood up for what they believed in?"

"I don't know, Sheila," said Windflower quietly. "I thought we were going to be spending our lives together.

What about the next time something else happens? Would you do it again?"

"I don't know," said Sheila, just as quietly.

Windflower sat for a moment in the uncomfortable silence that followed.

"Thank you for supper," he finally said, and then reached over and gave her a peck on the cheek. "Let's keep talking."

Sheila gave him a hug goodnight.

CHAPTER FOURTEEN

I t was early when Windflower got home, but he was exhausted. He tried to read for a while, but he couldn't keep his eyes open. He was sliding into bed when his phone rang. He hoped it was Sheila, but instead it was his Auntie Marie calling from his hometown in Alberta.

"How are you, my little rabbit?" his aunt asked, using the childhood nickname that she had for him.

"I am well, Auntie. How are you and how is Uncle Frank?" said Windflower.

"I am well too, but Frank has gone off on another of his adventures. I haven't heard from him in a few days. He started drinking again and when I confronted him about it, he got into a huff and said he'd find somewhere to go that actually wanted him. That's why I thought he may have shown up down your way."

"No, we haven't seen him around here. But he would certainly be welcomed back by the locals. He made quite an impression on them. Don't worry though, Auntie, he always surfaces at some point. He knows how to survive."

"I know. They say God looks after drunks and fools and Frank qualifies on both counts. But he's getting old now and after that time in St. John's when he got beat up, I had hoped he learned his lesson. Anyway, what's new with you, nephew?"

"Not too much," said Windflower, deciding not to burden his aunt with his current troubles. "We're surviving the winter so far."

"Any plans to get married yet? We are still waiting to cuddle your little ones. Soon it will be too late for us old ones."

"You are not so old. But no wedding bells yet for me. Sometimes I think that maybe it's too late for me too," Windflower said with a laugh.

"It is never too late to be happy. Until they throw dirt on you, you have a chance. Don't let your old ideas get in the way of your present and future happiness. Anyway, I will let you go. I have to go to bingo. Keep a watch out for Frank, please, Winston. Goodnight, my little rabbit."

"Goodnight, Auntie."

He wondered if she knew of his relationship troubles. And what did she mean by letting old ideas getting in the way of his happiness? Windflower thought about that until he fell into a deep sleep and didn't stir until he heard the wind at his window, which was a telltale sign of snow being drifted into his backyard. The forecast hadn't called for more snow but this might be one of those occasions in Newfoundland when a storm was sent back inland by the wind to pack another punch, after having already headed out to sea.

When Windflower went outside to carry out his morning smudging ritual it sure looked a lot like the last storm. He did his smudge and said a few quick prayers, adding his Uncle Frank's safe passage home. He thought about Sheila and laid down a few pinches of tobacco for her. His prayer for her was to find clarity and wisdom in her life. And while he was at it, he asked Creator for the same blessings for himself.

He went back had a quick breakfast, then shaved and put on a clean work uniform. He noticed that his red serge, the ceremonial dress of the Royal Canadian Mounted Police reserved for special events, needed cleaning. He put that over his shoulder to drop off at the dry cleaners, and went to work.

When he got there the door was locked, which meant the officer on overnight duty had gone to make one last round of highway patrol before their shift was over. Windflower unlocked the door and made his way to the lunchroom to make a new pot of coffee. Along the way he passed by the holding cell and surprised both himself and the sleeping dog lying on a blanket inside. The startled collie was aggressive until she saw who it was.

"Good morning, Lady." He would later tell others that this was the first moment he knew for sure he had a new dog. "Wanna go for a walk?" The dog's response was spontaneously joyful, as only a dog can be when they know something good is going to happen. Windflower grabbed her leash and a plastic bag from the lunchroom, which is when Evanchuk pulled up.

"Good morning, Sergeant," she said. "I see you've got a new friend."

"I'm talking her for a walk. Can you put some coffee on? I'll be right back."

"Sure," said Evanchuk with a smile. She went in to finish her paperwork and her shift.

"Let's go, Lady," said Windflower. They made a few stops along their route toward the wharf, and were soon back at the detachment.

Windflower could smell the coffee perking as soon as he opened the door. There was nothing quite like that aroma when you come in from the cold on a snowy winter morning. He put the dog back in the holding cell, grabbed a cup of coffee and waved his thanks to Evanchuk who was filling out her duty report. A few minutes later she popped in to say goodbye. Windflower was then alone to enjoy the rare peace and quiet of his office.

In less than an hour, that had completely changed. Tizzard had come by with a box of muffins to share along with the printout from the weather office. They were still predicting flurries for their area but both men knew that would change as soon as one of the meteorologists in Marystown stuck his or her head out the window. They opened the office snowfall pool. For five bucks you could predict the number of centimetres that would fall. Closest without going over would win. Tizzard bet 16 centimetres while Windflower guessed it would be higher, 21. They made plans to check in again after noon in case they had to put a storm plan into place.

Betsy came in with Windflower's correspondence and messages from the previous day. One that stuck out was from Brenda Ridgeway, Michael Ridgeway's sister. He could call her later because it was still too early to phone Ontario. When Betsy made it back to her desk, she buzzed him to say Laura Emberley was there.

The pharmacist sat in the small reception area next to Betsy, and Windflower led her back into his office. She refused his offer for coffee or tea and fidgeted in the chair across from him.

"So, Ms. Emberley, what did you want to see me about?" asked Windflower.

"I guess I didn't give you all the information when you came to see me the other day. I thought that since Michael was dead it was all over and I didn't want to speak badly about him. But there are some things that you, or somebody, should know. Everything was going along great with Michael and the pharmacy. He was working hard and saving money for a big trip. He was going on a round-the-world cruise with some friends, he told me."

"That sounds like fun," said Windflower, trying to encourage the woman to keep talking. "It also sounds like things were working out well at the pharmacy."

"They were, until the accident. As I told you before, Michael was a good guy whom the customers liked. He fit in well and although he didn't have a lot of friends he seemed to be relatively happy. Then he hurt his back in a skiing accident out at Marble Mountain."

"When was this?" asked Windflower, who by now had taken out a pad and was writing notes. He didn't intend to write her comments verbatim because it seemed to make people more comfortable when it looked like the officer was paying close attention to them.

"This was last spring, so I guess about 9 or 10 months ago. I think it was just before Easter, which was early last year. I remember because I was looking after Lady, his dog, and I had company coming for Easter. He called from Corner Brook and said that he hurt his back and would be a few days late coming back. That wasn't the end of the world and eventually, he came back."

"So what was so unusual about that?" asked Windflower.

"It wasn't unusual. But what happened after he came back was strange. He started missing time. I've told you about that. He also started getting multiple prescriptions for painkillers. I was doing checks of the opiate register one month. We have to account and report to the board about all our pain meds. I noticed his name appeared four times in one month, on prescriptions from four separate doctors, including two in Saint John's. And there were hundreds of pills in each prescription. I confronted him on this and he said he had lost one bottle and had to get a replacement."

"So you thought he was abusing his medication?" asked Windflower.

"He told me **that** part of his life was over," said Laura Emberley.

"What?" He had a history of drug abuse in the past? How did he get a job as a pharmacist?"

Chapter Fifteen

"I took a chance on him. Do you know how hard it is to get a regular pharmacist to come to work in Fortune? Yes, he had a history of drugs in his past. But he said he'd been five years clean, and that his issue was with cocaine and nothing else. I believed him because I wanted him to come here."

"What else is going on that you haven't told me about? Now is the time to come clean. Why didn't you report this when you first became aware of it?"

"Michael begged me not to, and I wanted to believe him. Once I figured out what was going on I cut him off, and made him promise to get help. He told me he would and I think he was going to the Narcotics Anonymous meetings at the clinic. Then I heard he was involved in selling some of the drugs on the street right here in Grand Bank," said Emberley.

"There were a few shady characters hanging around the pharmacy who seemed to be waiting for him. I guess I was naïve enough to think that I could manage this on my own."

"That was naive. We are now going to open an investigation into Michael Ridgeway's death and the circumstances surrounding prescription drug abuse at your pharmacy. I'm going to need you to sit with Corporal Tizzard to make a full statement."

"Okay. Can I make this statement later? I have to go open the store right now."

"The pharmacy won't be opening today. I can get a judge to order it closed while we carry out our investigation, but it would be better if you would cooperate." Emberley nodded her head in agreement. "Why don't you go over there and let the staff know and put a sign in the window? You don't have to say anything. People will think it's because of Michael Ridgeway's death. And get all of the records and reports ready. Corporal Tizzard will be over to see you later this morning."

Laura Emberley nodded again and left Windflower's office to head back to Fortune. Windflower didn't have much time to reflect on what he had just heard because as soon as the pharmacist was gone, Betsy called him on the intercom.

"Ms. Ridgeway from Ontario called," said Betsy. "She sounded a bit panicked. I told her you'd call her back."

"Thanks, Betsy," he said, picking up the message slip from yesterday and calling the number in Ontario.

"Hello," said a woman almost as soon as it started ringing.

"Good morning. It's Sergeant Winston Windflower from the RCMP Grand Bank Detachment. Is this Brenda Ridgeway?"

"It is."

"First of all, I am very sorry for your loss. A sudden death is always difficult."

"My mom is taking it very hard. Michael was always her favourite. She couldn't really tell me much. She said something about a car accident."

"Michael was involved in a car accident. But we have some indications that he may have actually died from heart failure. Did your brother have a heart condition?"

"No, not that I'm aware of," she said, sounding very surprised.

"We also believe he may have been abusing pain medication," said Windflower, leaving that last statement to linger a little. He could hear the woman sigh at the end of the line and after a lengthy pause he added, "Is there anything you want to tell me?"

"I thought all of that was over with Michael. Mom had been through so much with him."

"What do you mean?" asked Windflower.

"Michael was a cocaine addict. He struggled with it for several years and put all of us through the wringer. He stole from all of us. I had to get the locks changed on Mom's condo before she moved into the retirement home. Somehow he avoided going to jail, but he ended up in hospital and detox and a number of treatment facilities. Finally he got clean. He went to twelve step meetings all the time when he lived in Toronto. I even went to his one-year celebration. I was sure that part of his life was over."

"We suspect he may have been involved with dealing and distributing drugs from the pharmacy as well," said Windflower, deciding to lay all his cards on the table.

"I'm not surprised. When he was using he would do anything to get his drugs. But you know, he really did clean up his act. He went back to school and finished his pharmacy degree. He couldn't work in Ontario because he had a number of arrests, nothing serious, petty crimes really, but enough to give him a record. When the chance came to go east he was happier than I have ever seen him. So was Mom."

"Once again, I'm sorry for your loss. I also wanted to let you know that there will be a delay in releasing Michael's body. Either I or someone else will be in contact with you as soon as we know some more."

"There's no rush on that. Our family is not religious and we will arrange for a cremation and then have a private service later. I will probably come down in a few days to look after Michael's stuff."

"Okay. By the way, Michael had a dog, a collie. We're trying to put her in a kennel while everything gets sorted out."

"You might as well turn the dog over to the Humane Society. I'm allergic and Mom couldn't take it even if she wanted to."

"Thank you, Ms. Ridgeway. We'll look into that."

At least Michael Ridgeway's real story was coming out. Windflower knew the life of an addict is like an iceberg. Before he could delve any deeper into these thoughts, Tizzard was back with a suggestion to go to the Mug-Up for coffee.

"A grand suggestion," said Windflower as the two men bundled up against the heavily falling snow.

Chapter Sixteen

The Mug-Up was busy, but at least the ten o'clock crowd had cleared out by the time Windflower and Tizzard arrived. From their familiar corner table, they ordered coffee and raisin tea biscuits. Windflower waved good morning to Herb Stoodley who was still working the morning shift, and to the Mayor who was holding court in the tea room at the back.

Windflower gave Tizzard an update on his morning meeting and phone call.

"It sounds like the late Michael Ridgeway had his hands in a few things around here besides dispensing medications from the pharmacy. I wish MacDonald had clued us in about the break-in before now," said Tizzard.

"What did she say about the report?" asked Windflower as Marie, the waitress, dropped off their hot cups of coffee.

"She had the report done but didn't file it. She showed it to me. It was in the file but not recorded on the duty sheet and because of that, Betsy didn't add it to the weekly roundup report. So, MacDonald knew, and nobody else. I'm glad you're going to talk to her. She breaks down and cries whenever I start talking."

"I'll talk to her this afternoon when she comes in," said Windflower. "But what did the report say and what was MacDonald's conclusion or speculation?"

"MacDonald's report said that unknown quantities of pharmaceuticals were taken, which can be confirmed once we do the inventory. She also noted there was a broken window at the back of the building and the alarm had been cut. She interviewed both Laura Emberley and Michael Ridgeway. It also said Emberley had been out of town when the break-in occurred, and that Ridgeway had nothing further to add."

Tizzard stopped talking when their tea biscuits arrived.

Windflower continued when the waitress walked away.

"We have lots more to do on this file. I want you to go see Ms. Emberley when you get a chance. Get her to pull out all the inventories and reports for the last two years and bring them back over here so we can have a look at them. Can you also re-interview her? After that you and I will compare notes. There's something she's not telling me, maybe a lot of things, and that might help us get closer to the truth. Also, the Forensics guys are coming later. Is Fortier over at the pound?"

"Yup," said Tizzard in between bites of tea biscuits. "He's there till noon."

"And you'll need to make arrangements to take the dog to the SPCA in Marystown. The Ridgeways won't be taking it to Ontario," said Windflower.

"Why don't you keep her?"

"I've got quite enough to keep me busy, thank you, Corporal," said Windflower as he stood to leave. The Mayor saw him out of the corner of his eye and waved him over. Tizzard walked outside to warm up the Jeep.

"Good morning, Sergeant," said Mayor Sinnott. "Looks like another big blow comin'."

"Sure does, Mister Mayor," said Windflower.

"It'd be a shame to have someone drive into those craters on the side of the road on a stormy day like today."

"It would be. I'll have a look at that memo when I get back to the office."

"Thank you, Sergeant, enjoy the rest of your day," said Mayor Sinnott.

"You too, Mister Mayor."

Windflower turned up his collar to protect against the increasing snow and wind, and went out to meet Tizzard.

Tizzard dropped Windflower off at the detachment before heading to Fortune to see the pharmacist. He stopped at the reception desk at the front to talk to Betsy. "Can I have a copy of that memo from Mayor Sinnott?" he asked. Betsy scanned her computer quickly and then printed him off a copy. Windflower nodded to Betsy who was quickly back on the phone. He went back to his office to check his own computer for the latest weather forecast.

They had finally updated their predictions to 10 to 15 centimetres with the possibility of drifting and blowing snow along the southeast coast and the Burin and Avalon peninsulas. Plus, increasing winds later in the day, which was the perfect combination for a big mess. He decided to put the storm plan into action immediately after addressing the Mayor's letter. He read it once and then again, and had to agree with both the logic and the intent of the mayor's request. Windflower was not an engineer, but to him the ditches indeed looked unsafe. He went back out to Betsy and waited for her to finish her call.

"Betsy, will you fax this letter to Inspector Ford in Marystown and advise him that unless he has strong objections, I will be signing this letter in support of Mayor Sinnott's request. If we don't hear anything back in a couple of days, let his office know that it's okay to put my name on it. And Betsy, you might as well put the storm watch notice up. Corporal Tizzard will be back soon to coordinate it."

"Yes, sir. Corporal Brown called a few minutes ago. He said they were in Marystown but on their way."

"Thanks, Betsy. They're doing an investigation on a vehicle in Fortune. Can you also call Constable MacDonald and ask her to come in early to see me?"

Windflower went back to his office and started wading through his paperwork again. It never seemed to diminish. He had handed off most of the admin work to Tizzard when he had been made a Corporal, but a lot of things still got referred to him and both Inspector Ford and RCMP HQ seemed to write a lot of memos he needed to read.

Windflower's direct office line then rang. It was Sheila.

"Good morning, Winston. How are you?" asked Sheila.

"I'm well. A little crazy here at work, but well," said Windflower.

"So I've been thinking," said Sheila. "Maybe we should consider not spending as much time together for the next little while. It might make it easier for both of us until we sort things out."

Windflower listened carefully to what Sheila was saying. He had to admit to himself that he had been thinking the same thing.

"This will be a difficult time coming up," was his reply.

"It will. I'll have to go to court and I don't want to drag you through that. I'll also be continuing on the committee to save the fish plant. There will probably be less protesting, but it will be a public role."

"I don't have any problem with your public role. I have a problem with you getting arrested."

"I have no plans to repeat that experience. Not in the near future anyway."

"That's good," said Windflower. He paused for a few moments. He realized that for the first time in a very long time he was having questions about their relationship. Finally, he pushed those doubts aside and said, "Let's stay together through the next period of time and talk some more about how we are going to work this out going forward."

"Okay," said Sheila.

"We also might want to limit our public appearances though, maybe more for your benefit than mine," said Windflower. "It seems to me that at least 40 people in town are not happy with the RCMP. I know you and I haven't sorted everything out yet, but I don't want to make any decisions now we might regret later. Do you?"

"No. I don't want that either."

"Okay, I'll call you later to check in. I'll likely be working late by the looks of the weather."

"Be safe. I'll probably stay over at Moira and Herb's tonight if it stays like this. I don't like to be alone when we get a lot of snow, it makes me feel stranded."

"Bye, Sheila," said Windflower, and hung up the phone. Apparently he wasn't as mad at her as he believed. Or as afraid of Ford. Either way, it was a very interesting moment for Windflower, who wasn't really used to having more than one emotion at a time.

CHAPTER SEVENTEEN

Windflower didn't get much time to think about his feelings before a breathless and snowy RCMP Constable flew into his office.

"Why don't you take off your coat and get us both a cup of coffee? Mine is black, one small sugar," Windflower said as he handed over his battered RCMP coffee mug.

"Okay, sir," said MacDonald, still gasping for air, but looking a little relieved to have been given a short reprieve. She returned to Windflower's office a few minutes later with two cups of coffee.

"Thank you, MacDonald. Sit down. I know there have been a couple of instances in the last while where your judgment has been questionable. We can talk about them in more specifics later. But first I want to ask you, is there anything going on you want to tell me about?"

"What do you mean, sir?"

"I mean this is your chance to make a case as to why you shouldn't be disciplined because of your performance. It might be that you are ill, or there's something going on with your family, or some other reason why you seem distracted and are not carrying out your duties in a responsible manner."

It came out a little more forcefully than planned, but he let that sit with her because she looked like a deer stuck in the headlights.

Finally she spoke.

"No sir, I'm not sick or anything, and my family is fine," she said, almost in a whisper. "I don't want to disappoint you."

"Don't disappoint yourself," he said, again a little more sternly than he had intended. "I'm going to talk to Corporal Tizzard again about your performance and he will let you know how we plan to handle any discipline. But I can tell you Constable, if it doesn't improve, and quickly, you won't be in Grand Bank much longer. And your RCMP career will be much shorter than you planned. Dismissed."

MacDonald simply nodded and left the office, bumping into Tizzard on the way out.

"You're on the storm desk tonight," Tizzard said to her. "Go home and have a nap and be back here at 6." Once again MacDonald nodded and walked away. As she left, Tizzard stepped inside Windflower's office.

"How did that go?" asked Tizzard.

"I don't know what's going on with her, but there's something," said Windflower.

"Yeah," said Tizzard. "She had a great start and I thought we had another keeper like Evanchuk. But it's like a switch got turned off. She seems nervous and edgy."

"I thought she looked scared. Do you have a recommendation on discipline?"

"I think we should dock her a day's pay," said Tizzard. "It's kind of moot since she'll pick up tons of overtime this winter, but I think we need to send a message."

"Agreed," said Windflower. "I've already told her she's on her way out of here unless things get better, and fast. Let's hope this works. And I see you're already moving on the storm plans."

"Might as well. It looks like we'll be shutting down the highway before much longer. I talked to Laura Emberley. She's putting together the information for me and I'm going back over to talk to her again tomorrow."

"Great, you can give me an update while we go say hello to the Forensics guys."

On their way out Windflower asked Betsy to call the Mug-Up and put in an order for another tray of sandwiches for the evening and a half dozen cups of coffee to-go right away.

They cleared off their vehicle, and then headed to the Mug-Up.

"Brownie and the boys might appreciate a hot drink," Windflower said to Tizzard as they pulled in.

Tizzard ran in to get the drinks while Windflower waited outside. Tizzard put the coffees on the floor in front of him and jumped back in. "I think you are going to win the snow pool," he said.

Windflower smiled smugly. "So tell me about Emberley."

"She's definitely hiding something." But I can't figure out whether she's trying to protect herself or Ridgeway. But there's definitely something else going on here."

"I agree. That should be clearer once we see the records. There's a requirement to report all opiates on a monthly basis. Can you check with the clinic and confirm exactly what the rules are? Also, can you see if there have been any irregularities reported or found by the pharmacist's regulatory board, whatever it's called? Actually, let's get Evanchuk to do that running around. It's about time we brought her in on some of the other work," said Windflower.

"Good idea," Tizzard said, looking a little relieved. "I have enough on my plate right now, especially with Fortier leaving. Any word on a replacement yet?"

"No, but I'll raise it again with the Inspector when I see him on Friday."

The RCMP officers pulled up to the gates of the secured pound in Fortune, and punched in the entrance code. Inside, a big white van was parked next to an area that had been marked off by yellow police caution tape. There were four men in RCMP jackets taking pictures, measuring, and taking samples from the SUV that had been involved in the accident.

While they were watching, the ambulance from the Grand Bank clinic neared the gate and Tizzard went to let them in. Windflower walked up to the Forensics team and waved good morning. Two of the men waved back and one approached Windflower. "Good morning, Sergeant, not much of a day is it?"

"Good morning Brownie. We come bearing gifts," and he pointed to Tizzard who was already handing out hot coffee to the other men.

"Thanks," said Corporal Ted Brown. "We're ready to let the body go. We've got the inside of the trunk completely dusted for prints and plenty of samples of blood from the car and the carpet. By the looks of it, I'd say your dead guy was stabbed somewhere else, and then stuffed in the back to be shipped out later. There's just not enough blood here."

"So maybe at his place in Molliers?" said Tizzard.

Windflower turned to Brown.

"Do you have time to take a look at that place too? It's not too far from here."

"It doesn't look like we're going anywhere today. I guess we'll all need a place to bunk down tonight, too," said Brown.

"Well, you can stay with me," said Windflower. "I've got an extra room and I may be on duty tonight. I'll ask Betsy to see if there any rooms at the B & B. It's pretty slow this time of year."

"I bet," said Brown with a laugh.

"Tizzard, why don't you stay here and show these guys where Frankie Fallon hung out? Or better yet, I'll get Evanchuk to go with them."

Windflower went back to the car and called Betsy to check for rooms and get Evanchuk to come over to the pound. When he came back, Brown was showing Tizzard some of the other findings; clear plastic pouches the team had spread out over the Forensics van's floor.

"I don't know them all, but those patches are Fentanyl, those pills are Percocet, and there are at least ten cases of Tylenol 3's with codeine. There's also cough medicine and some stuff I've never seen before. A real pharmacy," said Brown.

Tizzard and Windflower made the snowy drive back to the detachment in silence, each processing the information they had received. A picture was being drawn but it looked more like a jigsaw puzzle with lots of pieces still missing. Windflower dropped his Corporal off at the detachment to set up the storm operation, then went home to grab a few hours of sleep. He would need it to get through the long night ahead.

Chapter Eighteen

Windflower awoke with a start. It took him a few seconds to realize where he was; daytime naps often shook him up. It was dark, but only because the days were much shorter this time of year. He took a quick shower and spent a few minutes tidying up the spare room for Brown. Luckily, nobody had stayed there since his Uncle Frank the past summer, so the sheets and linens were still clean. After replacing the towels in the bathroom and a quick vacuum of the living room, Windflower felt ready to welcome his guest.

He left the lights on in the kitchen and living room, and went back to work. The weather was no better and he wondered if the decision had been made to close the highway. He hoped so. It was really starting to pile up and out on the barren areas it would be whipping across the road drifts. There was no other traffic on the side-roads but when he arrived at the RCMP Detachment all the lights were on, and it looked like all hands were on deck.

Tizzard was directing traffic from the reception desk out front and MacDonald was in the storm radio chair. "We've just closed the highway," Tizzard said to Windflower. "Evanchuk and Fortier are on their way towards Marystown to set up the barricades. Forensics is going to ride with the snowplow operator down to Fortune."

"We might as well help out," said Brown as he came out of the back with two Styrofoam cups of coffee, and his crew. "These guys will do the early shift and Grainger and

I will come back after midnight. I was hoping to crash at your place for a few hours if that's okay."

"Sure, I'll give you a lift up there," said Windflower.

Brown grabbed his overnight bag and followed Windflower out to the car.

"So what did you find at Fallon's place?" Windflower asked Brown.

"The snow had covered up anything outside. Fallon was killed in the kitchen. There was tons of blood but it doesn't look like there was much of a struggle. Fallon was a big boy who probably would not have liked being stabbed. This suggests he may have been unconscious when it happened; asleep, passed out drunk, maybe. Unfortunately, the snow covered up any outdoor evidence," said Brown.

"Drugged?" asked Windflower.

"Given the amounts of pharmaceuticals around it might be a good guess," said Brown. "You can get the Coroner to check that out. Is it still Doc Sanjay? I love that guy."

"Sanjay is still around. He is a good man. Okay, this is your stop. Your room is the smaller one and there are food and drinks in the fridge. Help yourself to anything you want."

"Thanks, Winston. I'll see you later on. Be safe."

Windflower waited until Brown got into the house, and then headed back to the office. When he arrived, things were even busier than before.

"Froude's Taxi has gone off the road, just outside of town. Evanchuk and Fortier are on the scene. Multiple injuries. The ambulance is on its way," said Tizzard.

"Let's go."

Windflower and Tizzard ran to his Jeep.

"Do we know how many people were on board?" Windflower asked.

"Not yet," said Tizzard. "It's the middle of the week so probably not too many."

"Let's hope not," Windflower said.

The car radio then crackled to life: "Evanchuk in mobile one reporting in."

"Windflower, here, report, over."

"Four injuries, sir. Three serious, including the driver, over," said Evanchuk.

"Have you got everybody out, over?" asked Windflower.

"Negative, the driver is unconscious and one of the injured is pregnant. We're afraid to move her, over," said Evanchuk.

"Okay, we're almost there. And we have emergency services, over and out."

Windflower escorted the ambulance to the accident scene just over the hill.

Fortunately, the snow had seemed to dissipate but it didn't make the accident site any less chaotic. Fortier was talking to a man who was sitting on the ground a short distance away from the mini-bus that was tipped into the deep ditch at the side of the road. Evanchuk was half-ways inside the van talking to an obviously distressed woman with a small child.

Windflower ran to the vehicle and nodded to Evanchuk. "It's going to be okay, Ma'am," he said to the woman. "The paramedics are here. They will look after you now." The woman looked terrified, and very pregnant. A little girl holding a doll sat next to her, rocking back and forth. "Constable Evanchuk is going to take your daughter over to my warm police Jeep, right there."

Evanchuk took the little girl by the hand. She didn't want to go, and her mother really didn't want to let her. Eventually Evanchuk separated them, and got the girl over to Windflower's vehicle. One of the paramedics tended to the woman while the other ran to the driver.

"We'll need some help to lift him out," the one near the driver said to Windflower, yet Tizzard was already there. Together they lifted the unconscious driver out of the vehicle and onto the stretcher.

The other paramedic had somewhat calmed down the pregnant woman. Very gently he helped get her to her feet and out of the vehicle, and Windflower helped get her into Windflower's vehicle. "I think she may be going into labour," said the paramedic to Windflower. "She needs to get to the clinic ASAP."

"Tizzard," yelled Windflower. "Take my car and bring them to Emerg." Tizzard ran to Windflower's vehicle and was on the way to the clinic as fast as the roads would allow.

Meanwhile, both paramedics were huddled over the driver who was now out of the vehicle, but having extreme difficulty breathing. One of them yelled, "Trach!" and the other raced to the ambulance and came back with a kit. He pulled out a knife and a straw and made a quick incision in the victim's throat and stuck the straw down into the hole.

"That'll get us to the clinic," said the first paramedic to Windflower. Windflower helped lift the man into the ambulance and they took off back down the highway. As they were leaving, a second ambulance and the volunteer fire department were just arriving, which was when Windflower realized they had another patient. He went over to see Fortier and the man on the ground in the snow.

"Winston. Man, my head hurts," said the man.

Windflower silently stared for a second, not comprehending what was happening. Then he figured it out. "Uncle Frank, are you okay?"

"I got an awful knock on the head. What the heck is with these ditches? Someone is going to get killed. You need to do something about that, Winston."

"We're working on it. I'll listen to your story later. Right now Constable Fortier will take you to the ambulance to get you checked out at the clinic."

"Okay, Winston. Mario and I will get along fine. Don't worry about me."

Fortier smiled at Windflower as he led Uncle Frank to the waiting ambulance. Windflower and Evanchuk set up flares on the highway and barricades denoting the accident scene. Windflower left Fortier and Evanchuk to manage the area and went back to the detachment.

It was turning out to be quite a night. A snow storm, another serious accident, and his uncle was back. And it wasn't over yet.

CHAPTER NINETEEN

The detachment was lively as the various officers carried out their tasks through the night. The highway between Grand Bank and Marystown stayed closed overnight to allow the accident investigation to begin and to start clearing the debris. There were also numerous calls between HQ, the highways people, and media relations. But after a couple of hours, things calmed down long enough for Windflower to take a short trip to the clinic to check up on the accident victims, and to see his Uncle Frank.

Windflower met the duty doctor in his office and got the good news that Grand Bank had a new citizen. Tobias Francis Grandy was born shortly after his mother arrived at the clinic from the accident scene. Mother, baby, and big sister were all doing well and fast asleep in a room down the hall. The news about the driver of the taxi was not as cheerful, though.

Wilf Malloy was in stable condition, but not out of danger yet. He had sustained multiple fractures, and the extent of the internal damage still wasn't clear, or if there was any brain damage. Windflower knew all about that possibility because Sheila had been touch and go after her accident and they had to wait until the swelling went down to make an accurate diagnosis. She had even suffered a brain aneurism and a stroke, so Windflower knew how bad it could be, if the worst was to unfold.

Windflower headed to see his Uncle Frank.

The prognosis for his uncle was actually the best news of all. Windflower knew his uncle was okay even before he got the medical report because he heard laughter coming from Frank's room as he approached. Two nurses and the paramedics were laughing at something Frank had just said.

"Come in, Winston, and meet my new friends. I've been telling them all about you, the best Mountie in Newfoundland."

"That's what I was afraid of," said Windflower as the other people left the room. "I can see you're feeling better."

"My head still hurts but I'm in pretty good shape," said his uncle as he attempted to get out of bed to demonstrate his physical abilities.

"That won't be necessary," said Windflower, pushing his uncle back into bed. "Why don't you rest up tonight? Tomorrow, if you're feeling okay, we'll give you your old room at my house."

"Okay. To tell you the truth I am a bit tired. Good night, Winston."

Windflower had no doubt he was tired, and closed the door and bid goodnight to the duty staff. You never knew what Uncle Frank had been up to, but he was sure to have a few stories to tell about his adventures.

Windflower drove back to the RCMP office with the help of a full moon in the clearing sky. The detachment lights were all still on but Windflower could sense, even from the outside looking in, that the situation had calmed down considerably.

When he got inside Corporal Brown was sitting with Tizzard having a cup of coffee. Windflower got a cup and joined them.

"I sent MacDonald and Fortier home. They were both exhausted," said Tizzard.

"You must be too," said Brown. "I just got here a while little ago. I guess we missed all the excitement."

"It was an event, that's for sure," said Windflower. "A storm, a birth almost on the side of the highway, and one person still in serious condition."

"How's Uncle Frank?" asked Tizzard.

"Frank is going to be fine," said Windflower. "My aunt was right. God does look after drunks and fools."

Brown cut in.

"Why don't you guys go get some sleep? Grainger and I can hold the fort till morning and will call if something happens."

Windflower was about to object when Tizzard pre-empted him and said, "That would be great. These long nights are interfering with my beauty sleep."

Windflower thought about correcting his Corporal but looked at him and smiled instead. "We'll take you up on your kind offer. But make sure you call us if anything else happens, alright?"

"Absolutely. See you in the morning," said Brown.

A very tired but relieved Windflower and Tizzard headed their separate ways home.

Windflower remembered taking his clothes off and lying down in his bed, but slept so deeply it was like he didn't sleep at all because the next thing he knew his alarm blared its wakeup call.

Chapter Twenty

It was still dark as Windflower pulled his hoodie over his pajamas and went outside to do his morning prayers. He brought with him his eagle feather, a gift from his late grandfather who had been chief of his nation in Pink Lake in Northern Alberta. His grandfather was long gone, as were his parents, so this feather was one of his last connections to his family. He also took his medicine bag and poured a little of the mixture into his smudge bowl. When it was burning well, he took the feather and passed the smoke over his head and his body and the soles of his feet.

Then he offered up his prayers and intentions for the day. He thanked Creator for all the gifts he had already received, and for the end of the storm. He also gave thanks for those who were with him on this journey, both two-legged and four-legged. He asked for wisdom and guidance to stay true to his path, and at the end he laid down a little tobacco for the people hurt in the accident, and for the new soul brought into the world last night. When he finished his prayers he went back inside to shower and shave, and shortly after, left for work.

A few minutes later he was walking into the RCMP detachment. The first thing he noticed was the aroma coming from the lunchroom. It was the unmistakable smell of bacon frying in a pan. He could also hear raised voices and laughter. It had to be Tizzard.

"Good morning, Boss," said Tizzard. "You're just in time for round two."

Tizzard was standing at the stove wearing an apron and a large smile. Gathered around the table were Brown and his Forensics crew, happily engaged in devouring what Windflower suspected to be round one.

"We couldn't send them off empty-handed, or at least with an empty stomach," said Tizzard.

"He's doing a great job. I recommend Tizzard's kitchen to anyone," said Brown.

Everyone laughed, including Windflower, and he got himself a cup of coffee while he waited for his bacon and eggs. When breakfast was over, the Forensics guys packed up and headed back to St. John's. Windflower helped Tizzard clean up and then went back to his office to check his messages and e-mail. He was just getting started when he saw Tizzard walk by his office with the dog.

"I'm taking Lady out for a walk," said Tizzard, and as he spoke, the dog pulled away from him and ran to Windflower to get petted. "She certainly likes you. And she's great company around the detachment. At night when you're here alone she just curls up under your feet."

"Why don't you keep her then?" asked Windflower.

"That's not going to happen. I wouldn't be responsible enough. I have enough trouble looking after myself. But you, on the other hand..." and Tizzard let it hang there.

Windflower started to say no, but then he stopped himself. Tizzard could see the hesitation and went in for the kill. "Why don't you think about it today and if you decide not to keep her, you can take her with you to Marystown tomorrow?" Tizzard asked.

"Why not? You are much smarter than you look, Corporal. And that's a good thing. Now take the dog for her walk."

Tizzard smiled, made a mock salute and retrieved both the dog and the leash from Windflower's side. After he left, Windflower wondered if he really wanted a dog. What would Sheila think about the idea? Come to think of it, he hadn't talked to Sheila in a short while. She had spoken about staying with the Stoodleys last night, but it was too early to call. He could probably talk to Herb Stoodley though, because it was likely he was still on kitchen duty at the café.

Windflower jumped in his car and headed over to the Mug-Up, passing Tizzard along the way who was very clearly pleased with himself.

He parked in front and was soon standing at the counter talking to Herb, who was finishing up his shift.

"Go sit down and I'll bring us both a cup of coffee," Herb said.

CHAPTER TWENTY-ONE

"I hear that was a bad accident last night," said Herb.

"Yeah, the taxi went into the ditch pretty hard. It was almost a good thing it was stormy, because I'm sure that slowed him down. It could have been a lot worse, especially with a pregnant woman on board."

"Mayor Sinnott has been worried about that stretch of road ever since they fixed it up after the hurricane. He keeps saying someone is going to die out there."

"He may be right," said Windflower, deciding at least for now, to keep quiet about Sinnott's request that was sitting on his desk. "Did Sheila sleep at your place last night?"

"She did. We had supper and played a game of cards. I don't know what they were talking about, but she and Moira were still gabbing in the kitchen when I went to bed."

"I guess you know that Sheila and I have been having some discussions," said Windflower.

"'The whole town has been chatting about you two ever since Sheila got arrested at the protest. Everyone is trying to figure out how the arrested and the arrester can get along together," he continued with a smile.

"It's not funny," said Windflower.

"Agreed. But you have to admit that it's pretty good gossip for a small town like Grand Bank. And what **are** you going to do, anyway?"

"I don't know yet. But first I'm going to see how she feels about having a dog around. Thanks for the coffee, Herb."

Herb just shook his head at the last remark. "Say, why don't you both come over for dinner on Sunday? Moira's decided to shut the place early during the winter and if I can dig it out, I'd love to crank up the barbeque."

"Now, that's an offer I can't refuse. I'll check with Sheila and let you know."

Tizzard was walking into the Mug-Up as Windflower was leaving. They made plans to meet up later at the clinic to check in with Dr. Sanjay regarding his examinations.

Windflower drove the short distance to Sheila's house and was pleased to see her outside clearing the walkway to her back door. He followed her into the kitchen and sat at the table, and watched her put the kettle on for tea.

He had two simultaneous thoughts: one, this was an especially beautiful woman, and two, he really missed being around her.

Before he could tell her these things, she said, "So I've been doing some thinking."

In Windflower's experience that meant she had reached some sort of decision. He hoped it was in his favour.

"I realize that my protesting has impacted you and your work and I am very sorry about that. I do not regret my choice, nor my role in standing up for my community. I intend to be an activist in my community and I hope that doesn't mean having to get arrested again. I promise to talk you first before making any decisions that could lead to that in the future."

"Thank you. I can see you are trying to come as close to my side of the fence as possible and I appreciate that. I have always admired the way you stick to your beliefs and I want to support you. I can't support you getting arrested. That is a bit of a conflict with my policing role. But I do support you in every other way."

"Thank you, Winston. So does that mean we can be back together now?"

"That depends on how you feel about having a dog," said Windflower with a laugh. He then proceeded to tell her about Lady and his Uncle being back and the accident from last night. By the time they finished talking they were firmly back together and looking forward to some special time together later in the day.

"Oh, and we're invited to the Stoodley's on Sunday night for supper," yelled Windflower as he was heading out the door to go meet Tizzard at the coroner's office.

When he got to the clinic, he dropped in to see his Uncle Frank who was fully engaged in regaling the nurses with some of his jokes and stories about his adventures. He made sure his uncle had checked in with his wife to let her know he was okay, and then went down the hall where Tizzard was already talking to Dr. Sanjay.

"Good morning, Sergeant," said the Coroner. "Your Corporal here has been filling me in about the accident last night. I am sorry your uncle was involved, but he seems in fine spirits. He's quite a character, isn't he? He was telling me all about you."

"That's what I'm afraid of, Doc. What news do you have from your investigations?"

"I do have some things to report. Regarding the late Mr. Ridgeway, I am close to certain his death was heart failure brought about by other substances in his circulatory system. Until we get the toxicology reports it will be difficult to pinpoint exactly what those substances were, though. There is also a possibility he was poisoned."

"Poisoned? With what?" asked Tizzard.

"While we are waiting for the test results, we can't say with certainty, but I have a friend in the lab at St. John's who's agreed to take a look for both opiates and some known poisons to check my theory. The tox reports would normally take weeks, but since my contacts are making this a priority, I may have something as early as Monday," said Sanjay.

"That would be good. Can we release the body to the family? They're likely going to cremate," said Windflower.

"We have all we need from the corpse," said Sanjay.

"What about Frankie Fallon?" asked Tizzard.

"This may be a simpler case, but there might still be questions."

The doctor led the two men to the refrigerated area at the back of his office where Fallon's body was draped. The doctor then pulled back the sheet.

"As you can see, the deceased has a large cavity at the rear of his skull, which indicates a blow with a blunt object. That might have killed him. There are also at least a dozen points of entry from another sharp object, a large knife by the looks of it."

"So maybe he was hit over the head and then stabbed to make sure he was dead. Even so, he's a big man and there wasn't any sign of a struggle at the scene," said

Windflower. "Was there more than one person involved, and could it be possible he was drugged?"

"Possibly, but my simple medical examination wouldn't show that," said Dr. Sanjay. "The rest is lab and police work."

"That means us," said Windflower as he looked at Tizzard. "You head back. I'm going to stop by and see Uncle Frank."

Tizzard nodded and left.

"Thanks, Doc. Let us know as soon as you find out anything about Ridgeway."

"I will, Sergeant. By the way, do you have any time this weekend? Our Highland Park is waiting and my chessboard has become very lonely."

Windflower laughed. "I think so, but I'll let you know."

He left the Coroner's office and walked back to his uncle's room where the doctor was just leaving. "He's ready to go home," said the doctor. "He doesn't have any concussion symptoms and appears normal."

"Appearances can be deceiving," said Windflower with a smile. "Thank you, Doctor."

"So, Uncle, are you ready to come home?" asked Windflower.

"I am. And I'm starving. They couldn't feed a bird on what they give you here. I want a nice piece of fried bologna and eggs and some toast."

"I think you're going to be okay. Get your stuff together. I'll take you home and make you some breakfast," said Windflower.

His uncle's grumbling died down soon after they got to Windflower's house. He put on a fresh pot of coffee and made them both a late breakfast of fried eggs and bologna along with several pieces each of home-made toast and jam. Uncle Frank was out back having a cigarette and Windflower was in the kitchen cleaning up when Tizzard's vehicle rapidly pulled into his driveway.

Tizzard blew into Windflower's like a gust from a winter storm.

"What's going on?" asked Windflower.

Tizzard couldn't get the words out fast enough. "Boss, the Mayor's had a heart attack! They've rushed him to the clinic!"

CHAPTER TWENTY-TWO

"What happened?" asked Windflower.

"I was going into the Mug-Up when they were carrying him out. One of the EMTs said it was a heart attack. I gave them an escort to the clinic," said Tizzard.

"So what's going on up there?" asked Windflower. "Is he going to be okay?"

"They were working on him when I left, but it didn't look good to me. He wasn't moving," said Tizzard.

"Who wasn't movin?" asked Uncle Frank as he came in from the back porch.

"Mayor Sinnott," said Tizzard. "I think he's had a heart attack."

"That's too bad," said Uncle Frank. "He is a good man, a powerful force in this community. I hope he's going to be okay. Anyway, I have to go and see my friends. We'll see you later."

"Uncle Frank is right," said Tizzard. "He does seem to hold this town together."

"He is a good man. Keep me posted on how he's doing, okay? Now, I've got to go see a dog," said Windflower.

"See you later," said Tizzard.

Windflower spent a couple of hours at the detachment cleaning up files and correspondence until it was finally time to quit for the day. He took Lady out of the back cell and put her in the back of his Jeep. When he got home, he put out a bowl of food and a fresh bowl of water. He also spread an old blanket on the floor in the corner of the kitchen. "Here you go, Lady. Welcome to your new home."

Lady spent a few minutes circulating around the house, checking out all the new sights and smells. She seemed particularly interested in the room where Uncle Frank's stuff was sitting on the floor and circled around his bags a couple of times before plopping herself down on his luggage. "Okay, you can stay there for now. But your bed is going to be in the kitchen." She was pretty much asleep already though. He left her sleeping on the floor and went over to Sheila's.

When he got there he called out to her as he took off his boots and coat.

"I'm upstairs. I saved the bath for you. If you don't mind I think I'd rather have dessert first tonight."

Windflower didn't mind at all.

Later, in their robes, they ate some fish chowder that Sheila made earlier. It was full of thick pieces of cod, shrimp, mussels and clams. It also had a special tang that Windflower couldn't recognize as much as he tried. It was Sheila's secret ingredient; a big hunk of blue cheese mixed in with the fish and cream and vegetables. They shared chunks off a baguette along with a bit more of the blue cheese, and washed it all down with a cold glass of Chablis.

"A toast to the most beautiful woman in my world," he said, offering his glass up to Sheila.

"Thank you, Winston," said Sheila, raising her glass in return. "To our continued health and happiness."

"Speaking of health, that's terrible about Mayor Sinnott, I hope he's okay," said Windflower.

"Me too," said Sheila. "I'm not surprised he has heart problems with all that weight he's carrying around. But his shoes will be pretty big ones to fill if he can't continue."

"They would be. But I know someone who could do it."

"Who?" said Sheila as she reached for another piece of bread.

"You," said Windflower.

"Me? I thought you wanted me to maintain a low profile," said Sheila.

"No, what I said is I don't want you getting arrested. I think you have great leadership abilities and you would be a far better choice than any of the other possible candidates."

"I don't think we've ever had a female mayor in Grand Bank," said Sheila.

"That would make you the first," said Windflower. "Think about it. I would support you."

"Maybe you could start showing your support for me by drying the dishes while I wash up," said Sheila.

"Absolutely," said Windflower.

The pair had a comfortable and cozy evening lying on the couch watching an old movie on TV. This time it was The Great Escape, starring Steve McQueen. It was based on a true story about a group of POWs who managed to escape from what was thought to be an inescapable Nazi prison camp. But Windflower's and Sheila's favourite character in the movie was James Garner, who played a loveable type who could find anything that the big cheeses needed to make the escape possible.

Before they went to bed for the evening they planned out their weekend; on Friday night Sheila would be staying in Fortune weather permitting, and Windflower would visit with Doctor Sanjay. Saturday night was Fortier's going-away party at the Lions Club and Sunday night was dinner at the Stoodleys. Now that Windflower knew where his next food and drinks were coming from, and where he stood with his girl, he slept the sleep of angels.

Windflower awoke early and crept out of the bedroom. He dressed quickly in the bathroom and left the house swiftly and quietly, letting Sheila sleep in on her day off.

When he got home, only when he saw the bowls and the blanket in the kitchen did he remember the dog. He hoped she was okay. At first he didn't see her but when he passed Uncle Frank's he heard them snoring together.

Lady jumped up when she heard Windflower, but his uncle slept soundly on. Windflower wondered what kind of trouble he got into last night. Once she recognized who he was, she was very happy to see him and Windflower had to admit he was pretty happy too. He patted her on the head and she spun around on the kitchen floor in excitement. It reminded Windflower how long it had been since he had a dog and how much pleasure it brought.

He grabbed her leash and a plastic bag and headed out for a walk. That was one of the other things he'd always enjoyed about being a dog owner; you never had to worry about getting your exercise.

Windflower and Lady did the usual loop around Grand Bank; down to the brook and around the wharf. Things were pretty quiet around town and it was surprisingly mild for a December morning. He wondered if it was a Newfoundland chinook, like the ones back home in Alberta. One could almost hear the snow melt as the warmer air hit it, releasing mist into the air. Since there was really nowhere left to pile up the snow that had already fallen, Windflower felt lucky.

Mike Martin

Back at the house, Windflower re-filled Lady's bowl, had his shower and shave and did his morning prayers while the sun was just rising for the day. This morning he gave thanks to Creator for the gift of travelling with Sheila on his journey. He prayed for the strength and guidance to be a good partner to her. He was also grateful his uncle was safe after the accident. Finally, he laid some tobacco and said a special prayer for Mayor Sinnott to recover from his heart attack and to continue his work in the world.

No time for breakfast, Windflower grabbed a banana on his way out headed to his meeting in Marystown. He could get coffee and a breakfast sandwich there. The ride was peaceful and he only met one car on the highway, another RCMP vehicle. It was Fortier who was doing the final highway loop before his shift was over, and probably his last shift in Grand Bank. Mario Fortier was a good guy who would be missed. Windflower waved good morning and drove on to Marystown. That reminded him about Fortier's replacement and he made a mental note to talk to Inspector Ford about it.

CHAPTER TWENTY-THREE

L ess than an hour later Windflower was sitting in the Tim Hortons in Marystown eating his breakfast sandwich, drinking his double-double, and watching the small town come to life at the coffee shop drive-though. He was almost ready to leave when he saw two familiar faces coming through the entrance.

"Good morning, Winston, how the hell are ya, b'y?" boomed his old friend Ron Quigley. With Quigley was another smiling person he recognized quickly. It was Sgt. Carl Langmead of the Royal Newfoundland Constabulary, the provincial police force.

"Good morning, gentlemen," said Windflower in return. "I knew you were going to be here," he said to Quigley. "But I am surprised to see you, Carl."

"I've been seconded, some people say corrupted, to work with Ron and the RCMP on the opiate file," said Langmead. "Care for another coffee? Quigley tells me it's my turn to buy. But he always says that."

"Sure. Double-double," said Windflower, as the RNC officer went up to the counter to place the order.

"So what's new? Did you get snared with the marriage noose yet?" asked Quigley.

"No, but I can feel it tightening around my neck," said Windflower with a laugh. "I hear you've got something pretty serious going on yourself. That's what a little birdie told me."

"I'm still on the right side of the marriage bed," said Quigley. "Anything happening in Grand Bank?"

"Two dead bodies, a baby almost born in the ditch on the side of the road, and our Mayor is in the hospital with a heart attack. Plus it feels like we're working around the clock when we get a snow storm every second night. Other than that it's pretty slow."

"Ah, the joys of small town policing. I decided long ago that wasn't the life for me," said Quigley.

"He needs constant entertaining," said Langmead as he returned with a tray and three large cups of coffee.

"I'm a corner boy, a townie," said Quigley. "I could never be a bayman like Windflower here."

"That's funny," said Langmead. "Windflower, how does a guy like you, a Cree from Northern Alberta, get to be a bayman?"

"I think you start by getting a girlfriend from around the bay," said Quigley.

"Now you're treading on dangerous territory," said Windflower. "Don't be picking on the Newfie girls. They're da best kind, b'y."

"I told you he was a bayman. We better get a move on. Our meeting starts at 9:00 and it's ten to," said Quigley.

A few minutes later the three men were seated around the boardroom table in the large meeting room upstairs in the Marystown RCMP detachment. In addition to Windflower, Quigley and Langmead, there were two other RCMP officers, one from each of the other territories in Inspector Ford's jurisdiction. But interestingly, there was no Inspector Ford.

"Can you go check on the Inspector while I set up the presentation?" Quigley asked Windflower.

"Sure," Windflower responded, leaving the boardroom to go down to Ford's office. When he got there, his receptionist Louise was there, but there was no sign of the Inspector.

"Hello, Louise. Have you seen the Inspector?"

"Not yet," Louise said professionally, yet with a tinge of irritation that Windflower immediately recognized as disapproval. Somebody was in trouble with the real boss of the place.

"When he arrives, tell him we're in the training room upstairs," Windflower said as politely as he could. He departed quickly to rejoin his group in the boardroom.

Windflower gave a quick shake of his head to Quigley who picked up his cue and started the session. "Let's get going. We've got a lot to cover and Inspector Ford has been delayed and will be joining us later." He turned on his computer and started going through his PowerPoint presentation.

Quigley's presentation was deep, dark and disturbing to his fellow officers, each of whom had only a small piece of the picture when it came to opiate use and abuse in their areas. What started as prescribed pain medications had become the overwhelming drugs of choice of addicts in both the country and the province. The stats were startling: between 500,000 and 1,250,000 people were using opioids non-medically, the fourth-most prevalent form of substance use in Canada behind alcohol, tobacco, and cannabis. People were dying slowly from addiction and more quickly from overdose. The number of deaths related to prescription opiates had increased five to seven times, depending on the jurisdiction in Canada, in the previous 10 years. And it was still growing.

"What about the shift away from Oxycontin?" asked one of the officers as Quigley was going through his report. "Didn't getting rid of that help with the problem?"

"It did for a short period of time," said Quigley, referring to a federal government decision to ban the popular painkiller and replace it with a more tamper-resistant formulation, known as OxyNEO, which is difficult to snort, chew or inject. "But now we're seeing the addiction shift to Fentanyl and other non-Oxy opiates like hydromorphone."

"Canada is now the highest opioid-consuming country, per capita, in the world," said Quigley as he prepared to wrap up his presentation. "And it's a big problem right here in Newfoundland. Why don't you tell them what you're seeing, Carl?"

"In Newfoundland and Labrador we have an epidemic of opiate use and abuse," said Langmead. "We know from the general statistics the situation here in our province is no better than in other parts of the country. And in some ways it is much worse. Now grade school age kids are getting hooked by trying some of the prescription meds they're stealing from their parent's medicine cabinets. They are sharing drugs and needles and by the time they get to high school they are full-fledged drug addicts. We don't have nearly enough resources to deal with the impact this has in the larger centres like St. John's and Corner Brook, and we know the situation is sometimes worse in smaller communities."

One of the other officers, the RCMP rep from Stephenville, added, "Last month we had an operation where we seized over 500 Diluadids and 300 Percocets in one raid. That would be a year's prescription for somebody that ended up on the street in our little town."

"Exactly. We're making it harder to get drugs the conventional ways so now they're being more devious.

One of the ways that's showing up is in pharmacy hold-ups and break-ins. On the Avalon Peninsula, there have been incidents at almost every pharmacy in the area, from armed robberies to threats and demands from drug users. This past summer saw multiple armed robberies every weekend, including one pharmacy in Conception Bay South that got robbed twice in one day by two different robbers," said Langmead.

The other officers, including Windflower, just shook their heads at this news.

"There are some other factors at work that are leading to an even bigger problem, now and down the road," said Quigley. "We are working with both the medical community and the pharmacies to seal up the supply of opiates from those who don't have or require a prescription. But there are a few rogue doctors and even some pharmacists who are part of the problem."

"You all remember the doctor in St. John's, Brockingham?" asked Langmead. "He was convicted of 23 charges of providing women with prescription medications, such as OxyContin and Lorazepam, in return for sexual favours. He wasn't the only one. We know there are others but they got scared off when he got charged. Now we think some of them are not only over-prescribing but selling the scripts as well."

"There also appears to be an organized gang operating in the province that is orchestrating the illegal activity around opiates. They were headquartered in St. John's but the RNC put the heat on and we now think they are coalescing in both Western Newfoundland and right here on the southeast coast. That's why we brought all of you in together so we could talk about how we can cooperate. I know that's a lot of information to take in. Let's take a break and we'll get back together in twenty minutes to talk strategy," said Quigley.

Windflower's head was spinning with all the information he had just been provided. He needed a few minutes away from everybody to clear his head and process what he had heard. It looked like Michael Ridgeway may well have been a rogue pharmacist, albeit a dead one. But could he really have been involved with an organized group? He sounded like a bit of a loner.

Windflower thought some cool morning air might help, so he walked to the back of the building and stepped out through the entrance to the parking lot. On his way out he almost bumped into Inspector Ford, on his way into the building.

"Good morning, Inspector. We missed you at the meeting," said Windflower.

"I was tied up," Ford said gruffly, nearly pushing his way past Windflower to get into the building. He looked a bit worse for wear. Maybe even a little shaky.

"Are you okay, Bill? I'd like to talk to you about the replacement for Fortier when you have a chance."

"Talk to Louise," said Ford. And just like that he was gone, leaving Windflower a little stunned and surprised because Ford used to be his friend.

Windflower continued through the parking lot and walked around to the front entrance where Quigley and Langmead were standing.

"I should tell you what's going on over in Grand Bank," said Windflower. "It sounds to me like we have an opiate problem too. A big one."

"Let's go back inside and share our intel. Langmead here was telling me about an old friend of yours that is now involved again on the wrong side of the law," said Quigley.

"And who would that be?" asked Windflower.

"Shawn Parsons," said Langmead.

Chapter Twenty-Four

Windflower told the rest of the group about Michael Ridgeway and finding the body of Frankie Fallon in the trunk of his car. He also spoke about his discussions with the pharmacist in Fortune and their concerns about activities at that location.

"We have been monitoring all the pharmacies since the rash of robberies over the past year, yet we didn't receive any report about a break-in," said Quigley.

"The break-in report got mislaid," Windflower said without embarrassment, reminding himself to talk to Tizzard and MacDonald again when he got back. "But we're now doing a complete review of their inventory and opiate reports. I'll be able to give you more information about that later. So tell me about Shawn Parsons. How does he fit into all this?"

"You remember we had Parsons in custody last summer in connection with the double-homicide case involving his sister. We were investigating his involvement in dealing drugs in St. John's, but because he turned over on some of his former accomplices, he got out on bail. We've lost track of him but now think he's back into the business, big time."

"We think he's involved with the opiate ring in the province," said Quigley. "He's been spotted in Corner Brook and even right here in Marystown. We're starting to close in. Pomeroy's been assigned to track him. He couldn't be here today but we get regular reports."

"Why don't you just pull Parsons in?" asked an officer from Stephenville.

"We will, but we also want to make sure we get all his suppliers. That includes at least two doctors we already know about. The net is closing in, but we want to get everybody, not just Parsons," said Quigley.

The officers spent the rest of the morning together talking about the next steps, including a weekly conference call for the next few months. On the way out of the meeting Windflower excused himself and went back to Ford's office to talk to Louise about the replacement for Fortier. Ford's office door was closed and Louise didn't look any happier about the situation now than she did earlier. She promised to check up on Windflower's request and he left, still wondering what the heck was going on with Inspector Bill Ford.

Windflower headed back to Tim Hortons and bought a large black tea and a sandwich to eat in his Jeep on the way back to Grand Bank. It had been a long week and a lot had happened since he rolled out of bed on Monday morning. The solitary drive back would give him a chance to think about it all and reflect on what he'd just heard in the meeting, including the fact that Shawn Parsons was back on the scene. Windflower had a lot of things to sort out and luckily he had an hour and a half drive to do just that.

By the time Windflower re-entered Grand Bank, he at least had a short-term plan. First up was to see Sheila, and then talk to Tizzard about the pharmacist and MacDonald. After that he hoped to have a quiet afternoon followed by an evening of scotch-tasting and chess with his friend, Dr.

Vijay Sanjay. All of these things were reassuring, as he had hoped for a quiet Friday afternoon.

Before he even had his coat off, Betsy cornered him with a stack of messages and pointed towards his office. "Brenda Ridgeway is waiting for you in your office, sir."

Windflower took a glance at the messages, almost all of which were from media types, then looked back at Betsy.

"They want to know about the body found in the trunk of the car, sir," she said.

Windflower just shook his head. "Is Corporal Tizzard around?" was all he could say.

"He should be back any minute. He said he was going over to Fortune."

"Thank you, Betsy. Tell him to come see me when he gets back." He tucked the messages into his pocket and went back to his office.

Brenda Ridgeway was in her early forties, tall and slim, and dressed in a dark navy-blue pantsuit with a light flowery scarf. Her hair was jet black with a tinge of red highlights and her Michael Kors handbag was set by her feet. She rose to greet Windflower with a firm handshake.

"Brenda Ridgeway," she said. "You must be Sergeant Windflower."

"Sergeant Winston Windflower. Can I offer you some tea or coffee?"

"No thank you, Sergeant. I'm only here to make arrangements for Michael's remains. Your Corporal has been very helpful in that regard and I am on my way this evening to meet with the funeral home for the cremation."

"I'm pleased Corporal Tizzard was of assistance to you," said Windflower.

"Thank you. But I also wanted to talk to you directly. My brother Michael was an addict and when he was using drugs he was a completely different person, not a nice person. But he had cleaned himself up and was trying to start over here in Grand Bank, you know." She started tearing up and reached for a Kleenex from her purse.

Windflower smiled to acknowledge her emotions and she continued.

"I knew he was using again, almost as soon as it happened. We are close, we always have been, and Michael couldn't hide anything from me, even when he wanted to. I knew he was in trouble with drugs again. But there was more going on than just his addiction," Brenda said.

"What do you mean?" asked Windflower.

"I think Michael was being blackmailed."

As she said this, Tizzard burst into Windflower's office like a full-on gale force nor'wester. She was startled.

"Sit down, Corporal, Ms. Ridgeway is giving us some information which may be pertinent to our investigations. Go on, Ms. Ridgeway. You think that your brother was being blackmailed?" Windflower said in a calm tone.

Tizzard's eyes grew as wide as saucers but he managed to restrain himself.

"I do. When Michael was actively using drugs he would often ask to borrow 100 bucks, maybe even a few hundred. And you made you sure didn't leave any cash or your credit cards lying around near him. In the past few months he asked me to lend him $5,000."

"That's a lot of money. Did you give it to him?" asked Windflower.

"I did. I thought he might be doing drugs but he still sounded sane. He said he wanted to buy a snowmobile.

Maybe I shouldn't have done it, but I did anyway. Then he came back again, and this time he asked for $10,000, but I said no."

Windflower waited patiently as the woman paused. Finally, she continued.

"Then he started calling and telling me he had to have the money and that guys were after him. That something bad was going to happen. I thought he was just stringing me along so that I would give him the money. I stopped taking his calls."

By now the tears were streaming down Brenda Ridgeway's face and she was making no attempt to stop them. "I didn't know he was really in trouble. I would have helped him. I could have helped him," she said as she broke down, sobbing into her hands.

"It's not your fault," said Windflower kindly, but she would not be easily reassured.

He turned to Tizzard. "Why don't you take Ms. Ridgeway to the back and make her a cup of tea?"

"Corporal Tizzard will take your statement when you're ready. Thank you for telling us about this. It is very helpful and we will investigate it fully."

Tizzard lead her by the arm into the lunchroom.

Windflower didn't have time to really process all of this when he heard, "Inspector Ford on line 1," through the intercom on his phone. "Thank you, Betsy," he responded and picked up the phone.

"What's going on over there?" asked Inspector Ford when Windflower answered.

"What do you mean, sir?" asked Windflower.

"I mean the press is all over the Frankie Fallon death, even though we haven't released any info on the case. Do you know how stupid that makes us look? How did they find out about it?" asked Ford, his voice rising with each subsequent question.

"I don't know. It didn't come out of this office. We've barely had a chance to dig out from the snow we've had. I'm guessing it's somebody at the clinic. But not much we can do about it now."

"You can talk to media relations and at least give them a statement they can hand out. You got any leads on that yet?"

"Not yet, sir," said Windflower. "We had Forensics here yesterday and nothing back from them yet. We don't even have the Coroner's report."

"Well you better get cracking on it, Windflower."

CHAPTER TWENTY-FIVE

Before Windflower could respond the line went dead. Once again, Windflower was left thinking about what happened to his old friend Bill Ford. As he was thinking, he could see Tizzard walking out the door with Brenda Ridgeway. Tizzard waved and held up his five fingers to Windflower.

In less than five minutes Tizzard was back in Windflower's office, having dropped her off at the B & B. "I'll get her full statement tomorrow. She was too upset to talk today. That blackmail is something, isn't it?"

"If it's true then it makes Michael Ridgeway's death even more suspicious. How's your investigation going over at the pharmacy?"

"Evanchuk's been doing most of the work," said Tizzard. "I put the fear of God into Laura Emberley, so she's fully cooperating now. I think she was trying to cover up for Michael Ridgeway. Anyway, Evanchuk found that there are two missing opiate reports: July and October. She's checking the inventory reports now and should have something for us after the weekend."

"That's good. I should also bring you up to speed on the opiates situation."

Windflower spent a few minutes updating Tizzard on his meeting in Marystown.

"Do you think our stuff's connected?" asked Tizzard.

"Looks like it. We know that Ridgeway was mixed-up with opiates, but where does Frankie Fallon fit in? The name that worries me most is Shawn Parsons, though."

"I thought that scumbag was locked up," said Tizzard.

"Not anymore. I guess he's out on bail and up to his old ways by the sound of it. The RNC says he's involved with the opiate gang in this province. They recently had a big seizure on the west coast. Quigley says that the gang is moving into this area as well. We checked out Fallon's place, but never really had a good look at Ridgeway's. I may pop over this weekend to have a look around."

"Yeah, when MacDonald and I went over there, it wasn't a crime investigation scene. It might be now, said Tizzard."

"What's going on with her, anyway? You figure it out yet?" asked Windflower.

"Nope. I gave her the suspended pay letter but she didn't say a peep. I'll be keeping a close eye on her from now on, that's for sure. And in case you didn't hear, Mayor Sinnott's in bad shape."

"What happened now?" asked Windflower.

"He's been rushed to the heart institute in St. John's. He had a couple more heart attacks or seizures after they brought him in. The last I heard it didn't look good. They've got a prayer vigil at the church for him tonight."

"I hope we don't lose him," said Windflower. "He's kinda the glue that holds the place together right now."

"Well, it might be a good time to say a prayer, if you believe in that sort of thing," said Tizzard. "Anyway I'm outta here. I'm doing the overnight shift so I can be off tomorrow for Fortier's shindig."

After Tizzard left, Windflower doubted it'd be much of a party if the Mayor didn't improve. Windflower put him back on his prayer list.

Later that night, everyone but Evanchuk had left for the day when Windflower packed up his bags to head home. He said goodnight to her, got in his Jeep, and drove slowly up the road towards his house. Along the way he saw the lights on at Sheila's and dropped in to say hello.

"Hi, Sheila, it's me," said Windflower as he opened the back door.

"Come on in."

"I guess you probably heard the latest about Mayor Sinnott," he said.

"Yes, people have been calling all morning. We're hoping for the best, but preparing for the worst. All we can do now is pray. I'm glad they've organized the vigil. It's good for the community to be together."

"I can go too, if you'd like."

"No, you go on over to Doctor Sanjay's. I'll be fine."

"Okay, I'll call you later," said Windflower, and gave her a tight hug before leaving.

When he got home all of the lights looked to be on in his little house and music was blaring out of an open window in the kitchen. Inside, Uncle Frank was singing along at the top of his lungs to a country western song on the radio and Windflower was sure he was dancing with a broomstick too. When he saw Windflower he pretended to be sweeping.

"Thanks for cleaning up, Uncle," said Windflower. "You having a party of one?"

"I'm actually heading over to Jarge's for a meal of cod tongues. Then we're going to the lounge to listen to the band," said his uncle.

"Very good. Just don't get into any trouble in my town."

"That's what your friend in Marystown said," Uncle Frank replied.

"My friend?" asked Windflower.

"Bill Ford. I saw him in a bar in Marystown. Didn't he tell you that he saw me?"

"He must have forgotten," said Windflower.

"Anyway, I'm off. I'll see you later. I took Lady out for a walk so she's probably good for awhile.

"Thank you," Windflower said as he patted Lady's head. She was groggy because she just woke up from her afternoon nap.

After Uncle Frank left, Windflower thought about what he'd said. Frank saw Bill Ford in a bar in Marystown. Ford didn't tell him about it because Ford is an alcoholic and probably shouldn't be in that bar. Now he's grumpy and missing meetings at work, which might explain some things.

That was enough thinking for one day, so now it was time for rest and relaxation, which started with a soak in the bath and a good book. Luckily, Sheila had brought him back a book from St. John's. It was Newfoundland writer Michael Crummey's new book, Sweetland. It told the story of a small outport in Newfoundland facing relocation, or 'resettlement' as they called it there. Windflower was feeling pretty pleased with himself as he immersed himself in both the book and the hot water.

Half an hour later he was clean, refreshed and ready for Doctor Sanjay's offer of an evening's entertainment.

He knew there would be Scotch and hoped that samosas would be part of the package. He walked down the road towards the wharf and the fish plant and noticed that while the picket line and demonstrators were gone, there was now an aging freighter tied up at the fish plant berth.

He kept walking across the bridge over the brook and up to the beautiful green salt-box house where Doctor Vijay Sanjay and his wife Repa had lived for years. Windflower went in the back door and could tell immediately from the aromas that his hopes for samosas would be realized. "Good evening," he called out upon entering the small porch at the back of the kitchen.

"Come in, come in," came the response from Dr. Sanjay. "Welcome to our humble abode," he said as he came into the kitchen to greet his guest. "Repa could not be here to welcome you. She has gone to the prayer service for the Mayor. Whenever they have a multi-faith ceremony they always ask her to participate from the Hindu tradition. But she left us some snacks."

"My taste buds are already watering. I can smell samosas, but what is that other delicious smell?" asked Windflower.

"Ah, you will have to wait for that surprise. Come in and say hello to my chessboard first. It has been very lonely without any visitors."

Windflower smiled and followed Dr. Sanjay into his living room. Waiting for them as promised was the plate of samosas with the usual array of hot Bengali relishes. There were also three bottles of Scotch, two tasting glasses and a large carafe of water.

"Let us try the Highland Park before we begin our tournament," said Dr. Sanjay. He poured them both an ounce.

"Ah," was all that Windflower could say after he had smelled the bouquet of the Scotch and had a few sips. "That might be the most perfectly balanced Scotch I have ever tasted."

"Yes, it has that velvety smoke that we all desire and you can taste the honey and peat on the finish. It is expensive, but a small price to pay for ecstasy."

"Well said, my friend. Well said."

"Let the games begin," said Dr. Sanjay with a flourish as he sat on one side of the waiting chessboard. To Windflower's surprise, he won the first game and then the second. But it went downhill from there. Fortunately there was more Scotch and samosas to cushion the blow. They had another sip of the fabulous Talisker that Windflower had tried on his last visit and more of the silky smooth Glenrothe which both men savoured as liquid gold.

The last five losses in the chess game did not subdue Windflower's spirits nor his appetite, and when the doctor led him back into the kitchen he was more than ready to eat.

"This is our own special Bengali fish curry," said Dr. Sanjay as he spooned generous portions of the fragrant curry onto a plate of steamed rice and handed it to Windflower. He took a smaller plate for himself and sat at the kitchen table. "Repa made this before she left for the evening. It is one of our traditional dishes. Back home we would use bream or sea bass, but I like the flavour of cod."

"It is so good. It's almost hot and cool at the same time."

"That is the mustard and chili combination. In the Bengal we would cook it in mustard oil but that's hard to get here. So Repa uses some of the milder mustard seed she can find, and compensates by adding our own special chillies. Be careful of them, Winston. It is not impolite to pick them out. You are not Bengali."

"Too late," said Windflower as he grabbed for the carafe of water the doctor had brought from the living room. "It is really good."

"A little more, then," said the doctor as he scooped up another couple of ladlefuls of the curry and deposited them onto Windflower's plate. "It's sum good, b'y."

"It is sum good b'y," said Windflower as he happily cleaned his plate. He refused all offers of more, and once again graciously thanked his host. He helped Dr. Sanjay clear the table and load the dishwasher. The men made plans to get together again soon and shortly afterwards Windflower left for the short walk home.

It was a peaceful night in Grand Bank and Windflower enjoyed the opportunity to clear his head and to work off a few of the many calories he had consumed during the evening. When he arrived home, Lady was waiting for her nightly ritual and Windflower was glad for the opportunity to exercise. He took the route down through town that would lead him past Sheila's house, though there were no lights on and no car in the driveway. The night was growing chillier and the wind was picking up. Windflower hoped that didn't mean another storm was brewing, but sitting on the front step of the Atlantic meant that wind and storms were constant visitors. He pulled his collar up against the wind and completed his evening walk.

He was sitting in his living room reading his book, starting to doze off, when the telephone rang.

"Hello," he said, a little startled.

"Winston, were you gone to bed already?" asked Sheila.

"I must have fallen asleep while I was reading," he said. "What time is it?"

"It's about a quarter to eleven," said Sheila. "I invited a few people back to my place after the service and they're still here. People are pretty upset about Bill Sinnott. I was calling to suggest we not get together tonight. I'm not sure when everyone will leave."

"I understand. Why don't we get together tomorrow for por' cakes and pea soup at the Mug-Up? I haven't had them for ages."

"That sounds grand, Winston. I'll see you around noon tomorrow then. Good night."

"Good night, Sheila."

It was a little disappointing indeed, but with Lady snuggled up underneath his feet, at least he had some companionship. With that pleasant thought, he finished the chapter in his book, left a light on in the kitchen for Uncle Frank, and then headed to bed.

Chapter Twenty-Six

It may have been the absence of Sheila, or the spicy food he had just eaten, or his work stresses, but Windflower had a terrifying and horrible dream. One that woke him up in the middle of the night, sweaty and shaking.

He got up from bed, went to the kitchen and had a long drink of cool water from the fridge. That calmed his heart and slowed his breathing. He could hear Uncle Frank's snores coming from the other bedroom and went to close the door. When he did, Lady crept out from beside the bed and looked at him, as if to say 'Are you okay?' Windflower wasn't but he knew he would be once he had time to process this terrible dream.

The strangest thing of all was that although he was scared—more afraid than he could recall—he couldn't remember much about the dream. Only the woman's scream that woke him up. He went back to bed, and with Lady beside him for reassurance he managed to drift back to sleep, though a fitful sleep. At dawn he finally gave up his quest for more sleep and got out of bed.

When Windflower went out to the back porch to do his morning smudge he noticed the wind had picked up another notch. And it had grown considerably colder. It usually didn't get more than a few degrees below zero in this part of the world, but Windflower could tell it was colder than that by how quickly his hands seem to freeze as he struggled to light his smudge bowl. Shivering, he did his smudge quickly and his prayers even quicker. Regardless, he made sure to take a few moments to say a special prayer to Creator for Bill Sinnott. He prayed that he be given the support he needed for whichever route his journey would take him.

Even Lady had a low tolerance for the cold, so after she did her early morning business in the back yard while Windflower was smudging, she seemed quite content to go back into the bedroom with Uncle Frank. It was still early but not too early to get his laundry done. He gathered up the towels and tea cloths from the bathroom and kitchen and emptied them into his collapsible hamper. He grabbed a roll of quarters from the top of his dresser and took his laundry and detergent out to the car.

Minutes later, he had two loads of wash churning in the laundromat and was back home to make some coffee. When the coffee was done he filled up his Thermos and headed back to the laundromat, along with his Michael Crummey book. Three chapters later he switched the laundry to the spin dryers and sat back down to enjoy his book and his coffee. Another hour passed and he had all his laundry folded and was opening the door to his house. Uncle Frank was up and about, singing and drinking the last of Windflower's coffee. Plus, he had bacon frying in the pan, which was the most attractive aroma a hungry Windflower could imagine.

"Good morning Winston, how's she goin b'y? Want some breakfast?"

"It's going good, but no thanks. I'm going for por' cakes with Sheila. Did you behave yourself last night?"

"I've been off the booze since I got here," said his uncle indignantly. "I'm thinking about heading back home in a few days."

Windflower thought of telling him to stay as long as he wanted, but instead simply nodded. His uncle might take him at his word. "You're invited to come to Fortier's party tonight if you want," he said instead.

"Thank you, nephew. I was hoping you would ask. All my buddies are going. And I hear they've got a great band. I can show off my new dance moves."

With that, his uncle did a little pirouette in the kitchen. Windflower laughed and went to put his laundry away. By the time he got back Uncle Frank was opening the door to let his buddy Jarge in for breakfast. Windflower left the two men to their food and probably to practice their dance steps, and walked over to see Sheila about getting some por' cakes.

Sheila was on the phone when he arrived but dressed quickly. Soon afterward they walked arm in arm down to the Mug-Up café. It was cold and the wind was biting but at least there wasn't any snow. The café was warm and crowded and most people waved hello to Sheila and Windflower. He got them a table in the corner while Sheila made the rounds to say her hellos back.

"Two orders of por' cakes and pea soup," said Windflower when the waitress, Marie, came to take their order. "And two cups of tea." The tea came quickly as did the por' cakes.

Por' cakes—or pork cakes—were a Grand Bank staple and had been for as long as anyone around there could remember. They were cheap and easy to make, with the basic ingredients being minced fat back pork and potatoes, along with a little baking powder and flour to bind them together. Baked in the oven and served hot with molasses and a bowl of pea soup, this was the traditional Saturday morning lunch in Grand Bank.

Sheila came back just in time to savour the hot and thick pea soup, full of carrots and turnip, flecked with little pieces of salt meat. The por' cakes were cooked to a delicious-looking golden brown. When Windflower doused a medium sized piece of por' cake in the molasses, he smiled with satisfaction. All through lunch people came to talk to Sheila, mostly to check in about the Mayor, but also to pay their respects.

Windflower was happy to merely smile and enjoy his lunch. When the rush subsided for a minute he said to Sheila, "You have a lot of fans."

"People just need to connect. They are really worried about the Mayor and it's like they miss him already. He has so much respect in this community."

"It looks like you do too," said Windflower, as another couple came to their table to say hello to Sheila. After lunch the couple walked back to Sheila's where more people kept arriving. Sheila was the ever-gracious host but Windflower could see he was just getting in the way. He gave Sheila a peck on the cheek and they agreed to get back together later for the party.

Windflower walked home and now the snow had begun. He got to his house and opened the door. Before he could get inside Lady was at his feet. He grabbed her leash and together they did another circuit of Grand Bank, down towards the brook and up past the wharf. Once again Windflower noticed the ship at the fish plant dock, only now it was busily being loaded.

Windflower couldn't see exactly what was being put on board but it looked like rusty metal. He wasn't the only one watching this process. There were three pick-up trucks parked above the wharf with their motors running and their drivers intently peering through the now thickly falling snow. When he got back home Windflower and his new four-legged friend had a great snooze in the living room.

After his nap Windflower showered and shaved and took his red serge uniform out of the plastic bag from the cleaners. He hand-polished his brown boots and then, taking a look in the mirror, pronounced himself ready for the party. Lady was smiling up at him as if to agree. As he was leaving to pick up Sheila, Uncle Frank strolled in, smelling distinctly of beer and cigarettes.

"I'm going to have a bath and I'll meet you over there," he said to Windflower as he passed by.

"Okay," was all Windflower could think to say. It was clear that Frank's brief stint on the wagon was over. He wondered what that might mean for tonight's event. Frank was a grown man, though, and Windflower knew he wasn't his keeper.

The snow was still falling as Windflower went out to his car. Judging by the amount of snow on his windshield there must have been about 10 centimetres already on the ground. He started worrying about it. But then he decided to stop thinking, and just enjoy himself on a night out with his girl.

CHAPTER TWENTY-SEVEN

S heila was stunning when she walked downstairs to meet Windflower. She wore a long black evening dress that shimmered with sparkles, and her dark brown hair was up, just the way he liked it, which had a streak of red highlights that accented her caramel skin tone. Her jewelry was simple but elegant: short hanging pearl earrings and an old-fashioned brooch that Windflower knew to be her mother's. She carried her black high heel shoes in a bag.

At first he simply stared with his mouth wide open. Finally his tongue unfroze and he said, "You are gorgeous, Sheila Hillier."

She smiled and said, "Flattery will get you everywhere, Sergeant Windflower."

This time he smiled too, and he took a moment to take it all in. He then helped put on her knee-length vintage sealskin coat.

They arrived at the Lions Club a few minutes later and took their seats at a long table with Fortier and his family, Constable Evanchuk who came alone, and Tizzard and his date. Windflower and Sheila were introduced to Tizzard's date whom Windflower recognized as the girl from the checkout at the Fortune Pharmacy. Fortier's children were only here for the first part of the evening. Evanchuk had agreed to babysit them so the Fortiers could enjoy themselves at the party later on.

There was already a pretty good crowd, but Windflower knew nobody would stay late if this weather kept up.

The bar was open so Windflower took orders and invited Tizzard to come along and help him bring back the drinks.

"You work fast," said Windflower. "At least one part of your investigation in Fortune is going well."

"Thank you, sir," said Tizzard, deciding not to further engage in what might prove to be a sensitive discussion. He opted to try and switch the topic. "I'm hoping the weather shifts. If not we'll have another long night."

"Nice move," said Windflower, laughing. "You're smooth, Tizzard, very smooth."

Windflower and Tizzard carried the tray of drinks back to the table and by now the band was setting up to begin its first set of music for the evening. It was a four-piece group that Windflower had seen before at the folk festival in Burin. They played a combination of old country standards and traditional Newfoundland songs. Their accordion player was also a well-known story teller and a couple of times during any event he would be sure to spin a few yarns.

Tizzard and his date were some of the first on the dance floor when the band began. Sheila had left to make her rounds to say hello to her friends when the Deputy Mayor, Francis Tibbo, came by the table.

"Good evening, Sergeant. Since Bill Sinnott is indisposed I will be carrying out the official functions tonight. I have my speech ready whenever you are."

"Thank you, Mr. Tibbo. Corporal Tizzard is the Master of Ceremonies for the evening. I'll make sure to tell him you are here."

With that, Sheila came by and took him by the arm.

"Care to dance, Sergeant?"

"I would indeed, Missus Hillier. Excuse me, Mr. Tibbo, but my other duty calls."

Windflower and Sheila were soon twirling around the floor. "What did he want?" asked Sheila when they got far enough away from Francis Tibbo.

"He wanted to tell me that he's in charge now," said Windflower.

"He's an awful little man," said Sheila.

"He's a prince all right," said Windflower as their dance came to an end. When they got back to the table, Inspector Ford had arrived and was sitting with his arm around Fortier. He could hear Ford talking in a loud voice, and Fortier looked a little uncomfortable.

Ford nodded to Windflower and said hello to Sheila on the way up to the bar to get a drink. Meanwhile, the band was finishing up their first set and Windflower could see that his Uncle Frank and his buddies had arrived and were looking to having a very public party of their own near the back of the hall. Windflower nudged Tizzard. "You're on," he said.

"Good evening, everybody, and thank you for coming. We're all a little sad tonight to say goodbye to our friend and colleague Mario Fortier. But we're also going to celebrate the time we've had together and to thank Mario and his family for the contributions they have made to our detachment and our town. We have a few speakers and then lots of time for dancing and celebrating later on. I would like to invite Deputy Mayor Francis Tibbo to say a few words on behalf of the Town of Grand Bank."

Tibbo did have a few words on behalf of the town, but most of what he had to say was about himself and his unselfish role as a public servant of the people. He droned on for about ten minutes and while most people were content to ignore him, Inspector Ford blurted out, "Sounds like someone is running for something."

Windflower noticed Ford had somehow managed to get himself another drink while the Deputy Mayor was speaking, which wasn't a good sign. Mercifully, Tibbo wrapped up and Tizzard called on Ford to bring greetings from the District.

Ford rose from his seat, weaving a little, but hanging onto his drink. He got to the microphone and almost knocked it over. Then, slurring his words, he started to tell an awful and inappropriate story about a time that he and Fortier were stationed together in Northern Quebec. Windflower could see how this story would end and he walked up to the microphone. Tizzard took the cue and managed to shift the Inspector to one side and he thanked him for his comments and started the applause.

Then it was Windflower's turn to speak, and he began by acknowledging the absence of Mayor Bill Sinnott. That quieted down the crowd considerably. He then talked about Fortier and his good qualities and that he would be missed by everyone in Grand Bank. He then presented Fortier with a card and his gift from his fellow officers. It was a beautiful new salmon fishing line. "It's for your trips up the Miramichi," said Windflower as he called Fortier to the front to say a few words.

Fortier was a man of few words and he quickly thanked Windflower and the team in Grand Bank for their support. On behalf of his family, he acknowledged the community and how much they would miss it when they left. Tizzard was quickly back on stage afterward to close off the formal part of the evening, and to wish everybody a good time for the rest of the night.

For the RCMP officers that good time would not last very long. Windflower's cell phone buzzed and he went to the kitchen area at the back to answer it. It was MacDonald.

"Sergeant, we've had a call that the highway north of Marystown has been closed. The weather is getting bad out here. We probably should think about closing our section soon."

"Okay," said Windflower. "I'll talk to Corporal Tizzard and get back to you."

Windflower went back inside the main hall and found Tizzard. Together they went to the door and checked outside. "Let's close the highway," said Windflower when they saw the deteriorating conditions.

"I'll go back and get the storm centre organized," said Tizzard. "Evanchuk has gone home with Fortier's kids but I'll call her back in."

"Good," said Windflower. "I'll finish up here and give Fortier the news that we have to leave his party. I'll be over when I can."

Windflower stayed at the event for another set, but Sheila could see he was anxious to leave. He was grateful when she suggested he take her home. Before he could leave, however, Windflower had to deal with two more problems: Inspector Ford, and his Uncle Frank. Frank was less of an issue because he was a friendly drunk and his friends would look after him. It was embarrassing but there wasn't much Windflower could do as his uncle carried through on his promised dance presentation. Bill Ford, on the other hand, was getting louder, boisterous, and much drunker than before.

He had managed to knock over one of the band's microphones on his way to the washroom. Once he got back to the table, he spoke some form of drunken gibberish about the 'good ole days,' nearly falling asleep. Windflower had to get him out before he left, but a gentle hand on Ford's shoulder was not nearly enough. Windflower waited until the band was in full swing and people were dancing, to make his move. He and Fortier lifted the Inspector by the armpits and deposited him in the hallway at the front of the Lions Club.

Windflower ran and got his Jeep and pulled it up in front. He and Fortier literally poured Inspector Ford into the back seat. Ford protested vigorously but Windflower paid no attention to him until they got to the RCMP detachment where Tizzard, who had been alerted by Fortier, was waiting. Together they carried, pushed and cajoled Ford into the office and down the hall into the back cell. Only when the door was locked did Windflower speak.

"You will thank me later for this," he said and then walked out leaving Tizzard wide-eyed and speechless. Ford yelled what seemed to be an endless stream of obscenities in the direction of his Sergeant.

Windflower drove back to the hall and picked up Sheila who was now waiting for him at the entrance. "That couldn't have been easy," she said.

"No, but it could have been worse. Sorry for spoiling your evening," he said.

"Oh, Winston. I had a great time. We haven't danced like that since forever and despite it all, I think that the Fortiers had a nice time. Francine is such a nice woman. She is glad to go back to New Brunswick, but she said she will miss Grand Bank. They have great memories from here."

"Thank you, Sheila. You're right. Despite it all, I had a good time, too."

Windflower drove Sheila to her house and they said goodnight at her door with a long and warm embrace. Windflower would have much preferred to stay there for the evening, as would have Sheila, but duty and the storm awaited. By the time Windflower got back to the detachment, Tizzard had the storm watch in effect and was waiting for the snowplow operator to come by so they could take the drive to Marystown to make sure nobody was stranded before they shut the highway down. Inspector Ford was still howling in the back but everybody had more important jobs to do than pay any attention to that noise. Windflower closed the door leading to the back and went to work.

CHAPTER TWENTY-EIGHT

It was a long night, but when the snow mercifully ended just before dawn the officers on duty breathed a sigh of relief. It could have been worse; each of them had been holed up in the small detachment for longer periods of time when a particularly bad storm had wreaked its havoc on their part of the world. Windflower sent Fortier home first, since it had supposed to be his night off and he had to get ready to leave on Monday morning for the drive to New Brunswick. He was waiting for MacDonald to come in before letting Evanchuk and Tizzard leave as well. Windflower would continue until noon, if he could stay awake.

MacDonald arrived a little after 6 a.m. and he was able to let Evanchuk go (willingly) and Tizzard (under protest). There was no sign of life from the back cell so Windflower decided to leave MacDonald on the desk while he did the last highway reconnaissance before daylight. He also thought he might as well take the dog for a walk while he was out, so he drove up to his house.

Lady had been sleeping but wagged her tail happily when she realized it was Windflower, and that he was there to take her out. Windflower peeked into the spare bedroom but there was no sign of his uncle, which could be either good news or bad news. At least he wasn't in jail. Windflower and Lady traveled the one road that had been cleared in Grand Bank, which was a short but refreshing walk. After she had done her business and Windflower picked it up in his plastic baggie, they were good to head home.

Lady went back to her warm bed in the spare room where Uncle Frank had dragged her blanket from the kitchen. Windflower finally got to take off his dress uniform from the night before, and put on regular clothes before heading back to work.

The early morning tour was uneventful and when Windflower got back to the office MacDonald had thankfully made some fresh coffee and was heating up some muffins she had brought from home. She laid two of them on his desk along with a hot cup of coffee.

"Thank you very much," said Windflower.

"I'm not much of a cook," said MacDonald. "But it's pretty hard to screw up muffin mix."

"They're good. Maybe you should give yourself a bit more credit."

"Nah, I'm pretty much a screw-up. Do you have a minute to talk, sir?" she asked.

Looking around Windflower said, "I'd say my schedule is pretty clear."

MacDonald laughed despite her obvious nervousness. "Thank you," she started. "I'm thinking about resigning, sir. I may not be cut out to be a Mountie after all."

"Why do you say that? Yes, you've made some mistakes, but learning from them is just part of the process. We all make mistakes."

"Yes, I know that. But I am making errors in judgement and … anyway I just think it's better to leave."

"We're a little short-staffed right now with Fortier leaving, but once we get a replacement, why don't you take a few days and go visit your folks on PEI? Sometimes going home can give you another perspective, help you think more clearly. Don't make rash decisions now you may regret later," said Windflower.

MacDonald simply nodded and walked out of his office, leaving Windflower to wonder if anything he had just said to MacDonald had gotten through. He was still wondering that when Sheila called.

"Good morning, my love," said Sheila.

"Good morning, dear," said Windflower in return. "How's your day going so far?"

"It's good. I'm calling to remind you about supper tonight at the Stoodleys. Why don't you come by around six? How did last night go, and how did you make out with Inspector Ford?"

"Last night was quiet and I think the Inspector is still sleeping it off in the back. I just heard a noise. Maybe he's up and about. I'll see you later for supper," said Windflower.

"Okay. Have a good day."

"You, too," said Windflower as he hung up the phone and walked to the back. He got a cup of coffee for himself and an extra one for his Inspector.

"Good morning. Care for a cup of coffee?" he said to Ford who was still lying almost motionless in the bed in the small cell.

"Thanks," Ford muttered as he took the coffee from Windflower, his hands shaking so badly he could hardly hold it steady long enough to drink from it. He tried, but eventually just set it down next to the bed and lay back down. Windflower sat down on a chair and waited for him to speak.

"Am I under arrest?"

"No. You didn't commit any crime."

"I bet I made an ass of myself," said Ford sheepishly.

"That would be correct. Anyway, I've got work to do. If you need me I'll be in my office." He walked away, leaving the cell door open. If Ford wanted to talk he would listen, but he sure wasn't starting the discussion.

Half an hour later Windflower watched Ford leave the Grand Bank detachment, guessing they were going to pretend last night didn't happen.

It was just before 11:00 when Windflower decided to follow up on the idea to check out Ridgeway's house in Fortune. He decided to take his dog, figuring they could go for a stroll along the wharf in Fortune. She was overjoyed to see him, and they drove the short distance to Fortune.

It was quiet in the Fortune harbour this December Sunday. Windflower parked above the fish plant wharf where a Coast Guard ship was tied up, and walked along the ferry ramp towards the small cove that sheltered the multitude of fishing boats moored tightly together for the winter. There would be no fishing today, or for many months to come. But Fortune still had a semblance of what Newfoundland outports looked like before the great fall of King Cod. Fortune, at least for now, had a viable fish plant and a couple dozen long liners operating out of multi-coloured fishing stages along the water's edge.

Windflower and a very happy Lady strolled along the small boardwalk in between these stages until they made their way around the customs yard and back to Windflower's RCMP vehicle. Michael Ridgeway's house was in the middle of Fortune, near the community centre. It was a small bungalow, nondescript except for three large fake purple butterflies on one side of the house. Windflower thought it was a bit over the top, but not unusual, sadly.

He opened the door with the key he had taken from the office and Lady ran in through the open door. She ran about the house, frantically checking each room. "He's not here," said Windflower gently as the dog continued her search. Windflower started his own search in the kitchen and apart from a half-full dishwasher there was little to note. Certainly no sign of drugs or paraphernalia. But Windflower wasn't surprised because Ridgeway would have tried to hide that stuff as best he could.

He continued exploring but found little of interest. He was about to give up hope of finding anything significant when he heard Lady barking in the spare bedroom. He called to her to come, but she just sat on the floor. Either that was her usual sleeping place or she was trying to tell him something. Windflower went into the room and checked under the bed but still came up empty. Then he opened the closet door.

Inside was what he was hoping to find. There were cases of drugs and syringes and stacks of prescription pads. He put on his rubber gloves and carried the drugs and other stuff out to the car. He was about to leave when he noticed Lady sniffing around in the closet. There on the floor at the back was a small plush animal, which he thought to be her toy so he pulled it out and handed it to her. Then he noticed a small metal box with a lock on it, like a cashbox. He picked that up too, and then they both hopped back into his Jeep.

When he got back to the office Tizzard had arrived and he and MacDonald were sharing a box of chocolate croissants Tizzard had picked up along the way. Windflower showed them what he had found in Fortune and Tizzard agreed to go through it all that afternoon. Windflower grabbed a croissant and said his goodbyes. He and his bed had a long overdue appointment. He drove home and both he and Lady were fast asleep minutes later.

Windflower's ears opened first, which forced his eyes to come back to life as well. He could hear somebody, probably his uncle, out in the kitchen. He checked the clock and saw that it read 4:25. That was perfect timing. He could get up, have a shower and still be ready for supper in plenty of time. But first he had to deal with Uncle Frank.

"Afternoon, Uncle. How's your head today?" His uncle was nursing a cup of tea and gave him a dagger look in return. "You can do what you want. But this is not a good town for you to party in. I hear the local police can be pretty mean."

"I'm not hurting anyone," said Uncle Frank.

"You are hurting yourself, and me with your behaviour," Windflower replied. "You're a good man and you don't need to be making a fool of yourself. You have better things to do in the world besides getting drunk."

"I have to go out. I will be leaving as soon as I can get a ticket back home." And with that his uncle dumped his tea into the sink, put on his boots and coat, and left.

Windflower joked to himself to go into the counselling business. He then stripped off his old clothes which he'd napped in, then jumped into the shower.

After a nice, long and very hot shower, he felt refreshed and rejuvenated.

Chapter Twenty-Nine

Windflower picked up Sheila just before 6 and drove over to the Stoodleys for supper. Herb Stoodley had obviously been out with his snowblower because the driveway was clean and dry, as was the walkway out to the back door entrance and even right up to the outside shed where Herb was manning the barbeque. He waved hello to Sheila who waved back, who then went inside to see Moira. He motioned Windflower to come closer.

Windflower could see the smoke and smell the meat long before he got near to the barbeque. Stoodley opened the hood when Windflower drew closer and every pore of his body opened to let in the aromas. "That smells so good."

"Steak kabobs," said Stoodley. "It's my first time trying out this recipe. I got it from one of Moira's magazines."

"That's where I get mine, too," said Windflower as he peered over Stoodley's shoulder. He could see the browning meat on the metal skewers with alternating onions and red and green peppers. His mouth was watering and he hoped he wasn't visibly drooling.

"You're just in time to test the meat. I kept a few chunks of steak on the side to taste it along the way. He picked up a piece on the barbeque fork and passed it to Windflower. It was sweet and spicy and oh-so-tasty.

"It's perfect for me," said Windflower as he resisted the temptation to lick the fork before he passed it back. "Medium rare."

"That's what we're going for," said Stoodley as he popped a piece into his own mouth. "Perfect. Let's go eat." He put all the skewers on a plate and carried them into the house.

Sheila and Moira Stoodley were sitting and enjoying a glass of Merlot from a bottle set on the dining room table. Herb laid the steak on the table and poured the two men a glass. He then went to the kitchen to help Moira bring in the other dishes.

There were steamed carrots and broccoli and a steaming rice pilaf mixed with peas, raisins and chopped parsley. The women continued to chat throughout dinner but Windflower and his male companion focused almost exclusively on the task of eating.

When dinner was over the men did the dishes while the women got coffee and dessert ready. Dessert was Windflower's all-time favourite—peanut butter cheesecake—and even though he had eaten more than his share of the main meal, he was easily persuaded by Moira to take a second piece.

They started playing cards, and into the second game there was a knock on the door.

"Who could that be on a Sunday night?" Herb asked as he went to answer the door. He returned with Corporal Eddie Tizzard.

"Evening, everybody. Sorry to disturb you but I thought you'd like to know." Then he paused. "Mayor Sinnott passed away in hospital in St. John's a couple of hours ago. Somebody I know at the Health Science Centre was keeping an eye on him for me. She just called. I'm not sure who all knows yet, but I thought I would pass it on."

"Oh my God. Are you sure, Eddie?" Sheila asked.

"Yes, Ma'am. I guess we'll have to wait for the family to make the formal announcement, but he's gone."

"Bill Sinnott did more for this community than anybody I know. He will be missed," said Herb Stoodley.

Sheila looked shocked and devastated. Tizzard said goodnight and quietly left.

Windflower and Sheila left for home shortly afterwards.

"Are you okay?" asked Windflower when they arrived at Sheila's.

"Not really. I can't believe that he's gone. He was like a father figure to me and tons of people in the community. He was such a nice man too."

"He was a nice man," said Windflower. "Why don't you go sit down and I'll make us a pot of tea?"

A few minutes later Windflower was in the living room with his arm around Sheila. There wasn't much more to say but there was a comfort in just having each other to hold. After a little while the phone started ringing and soon people would be dropping in to visit. Windflower gave Sheila an extra big hug and left for home.

He drove over to the detachment before going home and the mood there was nearly as sombre. Evanchuk was out on patrol and Tizzard was sitting around and moping. Windflower knew his Corporal and the Mayor had grown close over the past few months and could see the younger man was still trying to process the news of his death. He stayed with Tizzard until Evanchuk came back and then left for home.

He had a quick walk with Lady before bedtime, and the night was chilly but clear. He could see the moon and all of the constellations out over the endless ocean. Windflower said a silent prayer in honour of the late Mayor and sent his hopes to Grandmother Moon to guide his spirit safely to the other world. It had been a long day and Windflower was glad it was over.

Both Lady and Windflower were asleep quickly. Windflower woke up before he could get answers to any of these questions. This time he could vaguely see the screaming woman due to a foggy screen between them. Who was she and what did she want? Windflower woke up before could get answers to any of these questions.

Just like the last time when he awoke after the bad dream, he was drenched in sweat and struggled to breathe. He checked the clock and saw that it read 3:59. He got up, went to the bathroom and went back to bed. Lady stirred a little when he first rose, and then settled down when he returned. Somehow, Windflower felt a little safer with the dog in his room, so despite his inner disturbance he was able to fall back to sleep. He woke again just after 6, feeling shaken but somewhat rested to begin his week.

Monday was a good day to review and plan the rest of his week, which he always took a little time to do before going to the office. But first he had to do his morning routine, which now included Lady. She was waiting for him at the back door and when he opened it she ran out to do her business. Windflower loved her energy and in his prayers he offered thanks for having a four-legged companion in his life again. He also prayed for the family of the newly passed Mayor to be strong in the face of this great loss.

He offered up his prayers as well for the community soon to be in mourning, and for the leaders, like Sheila, who would be called upon to help them. Both Inspector Ford and his Uncle Frank also came into his thoughts and prayers; for Ford to find his way back to a good path, and for his uncle to return to his greatness in how he offered gifts to the world. Finally, on this morning after a long week and a long night he prayed for wisdom and guidance from his ancestors and the spirit world, and Creator to help him on this journey.

Lady was already waiting to get back inside as Windflower packed up his medicine and smudge kit. He smiled as he filled her bowl with food and gave her fresh water. She seemed to smile back when he gave her a Milk Bone biscuit. It sure was nice to have a dog again.

He made a pot of coffee and sat down at the kitchen table to do his weekly review. First with the active investigations: were Frankie Fallon and Michael Ridgeway's deaths connected? Likely, especially since Fallon was found in the trunk of Ridgeway's car. Also, it was clear Frankie Fallon was killed. Murdered. And what about Ridgeway? Was it an accident or was he a victim as well?

The dead couldn't speak but maybe their remains could give up some information. Windflower made a note on his to-do list: check with Doc Sanjay on the preliminary tox reports. What was the motive here? Windflower thought there was always a motive, and more often than not, that motive was financial. So who could or would benefit from the deaths of either, or both, of these men? One person who was involved financially in this situation was Laura Emberley, the pharmacist. She may not have been directly involved with the deaths, but she was involved.

Accordingly, Windflower made talking to Tizzard and re-interviewing Laura Emberley the second and third items on his list.

What other evidence did they have or could they get? That reminded Windflower to put two other things on his list: call Brown in Forensics to see what they came up with from the vehicle and Fallon's place in Molliers, and check out the evidence he had collected in Fortune yesterday. What was in that locked box he found in Ridgeway's closet?

He also made a note to check on RCMP protocols for the death of a local dignitary. He wanted to make sure he and the Grand Bank detachment handled it with as much professionalism and respect as it deserved. They couldn't bring the Mayor back, but they could certainly give him a good send-off. He deserved it. Now that he felt organized and ready for the week, Windflower made himself a boiled egg and some toast and finished off the last of his coffee.

The only thing left to do before work was to take Lady for her morning walk, which was the most pleasant job in the morning. They walked down the road towards the brook and over the bridge. On the other side he noticed there was a lot more activity at the fish plant wharf. Workers were busily loading the boat with crates of metal, and noticed his friends in the pick-ups were back.

He walked down towards them just as they were unfurling a sheet hand-painted with the words "New Wave Fisheries are Stealing our Future" scrawled across it. They were tying the sheet to two metal poles they stuck in the snow bank outside the fish plant gates.

That can't be good. Lady was already tugging at him to go home so he didn't have time to stick around. As he turned back towards his house he could see more vehicles were arriving to check out the situation. Nope, that can't be good.

CHAPTER THIRTY

Windflower got to his detachment office early despite his busy morning. He put on a fresh pot of coffee and started going through his mail and e-mails when Tizzard and Betsy arrived at almost the same time. Windflower got Betsy to check with HQ about the protocols around the Mayor's death, and then got Tizzard to help him lower the Canadian flag outside the detachment to half-mast. "That's the least we can do," he mentioned to Tizzard, who heartily agreed.

Before he could get to his next task and his plans for talking about the on-going cases with Tizzard, Betsy beeped him to let him know Deputy Mayor Francis Tibbo was waiting outside for him. Windflower went to greet him.

"Good morning, Mr. Tibbo."

"It's Acting Mayor Tibbo," he returned.

"Oh, has the Council made that official?" asked Windflower.

"That's just a formality. I will be the Mayor and I wanted to get a few things straight."

"Okay. How can I help you?"

"Well, I think your priorities are all wrong," said Tibbo. "I expect, and the Council expects, that you should be spending your time catching criminals instead of doing public relations stunts. Like that community policing stuff. Focus on your job and leave the media relations to professionals like me."

Professionals? That's a bit of a stretch, but Windflower let it pass.

"And another thing. In case you haven't noticed, we have a drug epidemic in this town. People from outside are bringing in drugs and corrupting our youth. We want you to deal with that instead of having show-and-tell in the classrooms. We expect results," said Tibbo, pushing out his chest. "Or else we will be demanding changes."

With that, Tibbo strutted out of Windflower's office. He was still processing that outburst when Tizzard poked his head in. "Cup a coffee at the café, Boss?"

"Absolutely, Corporal Tizzard. I need a coffee after that exchange, and maybe a shower too."

The mood at the Mug-Up was subdued, even downright gloomy, and Windflower nodded good morning to the crew of locals who were nursing their coffee and sharing their grief. There was an empty chair at the Mayor's usual table. If anything, the people seemed even sadder in that grouping.

"It's a sad day today," said Marie as she brought them two cups of coffee. "But I guess we 'ave to go on."

"We do, Marie," said Tizzard. "We'll have a couple of tea biscuits when you get a chance."

"Mr. Tibbo is not very happy with us," said Windflower. "I don't think he's as much in favour of community policin' as Mayor Sinnott."

"He won't be Mayor, will he?" asked Tizzard.

Windflower shrugged his shoulders. "We'll work with anybody they select. We've got our hands full right now, though. I'm going to talk to Doc Sanjay this morning and see if he's got anything on the tox reports. And I'll check with Forensics to see if they found anything interesting out at Molliers. What about the stuff I brought back from Fortune? Did you have a look at it yet?"

"I've catalogued the drugs and have a list for you back at the office. But I couldn't open the box without breaking the lock. I wanted to check with you first. I also dusted it for prints and only found one set," said Tizzard.

"Bust it open if you have to. And what's the story on Laura Emberley? She must know more than what she's telling us if there are reports missing."

"I don't know for sure, Boss, but I'd agree. There's something else there. Maybe you should talk to her again. By the way, MacDonald didn't show today, so we're short a person, besides Fortier," said Tizzard.

"I'll talk to Ford again today and see if we can get somebody, at least on a temp basis. I don't know what to do if we have another storm. We can't keep pulling all-nighters," said Windflower as their hot tea biscuits arrived. There was silence as the two men buttered, then savoured their snack.

"Did you see the sign at the fish plant?" asked Tizzard.

"I saw it this morning. It looks like they're scrapping the place for metal now. I was hoping we'd get a bit of peace and quiet on that front, at least for a few days. You think the plant would have waited a while before moving to this level."

"You can see why people are upset. It's another reminder that the good old days are never coming back around here. I just hope the sign is the extent of the protest, but I get the feeling that something else is brewing. Maybe folks will be preoccupied with the Mayor's death."

"Anyway, we've got work to do," said Windflower as he went to the cash to pay. He saw Moira in the back and waved, yet saw no sign of Herb. On his way out he almost bumped into Sheila, who was on her way in.

"Good morning," said Windflower.

"Good morning, Winston," said Sheila. "I'm grabbing a coffee to go. I'm on my way over to the town office. There's a meeting with some of the town Council and a few concerned citizens. We're going to talk about the Mayor's funeral."

"Acting Mayor Tibbo has already been over to see me this morning," said Windflower.

Sheila raised her eyebrows at this reference and said, "I don't think any decisions have been made about that yet."

"I didn't think so," said Windflower. The two then made plans to get together at Windflower's house for supper.

As he was getting into his car, he saw Froude's taxi go by, a new van by the looks of it. He could make out his Uncle Frank in the front seat but the older man either didn't see Windflower or pretended not to. And in the back he saw a woman that looked like Constable MacDonald. But that couldn't be, could it?

When he got to work Betsy gave him an envelope she said came from MacDonald. So it **was** her in the taxi. He went back to his office and opened it:

Sergeant:

Thank you for all of your help. I don't think I can do this anymore. I am sorry for any inconvenience this might cause but I am thinking about resigning from the RCMP, and returning home today.

Sincerely,
Anne MacDonald

Tizzard came into Windflower's office with the lock box opened, ready to show his Sergeant the contents. He handed the box over to Windflower and got MacDonald's note in return.

"I thought you said you talked to her. Usually, when that happens, things get better and not worse," said Tizzard.

"It looks like I'm batting 0 for 2 in that regard," said Windflower. "I talked to Frank too, and he was in the same taxi."

"Should I go after her?"

"What are we going to do, arrest her? Let's give her a couple days and then contact her. She obviously needed a few days off. At this point I'm going to consider this a request for leave. What do we have here?" he asked, pointing to the box.

"Look inside," said Tizzard.

"A mini tape recorder..." said Windflower.

"And what looks like a couple hours of tape," said Tizzard. "I'm going to get Evanchuk to go through them. I'm hoping she'll agree to do a couple of extra overnight shifts. Speaking of which, I'm hoping you wouldn't mind doing a few nights too, till we get our replacement."

"I'll call Ford right now," said Windflower. "Pencil me in wherever we've got a hole." Tizzard nodded and went off to find Evanchuk.

Windflower called Inspector Ford's office in Marystown but Louise said he wasn't available. By her tone of voice, Windflower understood that to be code for 'Ford hasn't showed up for work yet and I'm none too happy about it.' He left a message for Ford to call and went out to see what Betsy.

"So, what did you find out about our protocol?" he asked.

"I couldn't find any official protocol policy. But I did find some newspaper reports about local RCMP detachments lowering the flag, and offering escorts in full dress uniforms to the funeral processions of local officials who died in office."

"If you can't find an official policy, then it probably doesn't exist, so I'm going to take your advice and appoint you as our local protocol officer," said Windflower. "Will you prepare a memo and post it on the board?"

"Consider it done, sir," said Betsy, who went off to carry out her first official duties as protocol officer of the Grand Bank detachment.

Matter resolved, at least for now, Windflower decided to pay Doctor Sanjay a visit. He told Betsy to beep him if Ford called but otherwise he would be back after lunch.

It was still fairly quiet on the roads as Windflower drove over to the clinic. He passed by the fish plant wharf and saw there were now a half dozen pick-ups parked alongside the makeshift sign. Not likely good news. But for now there was nothing he could do, and in actuality, nothing illegal was going on. One could only hope it would stay that way.

Dr. Sanjay was happy to see Windflower. "Come in, come in, my friend," he said when he saw Windflower's face in his office doorway. "I'm glad you came. I have some news for you, some very interesting news."

CHAPTER THIRTY-ONE

"I received a call from my friend at the lab in St. John's this morning. He put in a few hours of unpaid overtime on the weekend and was able to come up with a few preliminary findings."

Sanjay paused, then continued.

"First of all, Mister Ridgeway was a walking pharmaceutical emporium. The initial lab tests detected the presence of hydrocodone, oxycodone, morphine and codeine."

"Wow. Would this have caused his heart failure?" asked Windflower.

"Most certainly. Over any period of time, the use of these drugs in a great amount or in combination would result in damage to the heart vessels and arteries."

Again he paused.

"Is there something else?" asked Windflower.

"There is indeed. I don't think any of these drugs caused his immediate death. Michael Ridgeway was poisoned."

"Poisoned? With what?"

"The lab results detected a significant amount of nicotine. Enough to kill any human being."

"Nicotine? Did Ridgeway even smoke?" Windflower asked.

"Not from my examination of his lungs. That probably means the nicotine was given to him surreptitiously in some other compound or drink, or mixed with some other drug. He had over 60 milligrams of nicotine in his blood system, which is more than enough to kill him. And quickly. His breathing would have slowed, his heart would have stopped and he'd be dead within minutes of ingesting the nicotine."

"Is it hard to get nicotine in those amounts?" asked Windflower.

"Yes, unless you are a doctor or a pharmacist. We don't use it much here anymore because of the taboo on smoking. But in Europe and Asia, some doctors prescribe small amounts to treat _____ _____ ion. It is a stimulant, after all."

"Very interesting," _____ _____ g to get his head around this no_____ _____ hing on Frankie Fallon?'

"Ah, yes, Frankie Fallon, _____ Fallon clearly died of blood loss a_____ _____ nerous punctures on his body, preced_____ _____ to the skull. But in a short period of t_____ _____ h, he consumed a considerable amount of c_____ _____ ol."

"So he was drunk?"

"He was clearly impaired. But he a_____ _____ m pentothal in his blood. Something over 300_____ _____ e lab tests say."

"That's the 'truth serum', isn't it?" asked _____

"Yes, in lower doses it has been used to try and gain information from informants, but it is most commonly used to try and calm down psychotic patients. They might be given 50 milligrams or so, maybe 100 milligrams in an extremely violent case. 300 milligrams would certainly knock you out, and even a man as big as Fallon would be out cold in 20 minutes," said the doctor.

"Might he have taken too much by mistake?" asked Windflower.

"Yes, and then he ran into a wall of knives and bumped his head," said Dr. Sanjay with a laugh. "If I was a detective, which I am clearly not, I might suspect Frankie Fallon was interrogated and then killed, all while under the influence of a number of substances. By whom and why I would not have a clue."

Windflower thanked the coroner for the information and walked slowly back to his car. The **hows** were starting to become clearer, but the other questions were still pretty deep. Money, he thought. Money is the prime motivator in most crimes. Where is the money in all this? He was still mulling this question when he arrived at the door of the Mug-Up, almost as if by chance. And luckily, just in time for lunch.

Windflower went to the counter and ordered a bowl of turkey soup and a cup of tea. Then he went to a table to have a look at the local paper and wait for his order. While he was waiting he saw Herb Stoodley come in and waved him over.

"Herb, I missed you this morning. Did you get a shift off for good behaviour?"

"I was at the meeting at the town office. The family has set the funeral for Thursday morning and we spent some time talking about how that should be organized from the town's perspective. We're assuming you guys will be giving us an escort. And it looks like I'm going to be your interim Mayor and illustrious leader, at least until a new election can be organized."

"No problem about the escort. Anything we can do to help. But how did your promotion come about? What about Acting Mayor Francis Tibbo?"

"Tibbo gets to call himself Acting Mayor for one more day. The regular Town Council meeting is scheduled for tomorrow and a motion will be put forward to call for an election for a new Mayor, and to appoint me in the interim. No one who wants to run for Mayor is allowed to hold that position. It was the only way to keep Tibbo out."

"Well, that's good news. Congratulations."

"Maybe," said Herb. "It likely won't be easy with everything that's going on. I would have preferred if Sheila took over right now, but she said she wouldn't do anything without a vote."

"Sheila? My Sheila? She's agreed to run?"

Herb laughed. "It will be our Sheila now."

Windflower smiled at this last remark as the waitress arrived with his tea, piping hot soup and warm dinner roll with butter.

"I'll leave you to enjoy your lunch," Herb said, but just before he walked away he whispered something in Windflower's ear: "I won't be able to talk freely to you about this after today, but a heads-up about the fish plant. There's talk of a flotilla to stop the freighter from taking the scrap metal from the plant. But I didn't tell you."

Stoodley winked at Windflower and went back behind the counter to help out. Windflower waited a few moments for his soup to cool and thought about what Stoodley had told him. First of all, did he really say that Sheila would be running for Mayor? And secondly, what exactly was a flotilla? Since he thought better on a full stomach he savoured each drop of the delicious turkey soup and each crumb of his homemade roll. He wasn't thinking any clearer afterwards but he did feel better. Good enough to go back to work anyway.

When he got back, Betsy gave him a message from Inspector Ford's office. However, the message had come directly from Louise. It said Constable Harry Frost would be their temporary transfer until a permanent replacement could be found. Windflower remembered the name. It was one of Pomeroy's drug guys he'd worked with in the past. Frost had also worked in this area before which was good because with everything going on in Grand Bank they sure didn't have time to train a newbie.

Betsy also let Windflower know she had been in touch with the Town Council and had all the information on the wake and the funeral. Mayor Sinnott's body would be at the funeral home tonight and all day Tuesday. On Wednesday it would lie in state at the Masons Hall, where the former Mayor had been a member. The funeral would be on Thursday morning at 11 at the United Church. Betsy had assigned Evanchuk and Tizzard as vehicle escorts and reminded them to have their dress uniforms clean and ready.

Windflower thanked Betsy and asked her to phone Laura Emberley to come in as soon as possible for a follow up interview. He then went back to his office to return his phone calls and check his e-mails. There was a phone message from Ron Quigley in St. John's so he called that number first.

"Quigley, here," came the distinctive voice at the end of the line.

"Ron, how are ya, b'y?" said Windflower.

"If I was any better, I'd be dead. Thanks for calling back. Listen, Winston, what the heck is going on with Ford these days? I keep trying to call him and I need to get his approval on some stuff but he doesn't seem to be around. Some of the guys in St. John's are starting to ask questions about him. You used to be his buddy. What's going on?"

"Your guess is as good as mine," said Windflower, not wanting to give away what he saw happen with Ford over the weekend.

"There's talk here he's back on the sauce," said Quigley. "I don't really care, but I hear he's had some trouble for that in the past. I really need some action on my requests."

"I heard that too," said Windflower, again not wanting to volunteer the information that Ford himself had told him about his previous problems with drinking. "I can't seem to raise him either, but maybe you can talk to Louise in his office. She just got me a replacement for Fortier."

"Maybe I'll try that. Carl Langmead says hello. He said you'd want to know they're closing in on Shawn Parsons," said Quigley.

"That **is** good news," said Windflower. "Parsons deserves to be behind bars."

Quigley hung up and Windflower finished returning the rest of his calls and e-mails. The one person he couldn't reach was Brown in Forensics, so he left a message to call back. Then Betsy beeped him on the intercom to let him know the pharmacist from Fortune was here.

"Please bring her in."

Moments later, Betsy led Laura Emberley into his office and closed the door behind her.

"Good afternoon, Ms. Emberley, and thank you for coming in so quickly. I'm going to cut to the chase. We think you know more than you're telling us, and our patience is running out. We have two dead men and by the looks of it, they were both full of pharmaceuticals. We have missing drugs and drug reports and break-ins and reports that Michael Ridgeway was being blackmailed. It's all pointing back to your pharmacy so why don't you save us the trouble, and you a whole lot of pain, by telling us what you've been holding back?"

Windflower was surprised when Laura Emberley didn't blink an eye at him. She sat looking straight ahead as if she was pretending he wasn't there.

"Look, Ms. Emberley. We are going to close your pharmacy until we get to the bottom of this," he said, trying a new tactic.

"I've already decided to close the store. It's been losing money for a while, ever since the pharmacy opened up in the Walmart in Marystown. And with Michael gone I could never keep going on my own. I'm renting the building and the lease runs out at the end of the year."

"Did you know that Michael was being blackmailed? Were you involved with Michael?"

"I knew he was in trouble but I didn't blackmail him. Maybe you should be checking closer to home if you're looking for romantic involvements," she said.

"What do you mean?" asked Windflower.

"You didn't know? Your young Constable and Michael had it going hot and heavy for awhile. They tried to keep it a secret but I caught them in the storeroom one time."

"Who are you talking about? Evanchuk?"

"No, not her. The tall one. And I'm done talking to you like this. If you want to talk to me again, please contact my lawyer. Here's his name and number." She handed Windflower the information and walked out of the office.

MacDonald. Now he understood what she meant by an 'error in judgement'. And now he'd need to get her back to talk.

Chapter Thirty-Two

Windflower walked to the back where Tizzard was busy stuffing a plate-load of crackers and cheese into his mouth while reading a magazine.

"Having a light snack, Corporal?" Windflower asked.

"A growing boy's gotta eat, Boss. What's up?"

"It's hard to know where to begin," said Windflower as he recounted his day's activities to Tizzard. His Corporal was pleased with the news that they were getting help, surprised by the toxicology reports, and shocked by the information about MacDonald.

"I'll see what I can do about tracking her down," said Tizzard. "I think Evanchuk has been talking to her. I'll see if she will ask MacDonald to call me."

"Great," said Windflower. "It's also starting to look like Laura Emberley is more involved in this than she says. I just don't know how she fits in yet."

"Yeah, looks like it. Innocent people won't often talk about getting their lawyers."

"True," said Windflower. "You on tonight?"

"Yeah. I've got you penciled in for tomorrow night if that's okay. And we can get Frost for Wednesday. That way you and I and Evanchuk will be available for the funeral on Friday."

"Great," said Windflower. "Oh, and one more thing. I got a tip there might be some kind of protest happening around that freighter at the fish plant. See what you can find out."

"Will do," said Tizzard who went back to finishing up his cheese and crackers as soon as Windflower left for his office.

Windflower spent the last couple of hours going through his endless paperwork and initialling reports and memorandums from the Region and HQ. When he finally turned out his lights, he realized it was completely dark outside.

He packed up and was home quickly where Lady rushed to the door to meet him. He thought it was a nice welcome, and he patted her head and rubbed her rump. He took out a package of frozen cod from the freezer for supper, and then headed back outside for Lady's late afternoon stroll.

After the walk he put the fish in the microwave to thaw and peeled some potatoes. When the microwave beeped he took out the cod and dried it on a paper towel. Then he rolled it in flour and spiced it up with salt, pepper and a heavy hand of cayenne pepper. He cut up some fat back pork and heated it in an iron skillet to create the perfect medium for the fish. He gently laid the cod into the skillet and let it cook on a medium-high heat for five minutes on each side.

He was cutting up the broccoli when he heard Sheila come in. She came up from behind him and gave him a big hug.

"What's that for?" he asked.

"I just missed you," she said. "Do you have any of those Jamaican ginger beer drinks?"

"I think there's a couple in the fridge. Why don't you get us both one while I finish up here?"

Sheila rooted around the fridge and found the two small, stubby bottles she was looking for. She opened one and passed it to Windflower and took the other over to the kitchen table where Windflower had already laid out plates and cutlery.

Within minutes he was putting potatoes on each plate and poured a little of the pork fat from the frying pan over them. He then placed a portion of the fried codfish on the plates and covered it with the fried pork scraps, called scrunchions. He split the steamed broccoli between them and they sat down to eat.

"This fish is gorgeous," Sheila said as she forked a portion of the fried cod into her mouth.

"Hmmm," was all Windflower said in return as he dug into his plate of food. When they were finished, Windflower cleaned up while Sheila made tea and found some berries and ice cream for their dessert. They sat in the living room and caught up on each other's news. Windflower told Sheila about the abrupt departure of his uncle and MacDonald. Sheila talked about the plans for the Mayor's funeral on Thursday, and that she'd be doing one of the readings.

Windflower thought it was interesting she didn't bring up anything about her plans to be more involved in municipal politics. So he decided to go gently into that area by noting he'd seen Herb Stoodley at the Mug-Up.

"Herb's a great choice for the interim position," said Sheila. "He has the respect of just about everybody."

"Except for Francis Tibbo," said Windflower.

"Tibbo hoped he would automatically be named as the successor," said Sheila. "Luckily, saner heads prevailed and there will be an election held to replace the Mayor."

"Will you be throwing your hat into the ring?" asked Windflower, deciding to zero in on his real question.

"I haven't made up my mind yet. There are a lot of things to consider."

"Am I one of the considerations?" asked Windflower.

"Our relationship is," said Sheila. "But I won't make my decision based solely on my personal situation. The community has to be considered first."

Windflower thought of telling her he supported her in whatever decision she made, but that wasn't what came out of his mouth. What did was: "I hope you will consider my role in the community as well before you make your final decision." As soon as he spoke he knew by the look on Sheila's face he chose the wrong thing to say.

It was like he threw a match onto an oil-soaked rag. Sheila's eyes burned a hole right through him and before she even spoke he could feel her smoldering wrath. "All my life I've put other people first, what they wanted, what they needed, what I thought they wanted and needed. First when I was a child and then with Bart and finally again with my parents as they aged. I will not put any one person ahead of me ever again, Winston Windflower."

In a flash Sheila was up, dressed and out the door before Windflower had any chance to react, let alone respond. Even Lady looked at him as if to say 'What a loser you are, Sergeant Winston Windflower'.

Before he went to bed, he called Sheila to apologize but her call recognition system allowed her to ignore him. Finally, he gave up and went to bed. He read then tossed and turned, replaying the conversation and how he should have just said he supported her, until he exhausted himself and fell asleep. Sleeping would also prove to be unsatisfactory, because he soon after found himself back in the dream, the scary dream. The one with the screaming woman.

This time he forced himself to pay closer attention to the dream. He had learned from his Uncle Frank to look for the face of whomever was appearing in his dream, because they were usually messengers from the spirit world using the dream world as a medium to send messages back and forth. Both his uncle and his Auntie Marie were renowned for their dream work and both had helped Windflower hone his knowledge and awareness about the world of dreams.

When the screaming woman appeared, Windflower looked through the film that sat between him and the woman. The screaming was intense and frightening and he had to force himself to remain there so he could get a closer look. Finally, he could make out some features of the woman, and as he started to wake up he could clearly see that the woman in his dream was actually his own mother.

Windflower woke with a start and almost jumped out of bed. What did it mean and was she trying to tell him something? He had heard his Uncle Frank talk about screaming in dreams before and struggled to remember what he'd said. He knew if you couldn't scream in a dream when you wanted to, it meant you might be feeling powerless and frustrated about some situation in your life.

Then he remembered what his uncle said about hearing someone else scream in a dream: that some friend or family member was in need of help. But who could that be? Windflower didn't have that many living relatives he was close to. It could be Uncle Frank, but the dreams had started before his uncle had arrived. That only left his Auntie Marie. Could something be wrong with his aunt? Windflower checked the clock and saw it was 2:30 in the morning. That meant it was still fairly early back in his hometown of Pink Lake but not too late to call his aunt.

He called the number and let it ring for a while, but no one answered. Finally, the message came on and his cheerful aunt asked the caller to leave a message. Windflower did leave a message, but it was not like his aunt to not be home at this time. Maybe she was visiting someone or out of town, though. Windflower wasn't sure what was going on, but both his dream and his aunt's absence bothered him. Maybe he would try and call someone he knew back home in the morning, just to be on the safe side.

In any case, there was little more that he could do about it tonight so he picked up his book again and started reading. It was dramatic and riveting. It served Windflower well, first to get his mind off worrying about his aunt, and then tiring him enough to get to sleep.

Windflower still awoke early, but when he realized he was working the night shift and didn't have to get up quickly, he didn't. Both he and Lady were content to have a little lie-in until well after the sun had risen. He got up and pulled his RCMP hoodie over his pajamas to let Lady out and to carry out his morning rituals. This morning he had a lot to think about and many people to pray for. This included his aunt and uncle, who both seemed, at least to Windflower, to be in some form of trouble.

He also prayed again for Bill Sinnott and his family, which caused him to include the whole community of Grand Bank in his prayers. There were many in the community who were hurting because of his passing and who would miss his wisdom and guidance.

That reminded him about Sheila, and while his first thoughts were about their relationship, he decided to pray she would make the right decision for herself and the community. For himself he asked for the continued support of his friends and allies in this world and beyond, to be a good person, and to always walk a good path.

Lady was ready before Windflower, so he let her in and got her fresh food and water, and then finished his prayers. He put on the coffee and made his plans for the day.

CHAPTER THIRTY-THREE

It was just after 8 Windflower finished his breakfast and reviewed his list for the day. First up was to call Betsy and check in.

"Good morning, Betsy, how are you this fine morning?"

"I'm just grand," she said, clearly pleased her superior officer was in good spirits. "Corporal Brown in Forensics already called for you this morning. And Corporal Tizzard said he would like to talk to you if you called."

"Thanks, Betsy. I'll phone Forensics right away. Would you tell Tizzard I'll talk to him later?"

After hanging up from Betsy, Windflower called Brown in St. John's.

"Good morning Brownie, how are you today?"

"Sergeant Windflower, how are tings around the bay, b'y?"

"Tings are good, b'y," said Windflower with a laugh. "What have you got for me?"

"We're still going through the drugs and equipment, and we'll send you an inventory report later on that. The most interesting thing we've found so far is with the prints we lifted from the vehicle and the residence in Molliers. There appears to be four sets of prints at each location. One is clearly Fallon and the other is Michael Ridgeway. His file popped up when we ran it through the system."

"Yeah, he's got a history with drugs so that's not surprising. Who are the others?" asked Windflower.

"That's where it gets interesting. One of the other sets of prints belongs to Shawn Parsons. He's got a lengthy file and is flagged as a person of interest in a number of investigations here in St. John's."

"That is interesting. I've had some dealings with him in the past, but I didn't realize he had been in this area. What about the last set?"

"Well, it's not a full set, just some partials," said Brown. "But judging by the size of the ones we got I'd say it was probably a woman. There was nothing matching in the system but that could be because it's only a partial."

"Even more interesting. Thanks, Brownie, very helpful as usual. Anything else?"

"Not for now, but I'll send over that inventory when we get it ready," said Brown.

"Okay, Brownie, thanks. We'll talk soon."

After he hung up Windflower thought about what he'd learned from Brown. Shawn Parsons, that scumbag, was his initial thought. And then he thought about the other news he'd received, and the possible news a woman might be involved. Emberley, possibly. There was one way to find out: get her prints and see if they were a match. He called back to the RCMP office and got Tizzard on the line.

"Good morning, Boss. What's up?" asked Tizzard.

Windflower gave him the news he'd received about the fingerprints and the possible involvement of Shawn Parsons.

"That piece of garbage," said Tizzard.

"My thoughts exactly. But there's more. Forensics also found some partials they believe to be a woman's."

"A woman? What woman?"

"I'm guessing Laura Emberley," said Windflower. "I want you to go over and pick her up and take her prints. If she protests, tell her she's being investigated for fraud and obstruction of justice. If she starts squawking about a lawyer, tell her she can have one after she comes to the detachment."

"Okay, will do. I'll call you back once I get her back in," said Tizzard.

"Great, thanks," and Windflower hung up.

Windflower looked at the clock; it was just before 10. A little early, but he could still make his call to Pink Lake. If Windflower could reach his old friend Brandon Pelletier who was the Chief of the tribal police in Pink Lake, Brandon could go and check up on his aunt. He phoned back to the office and got Betsy to look up Brandon's number, and she quickly did. Betsy could find anything!

Windflower dialed the number and waited as it rang several times. He was about to hang up when a gruff voice answered. "Tribal Police, Pelletier here."

"Brandon, my old buddy, did I catch you sleeping on the job?" said Windflower playfully.

"Who is this?" the voice at the other end of the line demanded.

"It's Winston Windflower."

"Windflower. What the heck are you doing calling here at this hour of the morning? You've disturbed my beauty sleep. And God knows I need it."

"Sorry for waking you Brandon, but I have a favour to ask. Could you send somebody round to my Auntie Marie's house? I've been trying to reach her but there's no answer and I'm kind of worried about her," said Windflower.

"Sure, Winston, I can do that. I'll send one of the boys over as soon as they come in this morning. I hear her husband is wandering around your parts. Any sign of him?" asked Pelletier.

"Uncle Frank left here a day or so ago. He didn't take too kindly to my suggestions about behaving himself and keeping a low profile."

"I have the same problem," said Pelletier laughing. "Anyway, we'll check on your Auntie and let you know. Can I call you back at this number?"

"No, call the RCMP in Grand Bank. And if I'm not there, just leave a message. Thanks very much for this, Brandon."

"No problem. It's always good to have the RCMP owe you a favour."

Windflower hung up and made one more call: Sheila. Yet again there was no answer. He wondered if she was ignoring him. Maybe Herb would be there give him some advice over coffee. He hoped so. One more walk with Lady before he left, this time a quick one down to the end of the road and back. Lady would have liked more, so Windflower appeased her with two Milk Bones when they returned home. He then headed to the Mug-Up.

There was still a large group of men sitting around the coffee klatch when Windflower arrived and he noticed the room got noticeably quieter when he entered. He ordered a cup of coffee and read a copy of the Southern Gazette, last week's edition, while he waited. He looked at a picture of Mayor Sinnott and read an article about how one other small community was working through the loss of their fish plant and major employer by moving into something called 'secondary processing'. He didn't have time to finish the article before Herb Stoodley sat down beside him with two cups of coffee.

"It looks like you could use a cup," said Stoodley.

"Thanks. I've got a lot going on."

"I understand. Including on the home front."

When Windflower quizzically raised an eyebrow, Stoodley continued.

"Sheila was over last night. I didn't hear much, but your name did come up a few times. She and Moira were still at it when I went to bed."

"I was just trying to help. You have to look at things sensibly."

"Ah, that might be true, but the truth, reason and love keep little company together now-a-days," said Stoodley.

"Shakespeare?" asked Windflower.

"The bard still gets most things right, even today. The way I see it, Sheila has lots of people to give her advice, but very few who just love her. So that might be something to think about. It doesn't matter how many dances we have, what's important is who goes home with the girl."

"And all's well that ends well," said Windflower.

"Now you're thinking right. And remember nothing works best like restraint of pen and tongue."

"Shakespeare?"

"No," laughed Stoodley, "But I'm sure he would have approved."

Windflower finished his coffee and was leaving when Tizzard hurried into the café. "She's gone," he said breathlessly, even before he sat down.

"Who's gone?" asked Windflower.

"Laura Emberley. I went to her house and the pharmacy and there's no sign of her. Her car's gone, too, by the looks of it."

"I guess we may have been getting too close. Go home Corporal, you've been up all night. I'll get Betsy to start tracking Ms. Emberley. Unless she has a personal helicopter she's likely somewhere between here and Gander or St. John's."

"Okay. I'll go home and have a nap, but I'll be back in later."

Windflower nodded. He left his young Corporal at the Mug-Up and went over to the Grand Bank detachment.

"Morning, Betsy," he whispered on the way in. She was on the phone but he signalled for her to come see him. He picked up his messages from the slot and started going through them. One was from Louise in Inspector Ford's office in Marystown. It was marked in red, 'URGENT'. He picked up the phone and called Marystown.

A very distraught Louise answered on the very first ring.

"Good morning Sergeant. Thank you for calling me back. I don't like to do this but I think Inspector Ford is in trouble. He's been drinking a lot and he hasn't been here since the weekend. I'm trying to hold things together but it can't go on like this."

"Okay," said Windflower, trying to help the woman to relax a little. "When was the last time you talked to him?"

"He phoned in Monday morning to say he was ill. One of the other officers said they saw him in the bar talking with an older gentleman. He's not picking up his cellphone and I've tried calling his house but there's no answer. I'm really not sure what to do next."

"Let me see if I can find him. I can come over tomorrow morning. Is there anything urgent?"

"There's a couple of files that really need action, like your permanent replacement, but so far we've been managing."

"Okay, if there's anything else I can deal with it when I come over."

"Thank you, Sergeant, I really appreciate your help."

After Windflower hung up an eager Betsy Molloy was standing in front of him with her notepad in hand. I love Betsy, thought Windflower.

Chapter Thirty-Four

"Betsy, I need you to put a full trace on Laura Emberley. Tizzard has a file with her basic information. Hopefully he also has her vehicle information on it as well. She is wanted as a person of interest in the death of Frankie Fallon. Put it on the wire and alert all RCMP contacts in the province. I'm not sure we have a photo of her, so see if you can find one to attach. Also alert the Constabulary in St. John's and the airports in Gander and St. John's, as well as the ferry terminals in Argentia and Port aux Basques. She is to be detained and held for questioning by the Grand Bank RCMP."

Betsy took down all of this information. "I'll take a look at Corporal Tizzard's file and draft up the initial alert first and bring it back to you. Is that all?"

"Thanks, Betsy, that's it for now," said Windflower.

"By the way, did you see the message from Constable MacDonald?" asked Betsy. "It came in on the machine last night. It just said she wanted to talk to you."

Windflower looked down and found the message in his pile. It was from A. MacDonald and it had a 709 area code number, which meant she was still in Newfoundland. "Thanks, Betsy."

Windflower dialled the number.

"Hello," said a timid voice when the call went through.

"Constable MacDonald, it's Sergeant Windflower."

"Yes, sir, sorry, sir," said Macdonald.

"What's going on, Constable?" asked Windflower as calmly as he could.

"I'm in St. John's. I know I'm in a lot of trouble but I felt like I had to get away. I was planning to go home but I think I'd feel worse if I did that."

"Why don't you just come back? You can only clear things up by coming clean. Tell the truth, and maybe we can find a way to help you."

"With all due respect, nobody can help me now, sir. I think I royally screwed things up," said MacDonald.

He let her bad choice of words pass. "I'm still your best shot. There aren't many good options for you if you keep running away. I'm not sure what your story is, but I'm willing to listen. But let me be clear. This is your last shot with me. Either come back and tell the truth, all the truth, or I will issue an order for your arrest."

He could almost hear MacDonald thinking about her options over the phone line.

Finally she spoke. "Okay, I'm prepared to make a statement and prepared to resign from the RCMP afterward. Do you want me to come to Grand Bank?"

"Meet me at the RCMP detachment in Marystown tomorrow around noon." He suggested Marystown because if it were necessary to detain her it would be easier in Marystown because it had more room and a special unit for women.

"Okay. I'll see you tomorrow."

Windflower knew it'd be a doozy day tomorrow. He put down the receiver just as Betsy walked back into his office. She had a printed 'Alert' notice done up with a surprisingly new picture of Laura Emberley on top. "Where did you get the pic?" asked Windflower.

"Facebook. Social media makes tracking people so easy anybody can do it now."

"I see you got her auto info too."

"That's D.O.T. A bit harder to get access than Facebook, but if you know where to look..."

"Thank you, Betsy, good job," said Windflower to his now-beaming administrative assistant. "Put it up and keep me updated."

"Will do," said Betsy as she happily went off to post her notices.

It made Windflower pleased as well to think that at least one person in his life was happy with him. Now, if he could only do the same with Sheila. He called Sheila's number, and to his surprise and pleasure, she answered.

"Good morning, Sheila, how are you this morning?"

"I'm well," she said.

"I wanted to talk to you about last night," said Windflower.

"I'd like to talk too," said Sheila. "But I don't want to do it over the phone. Let's get together for an early supper tonight at my place."

"Okay," said Windflower. "I'll come over right after work."

There may be hope for redemption after all. Windflower reflected upon Herb Stoodley's advice and Shakespeare's wisdom that 'The course of true love never did run smooth'. As long as it didn't turn out to be 'Hell hath no fury like a woman scorned', he might be okay. That wasn't the bard but it was enough to shake him up. Time for another cup of coffee.

When he went to the lunchroom at the back, Evanchuk was sitting quietly, drinking a cup of tea. She was also reading a notebook.

"Evanchuk, what are you reading?"

"Oh, hi Sergeant. I found this at the bottom of the metal box Tizzard gave me. It was underneath the pile of tapes. It looks like a record of times and dates and there are a lot of initials like SP and FF. I think the FF might be Frankie Fallon, sir," said Evanchuk.

"Let me see," said Windflower. He glanced down at the notebook and took it from Evanchuk. He flipped through some of the pages. He could see a number of dates and notations and numbers and also a few more initials. "SP might be Shawn Parsons. "We've got some information indicating he was in the area. His prints are on Ridgeway's car and at the house in Molliers."

"That dirt bag," said Evanchuk, making that the majority and unanimous opinion of Shawn Parsons. "I saw another one too: LE. Is that Laura Emberley, the woman we just posted about?"

"Might be. It's starting to look like she's much more involved than we first thought, or made herself out to be. Once we nab her we'll find out more. Have you listened to any of the tapes yet?"

"Not yet. I'm going to start tonight as my bedtime listening. By the way, I talked to MacDonald. I suggested she call you."

"Thank you, Constable. I did talk to her. I'm going to interview her tomorrow in Marystown. Did you know she was involved with Michael Ridgeway?" asked Windflower.

"No, I didn't. I knew she was seeing somebody, but we didn't talk about it much. I can see now why she wouldn't say who it was. How much trouble is she in?"

"I don't know. I'll find out tomorrow."

Windflower got his coffee and walked back to his office. He worked his way through his messages, e-mails and correspondences and a little after 1 drove back up to his house for lunch. Lady seemed a little anxious, so he took her out for a stroll. He decided to take his normal longish route around the wharf. As he turned the corner to go down to the main wharf he could see that on the other side, at the fish plant entrance, there were now at least a dozen vehicles parked by the homemade protest sign.

It didn't appear the people involved were doing anything more than milling around and since there was nothing coming in or out of the fish plant, they couldn't be accused of obstructing anything. Windflower briefly thought about going over to talk to them but instead followed Lady as she pulled him along the harbourside. There were a few more fishing boats moored at the dock, more than usual anyway. Nothing really wrong with that either, though.

Sometimes people pulled their small boats into the harbour to get a little work done on them. It seemed strange to have that happen in December, but what did Windflower know about fishing boats? There certainly weren't many of them where he grew up in Pink Lake.

Lady let Windflower know when she'd had enough by another tug on her leash, and soon they were back home for water and fresh food for both of them. Lady had to settle for the contents of her bowl, while Windflower made himself a ham and cheese sandwich on some nice bread he'd picked up at Sobeys. He cut it thick and smeared it with Keen's hot mustard. With a handful of baby carrots and a few bread and butter pickles, it turned out to be a great lunch. Windflower tidied up and gave Lady one more pat on the head before he left for his afternoon and overnight shift.

When he got back to the office Betsy handed him a message as soon as he entered. It was from the Pink Lake Tribal Police about his aunt. Windflower went to his office and made the call.

"It's Winston Windflower here. Someone called me about my aunt, Marie Pendleton."

"Yes, one moment please, I'll find the officer who is looking at that case," said the woman who answered the phone.

A few moments later a man came on the line. "Sergeant Windflower, it's Maurice Desmarais. The Chief asked me to go and check on Missus Pendleton. I'm glad we did. It appears she has had a series of strokes, at least that's what the doctor at the clinic said. She can't talk and has some partial paralysis, but it looks like she's going to survive and eventually should be okay. She indicated she had trouble walking and was getting anxious because she couldn't let anyone know she was in trouble."

Windflower thought it was just like Uncle Frank to be missing in action when there was an emergency.

"Have you seen her? Is she okay now?"

"Yes, I found her this morning. Like I said she has some trouble walking and can't talk. Her left side looks like it's frozen, but apart from that she is doing fine. She is at the clinic now and they are going to run some tests. Depending on that, they may have to take her to Edmonton, but there's no word on that yet. She seemed very relieved to see me this morning, and when I left her she was eating and laughing with the girls at the clinic," said Desmarais.

"Do you have a contact I can follow up with at the clinic?" asked Windflower.

"Yes, the doctor is Mark Stone, but your best bet would be to talk to the nurse, Linda Lalonde. She's easier to reach and she would have the latest information. I told her you might be calling," said Desmarais.

"Thank you very much," said Windflower. "And say thank you to the Chief, too."

"Will do. We're just happy she's okay. Auntie Marie is a special lady."

She certainly was, especially to Windflower. Since his own mother died young, Auntie Marie had been like a mother to him, including her constant prodding about his unborn children, whom she had already pre-adopted as her own grandchildren. She was a very special lady.

Mike Martin

CHAPTER THIRTY-FIVE

The rest of the afternoon flew by until it was time to take a break and go over to Sheila's for supper. Windflower drove quickly through the dark and silent streets with lights shining from within almost every house. Each house looked so comfy and cozy and warm. So too was Sheila's as he turned up into her driveway and parked behind her car.

He said hello from the porch and Sheila answered him from the kitchen where Windflower's nose told him supper was well underway. His scent buds did not lead him astray and Sheila directed him to the kitchen table where a place had already been set for them both. Windflower sat down and poured them each a glass of water from the jug that lay in the middle of the table.

"Smells like fish," said Windflower.

"You would be correct," said Sheila. "I thawed out a bit of salt fish and I've had it soaking all day so that I could make a few fish cakes."

"They smell delicious. So how do you make fish cakes anyway?"

"Well it's pretty simple if you've got the salt fish and a few potatoes. I mash them up with some flour, add some chopped onions and salt and pepper, then fry them up in fat back and here they are," she said, as she laid two perfectly round and browned fish cakes on a plate in front of Windflower. She also reached into the oven and pulled out a casserole dish with some roasted potatoes. She served them each a helping and along with some homemade pickle relish, their supper was ready to go.

Windflower said little, but the smile on his face grew with each bite of the delicious fish cakes. It was so good he had second helpings of both the fish cakes and the potatoes. At the end he sat for a moment to silently savour the meal he had just enjoyed.

"That was wonderful, Sheila. I think fish cakes are moving up on my top ten list."

"Lucky for you I already packed a few away for your midnight snack."

"Thank you so much. That will be greatly appreciated later tonight. Why don't you make some tea and I'll clean up the dishes?"

They were quiet and pensive as they carried out their tasks until both sat down at the table with a pot of tea and a plate of date squares in front of them. "I didn't tell you about Auntie Marie," Windflower said, and he told Sheila both about his foreboding dream and what happened afterward.

"I hope she'll be okay. She is such a nice and kind woman. So is your uncle by the way, when he's not drinking."

"Uncle Frank," said Windflower with a sigh. "That's another story. He will likely surface again soon in some new jackpot. That's usually what happens. He is either the luckiest or unluckiest person I know. Lucky because no matter what hole he falls into, he always seems to find a way out. Unlucky because he keeps finding new holes to fall into."

Sheila laughed, but soon grew a little more serious. "I guess we should talk," she said.

Windflower nodded and she continued.

"I have been thinking a lot about what is happening around me and within me and I have come to a few conclusions. First of all, I love you very much and I want to be with you. That is true and clear for me. But I also have to act in a way that preserves my own integrity."

She now had Windflower's complete attention.

"There are three questions I believe we have to ask ourselves to do that, answered in order. They are: Who am I? Where am I going? And who is going with me?" Sheila paused and poured them each a cup of tea. "You can have a date square, Winston. It would make me more comfortable if you were eating."

Windflower laughed and popped half a date square into his mouth. Sheila took a sip of tea and continued.

"Despite my age and experience, I'm still figuring out who I am. But I know inside what feels right, and what is pulling me towards that is service, particularly service to the community. I am also an informal leader in this community and I am being called to be a formal one. That is particularly important to me as a woman, because there are few prominent female leaders in this community, few role models for young women to follow. If I run for Mayor and win, I will be the first female Mayor in our town's history."

"Wow. You really could make history."

"I would not want to be elected just to be the first. I would want to be elected on my abilities and competence, but yes, that is part of the consideration. It is also where I think I am going. So I have now at least a partial answer to the first two questions. The third is up to you."

Windflower paused and looked straight at Sheila. "I love you and support you. I will follow you wherever you are going."

"I will need that support, but I also want to know I can make my own decisions, about my career choices and political ambitions, without needing your approval in advance."

"I just want to be consulted on decisions that affect me, Sheila. I don't expect you to tell me everything about your work. I really just want us to build a partnership that can help support each other."

"Oh, Winston, you are the best," said Sheila. She came around to hold him and he stood to hold her tightly. They stayed in that embrace for only a few moments, but it was certainly the best part of Windflower's day. They kissed, long and passionately and deeply. "Unfortunately for me, I have to go back to work," said Windflower.

"That's unfortunate for me too," said Sheila with a laugh. "But I think we have many more evenings to spend together."

"I think so too," said Windflower as he hugged her close one more time and left to go back to the detachment.

The night was clear and the wind had taken a bit of a break. Windflower stared up at the sky and gave thanks to Grandmother Moon for guiding him through this difficult passage. And for the dreams that enabled him to help his Auntie Marie.

He prayed quietly. "Please help me find my uncle now. My aunt will need his help and support to recover and heal."

Windflower was back at the RCMP building in no time. He put on a pot of coffee to help him get through the long night alone. He checked the messages on the phone and on the internal RCMP website that gave a continuous rolling report of activities in the region. No new reports, which meant nothing new on his search for Laura Emberley. Not much even on the weather front. The forecast was for clear skies overnight, lasting until noon Thursday, which would make for a good trip to Marystown tomorrow, and to the Mayor's funeral on Thursday morning.

It was a quiet night on the midnight shift. Windflower kept busy and alert by doing a health and safety inspection of the detachment. This was supposed to be done monthly, but it was more like whenever he remembered to do it. The last time might have even been about 6 months ago. In any case, it had to be done and it took him close to 3 hours to check all of the equipment and machinery for broken or missing parts and to identify any possible electrical or mechanical hazards. Once he was done with that task, he heated up his fish cakes and had his late evening meal. Then he went out on the first of his driving tours of the town and the surrounding highway.

He actually liked that part of the overnight shift. Driving through Grand Bank in the dark was like going through a ghost town, with only a few glimmering lights breaking the darkness. He especially liked being on the highway alone with the moon as his lantern and the stars shining out over the ocean. It was as quiet on the road as it was in town and Windflower enjoyed the silent beauty and majesty of the December night before heading slowly back to his office.

The remainder of the night was uneventful and at 6 he locked up the office for the final tour of his district. By the time he got back, Evanchuk was sitting in the kitchen drinking her first cup of coffee.

"I've got more stuff from the tapes," she said excitedly to Windflower.

"That's great. But I'm knackered. I've got to get a nap in before I go over to Marystown. Maybe you could go through it with Tizzard when he gets in." Seeing her disappointment he added, "Good work, Constable, I knew we could count on you to do a good job."

Her ego and pride restored, Evanchuk smiled and said, "Thank you, sir. We'll give you a full report later."

Windflower left and dragged himself home. He let Lady out for her business in the backyard and refilled her food and water bowls, but that was the extent of his energy supply. He threw off his clothes, set the alarm for 10:30, and was fast asleep within a minute.

The alarm shook him awake, but he had to struggle to remember what day of the week it was. He had a hot shower and shave and by the end of that, he felt refreshed and part of the world again.

He took Lady for a brisk walk which included a stop by Sheila's to say a quick hello and to steal a kiss.

When he returned home, he grabbed a banana off the top of the fridge and gave his other girl, Lady, a biscuit and a pat on the head. "See you tonight, girl," he said as he closed the door and drove quickly through town to Marystown. The drive would give him a chance to unwind a little and to think a lot.

He was so hungry it seemed like his RCMP Jeep automatically made the turn into the Tim Hortons parking lot. He went inside and ordered a large coffee and an 'everything' bagel, toasted with butter and cheddar cheese. Not very good for his waistline, but perfect for his appetite. He hopped back onto the road to Marystown.

He had finished his bagel and half his coffee when he arrived at Louise's desk outside of Inspector Ford's office. Sitting in the chair opposite of the administrative assistant was Constable Anne MacDonald, looking very much like a Maritime girl in her jeans and flannel jacket.

Windflower said good morning to both, and nodded to MacDonald to stay put while he went inside Ford's office with Louise.

"Thank you for coming, Sergeant," said Louise. "I'd really appreciate if you'd have a look at these documents. I have been holding them, but most are past due and getting urgent at this point. I have initialed them as being correct, but I just don't have the authority."

Neither did Windflower, but he kept that to himself. "Okay. Will you get Constable MacDonald a cup of tea and tell her I'll be about half an hour?"

While Louise went to look after that, Windflower went through the file folder. There seemed to be almost a month of requests, some minor, some looking substantial. Windflower approved as many as he thought looked reasonable enough, including his own request for a permanent replacement in Grand Bank. He left the major ones in the file folder. He didn't mind helping Louise out a little but there was no point of trying to stretch this non-authority too far.

After he finished his review he called Louise on the intercom to give her back the folder and to explain what he had done. Louise—who had been around the RCMP forever—understood completely. They agreed to talk more before he left for the day, and he asked her to send in Constable MacDonald.

Chapter Thirty-Six

MacDonald didn't just look nervous, she looked drained. Windflower asked her to sit at the small table in the Inspector's office, and he sat across from her. No point in trying to make her feel even more intimidated by sitting behind his desk. He knew he wasn't supposed to, but he felt sorry for MacDonald, and if he could he would try and help her.

"So, go ahead, Constable. You might as well tell me what's going on and we'll see where we go from there."

MacDonald sighed and began. "I didn't mean for it to happen. I guess I was lonely or homesick or something. I wasn't looking for anything, but Michael had an interest in me and since I wasn't feeling particularly good about myself at the time, when he made his move, I accepted."

"We're talking about Michael Ridgeway?" asked Windflower, just to be sure.

"Yes, I met him when I went to Fortune to get a prescription filled. He seemed nice and funny and when I went back to have it refilled, he asked me out. At first I told him I couldn't because I was concerned what it would look like. And also because I didn't want any more complications in my life. But he persisted and eventually, I gave in," she said.

"When was this?" asked Windflower.

"I began seeing him in June and it went on for about three months. We would mostly meet at his house in

Fortune and sometimes we would go for walks up on the Cape. In September, Laura Emberley caught him and me together in the back room at the pharmacy, and I told him it had to end," said MacDonald.

"How did he take it?" asked Windflower.

"Michael was pretty upset. He confessed he had been using prescription drugs intravenously and hiding it from me. He said he was trying to get off them and wanted me to stay with him as he went through that process." MacDonald paused and took a sip from her tea. "That actually convinced me it was over and I told him that. He didn't like it but we agreed to stay friends and he seemed okay about it."

"So was that the end for you and Michael Ridgeway?" asked Windflower.

"It was as far as our relationship went, but it wasn't the end of my dealings with Michael," continued MacDonald. "In fact things got more intense. Michael told me he was being blackmailed at the pharmacy, and being forced to pay money and hand over prescription drugs to the people threatening him. He said they knew he was using drugs and threatened to expose him. I suggested he report the matter to Tizzard, but he said the police would never believe him."

"Do you know who was involved in this blackmailing? And why didn't you report him and these activities yourself?"

"I guess that was my biggest mistake. Michael begged me not to say anything. But the truth is that I was afraid, afraid for myself. I stayed quiet to protect myself. I really didn't know how much to believe Michael. He was getting more erratic and paranoid through the Fall. He said he would get killed if he didn't deliver. I didn't believe him, until it was too late."

After this last statement, MacDonald buried her head in her lap and started crying. Windflower decided to take a break.

"I'm going to take you downstairs to the holding area. We can continue this conversation a little later."

When MacDonald started to protest, he simply raised his hand to signify there would be no debate. MacDonald sniffled, and although still crying, allowed herself to be led out into the reception area.

"Louise, I am going to escort Constable MacDonald down to the holding area. Could you please call down and let them know we're coming? I'll be back in a few minutes to continue our meeting. Thank you, Louise."

Windflower walked with MacDonald downstairs to where the holding cells were located. The woman's section was near the back, separated from the men's area by a metal gate. Windflower said hello to the guard at the front and walked right up to the gate where he was met by a female RCMP Constable.

"Good afternoon, Sergeant. I'm Constable Newsome. I understand you would like us to look after Constable MacDonald for a while."

"Thank you. Constable MacDonald is being held in protective custody. I will be back later today to talk to her."

"Yes, sir," said Newsome as she guided MacDonald—who was in a bit of a fog and still crying—back to a quiet cell.

Windflower was relieved to drop MacDonald off, and he walked back upstairs to where Louise was waiting for him.

"Have you heard anything from Inspector Ford?" he asked.

"He called in this morning to tell me he wouldn't be in this week. I think I may have to file a report with the Region. I don't want to do it, but it looks like I may not have a choice."

"You have to do what you need to do. But wait until I have a chance to talk with him. I'm going to go over to his house right now to see if I can find out what's going on."

Louise nodded, and Windflower left to drove through Marystown to Ford's house on Smallwood Drive. Windflower knew the way because he had stayed there while he was helping out the past year.

Windflower pulled up in the driveway behind Ford's pick-up. He rang the doorbell and received quite a shock when his Uncle Frank opened the door.

"Come in. I've been expecting you."

"What are you doing here? And what do you mean, you were expecting me?"

"Come in, Winston, and have some lunch. I'm making up some bologna and beans. Your friend can't eat a lot yet, but I'm starved. To answer the first of your questions, I've been looking after Bill. He had a hard time getting sober but the worst is over now. I just kept making him weak tea with some of my medicine. I think he's going to make it now."

"Did you hear the news about Auntie Marie?"

"I did, but we can talk about that later," said his uncle. "You better go talk to your buddy first."

Windflower followed his uncle into the kitchen where a very tired and drawn looking Bill Ford was sitting unshaven in his pajamas, nursing what Windflower assumed was a cup of his uncle's tea.

"Winston," he murmured. "I would have died without your uncle. You'll have to excuse me though, I have to go lie down. I still can't take the smell of food. I'll talk to you when you've finished eating."

Ford dragged himself to the living room where it looked like he had made a makeshift bed for himself.

"Sit down," Frank said to Windflower. "I'll dish you up some beans and bologna."

Windflower sat down as directed and only then did he realize how hungry he was. He finished off his plate in no time and was ready for more when Frank dished them up. As usual there was little talk while the two men ate. Afterward, Frank put the dishes in the sink and went out for a smoke. Windflower followed him.

"So how did all of this come about?" Windflower asked.

"I saw Bill at the bar at the motel when I got in on Monday afternoon. I had already made up my mind to quit drinking again when I walked by the bar and saw him sitting in there by himself. He was in bad shape, nursing a hangover and pretty desperate looking. I offered to help him dry out and that's what we've been doing since. Sometimes you are just put in someone's path to help. This was my turn."

"And how did you know I was coming?" asked Windflower.

"A little rabbit told me," said his uncle as he stubbed out his cigarette and went back inside.

Windflower followed. "What do you mean?"

"I told you already. Don't you remember your Auntie used to call you her little rabbit? Well, a little rabbit came right up to me in the backyard here. That's how I knew you were coming. It was a sign. You've got to be watching out for the signs, Winston."

"You saw a rabbit in the backyard in the middle of winter?" questioned Windflower.

Ford had slowly come back into the kitchen and laughed at this last statement. "The neighbours next door have pet rabbits. Sometimes they get out."

While his uncle feigned indignation and started doing the dishes, Windflower nodded to Ford and indicated they should move out to the living room so they could talk.

"I guess I owe you an explanation," said Ford.

"I'm listening," said Windflower. "There are more people than me that need an explanation. A lot of people out there are depending on you, including your office."

"Yeah, I know. I'm a real screw-up. You know I really didn't want to get back to this place. I was doing okay here in Marystown, even dealing with that crazy Inspector Arsenault. I had a program then. I was going to meetings and I had a sponsor. When I went out to the west coast, I thought I was okay. I thought I could do it on my own."

"You were sober for a long time," said Windflower.

"Eight years, going on nine. I knew what to do, I just didn't do it. I started hanging around the wrong people. When things got hectic and my life got stressed out, I was ready for a drink. And when it was offered to me one more time, I had no will to resist. At first it wasn't too bad. I would only drink when I was out in the woods, then only on weekends. But it went downhill fast. I was drinking daily again in a month. Once an alcoholic, always an alcoholic."

"So where do you go from here? What about the Member Assistance Program?"

"I guess that's one of my first calls," said Ford. "I'm going to need some help. I'll call them this afternoon."

"And the Region?" asked Windflower.

That's my second call. I know they won't be happy but I guess I have to face the music. I probably wasn't cut out to be a big wheel," he said with a wry smile.

"As soon as you know anything you need to talk to Louise. She's looking after the whole shop right now. As a matter of fact, you should probably call her first. She's been holding down the fort by herself."

Ford nodded again weakly as Frank came into the living room. "I'm going to be on my way now. The taxi will be here soon and then I'm off to Edmonton."

"How did you hear about Auntie Marie?" he asked his uncle.

"I had the same dream as you. Once I stopped drinking my dreams came back. I knew right away there was something wrong at home. I called the house but there was no answer so I got a neighbour to go find out what was going on. I think they got there just after your policemen friends. Anyway, Marie is getting better, but they shipped her to Edmonton to do some more tests and to start her rehabilitation plan. I'll see her tonight."

"You never cease to amaze me, Uncle," said Windflower as he heard a car horn sound from outside. "That will be your ride."

"Pay attention to the signs, Nephew. They are all around you," said Uncle Frank as he gave Windflower a hug. He also went and embraced Bill Ford who was shaky but standing to thank his new friend. He started to speak, but Uncle Frank cut him off. "There is no need for thanks in a family," he said. "Just be grateful because the blessings are already on the way."

Uncle Frank then left, with Windflower heading back to the RCMP offices in Marystown shortly thereafter.

Chapter Thirty-Seven

When Windflower returned, Louise was already on the phone with the Regional people. Ford had called her and given her an update. She was putting the wheels in motion to advise all the necessary personnel Acting Inspector Ford was on indefinite leave and to get a replacement Inspector named as quickly as possible. So she looked a little better, and almost relieved when Windflower showed up.

"I think we'll be okay now," she said. "Thank you for coming over and getting him to move. It really helps. It's so much easier this way. Now I can report on all the matters that have been held in abeyance and hopefully, we'll get a new commanding officer soon."

"No problem. I'm going down to see Constable MacDonald and then I'll be heading back home. If you need me, you know where I am."

He went to check on MacDonald, and Louise continued putting her universe back together. MacDonald was still pretty upset when the female guard brought her out to the small interview room at the edge of the holding cells. "I have a few more questions for you today and then I am going to ask you to give a full written statement, okay?" asked Windflower. MacDonald nodded her agreement.

"Who was blackmailing Michael Ridgeway?" Windflower asked.

"I'm not really sure. Michael kept talking how this thing was bigger than him. He said the operation was being run out of Nova Scotia, but I thought he was just being paranoid. Frankie Fallon was hanging around the back of the pharmacy sometimes and I saw him talking to Michael once, but I just figured Fallon was just a low-life trying to sponge off Michael, not threatening him."

"What about the break-in? What was the story around that, and why didn't you file your report?" asked Windflower.

"Fortier and I went over to investigate the report by Laura Emberley, and he interviewed Michael and Emberley while I took a look around. There was a broken window at the back of the building and the alarm had been cut off. But there was nothing disturbed or strewn around inside like there usually is when there's a break-in. It was almost too clean, if you know what I mean. Emberley had a list compiled of what she thought was missing but that looked too simple."

"So you thought something fishy was going on?"

"I did. So did Fortier. He said he thought Emberley was lying but he wasn't sure about what. Later Michael told me he didn't think there was a break-in at all. He said he had been told by Emberley to stay away from the pharmacy on the night of the break-in. I wanted Michael to come forward with his concerns, but he said Emberley would fire him if he did. So I held onto the report and kept it in the file without recording it. I was hoping to convince him to change his mind. But we ran out of time."

"When was the last time you saw Ridgeway?" asked Windflower.

"I saw him the day before he died. I asked him again to come forward and make a statement, but he said it was too late. I didn't know what he meant by that. But now we know it was true."

"Okay. Do you still have a place to stay in Grand Bank?"

When MacDonald nodded he said, "I'm going to bring you back with me to Grand Bank. If you agree, I will release you in modified house detainment. You are to stay in Grand Bank and report to the detachment daily until we settle this matter. If you don't want to do that, I'll have to leave you here," said Windflower.

"I'll come back to Grand Bank. I just have to go over to my friend's house to pick up my stuff. Then I'll be ready to go."

"I'll drive you over."

Windflower thanked Constable Newsome and said goodbye to some of the other staff he knew or recognized from previous visits. He drove MacDonald to her friend's house and waited for her to pick up her bags. Then he stopped at the Tim Hortons drive-through and picked up two large coffees.

It was getting darker and darker as they drove back to Grand Bank and MacDonald was deathly quiet along the way. That suited Windflower just fine, though. He was quite content to have an hour or so of peace after the turmoil of the day. When they got back, he dropped MacDonald off at her house and went to see if Sheila might be home. And maybe, just maybe, if there were any chance of supper around her place.

As luck would have it, Sheila was just getting back herself and she suggested heating up some chicken stew she had in the freezer. Windflower ran over to Sobeys and picked up a salad bag and a loaf of freshly-made multigrain bread. He added a few carrots, a chopped red pepper and some raisins to the salad mix and sliced up about half of the bread. By the time Sheila had the table set, the chicken stew was bubbling on the stove and their feast was ready. Windflower got them both an India beer out of the fridge. It was a local beer that had a picture of a Newfoundland dog on the front.

When Windflower saw the picture, he remembered Lady, and begged 15 minutes from Sheila for a quick walk with the dog.

Lady was as pleased as always with her master's return, but kind of surprised with his quick pace on their mini-walk. But there was dinner waiting for him at the end of his trek and Windflower was certainly ready for his meal. As promised, he was back at Sheila's 15 minutes later digging into his hot bowl of chicken stew.

A second helping and several thick slices of bread later, he was finally able to speak. "That was so good, Sheila," he said. "So what's new with you?"

"I had a good day. I've been meeting with people to talk about the community and where they see it going. There are some great ideas out there."

"Have you made a decision yet about running for Mayor?"

"No. Lots of people are encouraging me, but I want to figure out what I want to do as Mayor before I commit. I don't want to just have the title; I would like to accomplish something."

"That's good. It seems to me that far too many people just want the glory without doing the work."

"Besides, the Council hasn't even set a date for an election, and won't until after the funeral," she said.

"That's very respectful to Mayor Sinnott," said Windflower.

"He deserves at least that much. Dessert?"

Windflower thought about saying he was stuffed, which was true, but when he saw Sheila reach into the fridge and pull out a small white cake box, his resolve was broken.

"I'll clean up the dishes," he said.

Soon, Windflower was sitting and savoring his most favorite dessert. He tried to make his peanut butter cheesecake last, but it seemed to melt away on his fork and within seconds his large, very large, piece was reduced to a few crumbs on his plate. "Ah, he said. "That was very good, Missus. Hillier."

"You're welcome. I hope you're staying tonight. You can thank me properly later."

"I would love to do just that," said Windflower. "Let me just check in with the office for a few minutes and walk the dog. After that, I'm all yours."

Windflower grabbed his hat and coat and headed back over to the Grand Bank RCMP building.

When he got there, he found Tizzard in the back having a snack, as usual.

"Hey, Boss," said Tizzard. "You remember Kevin Frost," he said, introducing the other man who was also greatly enjoying some cheese and crackers.

"Sure. Welcome to Grand Bank, Constable. You've been around here before, right?"

"Yes sir. I did that piece with the drug squad you were involved with. I spent a few nights in enemy territory down around Lamarra."

"It's getting better now," said Windflower. "Tizzard and the late Mayor have done a lot of work trying to get the locals on board. They're still distrustful at times but it's improving. Speaking of the late Mayor, are we all set up for tomorrow morning?" he asked.

"Yup," said Tizzard. "Frost will look after the shift tonight and stay until after the funeral. Evanchuk is going to do the escort and I thought you and I could be at the church. Funeral is at 10:00, so we should be there by 9:30."

"Perfect. There's a few things I need to talk to you about," Windflower said to Tizzard, motioning him to come with him. "Have a good night, Frost."

"Evanchuk told me we may have some sort of code book to go along with the tapes," said Windflower when they got back to his office.

"Yeah, we're able to track the dates and people and what looks like money and amounts of drugs being transferred in and out of the Fortune Pharmacy," said Tizzard. "Ridgeway may have been a drug addict, but he would make a pretty good accountant."

"Did you say transfer in and out of the pharmacy? Why would anybody transfer drugs in?"

"I know, it's weird, isn't it? It must be some way for them to get around the reporting system when it comes to the opiates. Anyway, we're still going through the tapes, at least Evanchuk is. I'm hoping to have a full report for you by Friday."

"Good," said Windflower. "MacDonald is back. I picked her up in Marystown. I am holding her on administrative detainment."

"Is there any such thing as administrative detainment?" asked Tizzard, looking puzzled. "I never heard of it."

"No. But I didn't want to arrest her. This way we get to keep her around until we figure out what to do with her."

"What do you mean?" asked Tizzard.

"She had an affair with Michael Ridgeway and it looks like she compromised the investigation of the break-in at the Fortune Pharmacy, and maybe more. I told her she had to stay in Grand Bank and report here every day. And I want you to interview her and get a full written statement. Okay?"

"Okay. But what about—"

"It's been a long day, Corporal. I've got a date with two beautiful females. I'll see you in the morning. Oh, and by the way, Ford is out in Marystown. Bye."

Tizzard was left standing in Windflower's office with his mouth wide open and a very blank look on his face.

"Tomorrow," Windflower shouted back to him as he left the office for his first date: a beautiful collie.

Windflower and Lady had a lovely long walk all over Grand Bank. It was getting warmer, and he unbuttoned his jacket as they walked along. That might be welcome in some places, but around here it usually meant more snow was on the way.

Windflower finished the loop with Lady and settled her in for the night with fresh food and water. He drove over to Sheila's where she was waiting for him on the couch in the living room. They were both too tired for TV and too eager for each other to spend much time there. They had a loving and wonderful time upstairs and with Sheila nestled tightly into the crook of his arm, Windflower fell quickly into a peaceful sleep.

Chapter Thirty-Eight

Windflower awoke, dressed and drove back home in the darkness of the early morning. Lady quickly came to see him when she heard the door open. He let her out the back door and stood for a moment on the porch to breathe in the fresh Newfoundland air. The wind was definitely coming in from the south, which meant milder temperatures. But it almost certainly meant snow, as well.

How much was anyone's guess, and Windflower had long ago given up guessing about the weather. There was no certainty to the weather in this part of the world, only that it was unpredictable. Windflower smudged with his grandfather's eagle feather and allowed the smoke to envelope him in the darkness. He always felt clean and refreshed after he smudged.

This morning he had many things to give thanks for. His Auntie was in good hands in Edmonton and his Uncle Frank was likely there with her now. He had good relations with the love of his life, although he knew that was more probationary, dependent upon his good behaviour. And he had Lady, a friend for life, who didn't care what he said or did, as long as he came home to see her. For all of these gifts he gave thanks. He also prayed again for Bill Sinnott's spirit to be guided safely to the other world. And he prayed for his friend Bill Ford's return to a good path in the world. Finally, he asked for the strength, wisdom and guidance to carry out his own responsibilities and be a good person in this world.

He put an egg on to boil and then added another one. He showered and dressed in his red serge uniform and shined his boots. They didn't really need it, but this was a special day and he wanted to look his best. He ate his breakfast standing at the kitchen counter and then drove over to the RCMP office. There was definitely snow in the air.

He was the first one there for the morning shift. Frost wasn't there either, so that meant he was out on his highway round. Windflower put on a fresh pot of coffee and sat in the lunchroom until it started to perk. Once it began, he removed the glass carafe and put his cup underneath the spout. It was sneaky, but Windflower loved the first few drips of freshly made coffee.

He had just filled his cup and replaced the carafe when he heard Tizzard and Evanchuk coming in together. He said his good mornings and then went back to his office to do some paperwork before the day got too hectic. One thing he absolutely had to do was to formally suspend MacDonald. He did up a draft and e-mailed it to Betsy. She would clean it up and add the correct formal terms. There was nothing like a good admin person, and Betsy was one of the best.

He finished his report on MacDonald and was happily enjoying his coffee when the phone rang. It was Langmead from the Royal Newfoundland Constabulary in St. John's.

"Good morning, Carl. How are things in the big city?"

"Good morning, Winston. It's foggy this morning at RNC headquarters and drug addicts are still trying to steal the eyes out of people's heads to feed their habits. But other than that, things are good. I want to let you know we have Shawn Parsons in custody."

"That's good news. I hope you'll keep him there this time."

"If it was up to us, he never would have gotten out," said Langmead. "But, as usual, Mr. Parsons has a story and it involves other people. It's funny how his life of crime is never his fault."

"Yeah, I remember his stories. Always somebody setting him up."

"Right now we're holding him on breach of conditions, which is good for a year inside, but we'd like to get more. We're likely going to charge him with suspicion of trafficking a range of prohibited substances, and we have some surveillance of him in the activity of moving said items around. But he's always been smart enough not to have a major supply in his possession. He has other people doing his dirty work for him. And he's already trying to shift the blame."

"Who's he trying to set up now?" asked Windflower.

"That's why I'm calling you. He says Laura Emberley, the owner of the Fortune Pharmacy, is the one calling the shots. And that she's hooked up with a gang in the Halifax area."

"It's not the Russian guys again, is it?"

"I talked to your man, Quigley, and he thinks it might be," said Langmead. "He's following up in Nova Scotia."

"That's interesting. But here's some interesting stuff for you. Emberley is on the run and we have Shawn Parsons's fingerprints on a murder scene here in Grand Bank."

"It'd be great if we could hook him up on that," said Langmead. "Maybe you should come talk to him about it."

"I'd like to get Emberley first," said Windflower. "But yeah, sure, we can talk about that. Thanks for letting me know. I'm going to try and talk to Quigley too to see what he knows. I'll get back to you. And keep an eye out for Laura Emberley, would ya? If she's still on the island, I bet she's in St. John's."

"Will do," said Langmead, and then hung up.

Windflower hung up the phone and was sitting there thinking about what he'd learned when Tizzard showed up in his doorway.

"Puzzled about something?" asked Tizzard.

"They've got Shawn Parsons in St. John's," said Windflower.

"That's good, right?" asked Tizzard.

"It is. But they think he's trying to shift the blame to Laura Emberley, and maybe even that Russian crowd in Halifax."

This time Tizzard looked confused.

"Let's get a fresh cup of coffee and see if we can't make sense out of this mess," said Windflower. "'Oh what a tangled web we weave when we first practice to deceive.'"

"Shakespeare?" asked Tizzard.

"Many people think so, but you and I know of course it's Sir Walter Scott," said Windflower. Tizzard shook his head and followed his Sergeant into the lunchroom.

Frost was back from his morning tour and sitting with Evanchuk when Tizzard and Windflower came in. This was a good time to talk to everybody at once so Windflower filled his cup and sat down with his staff. He let Tizzard take the lead in talking about the routines in the office and scheduling and Windflower brought everyone up to date on the investigations. He also told them what he knew about MacDonald and the arrangements he had made for her to check in at the detachment.

When Windflower finished his updates, Evanchuk asked, "What's going on with Inspector Ford?"

"Inspector Ford is on indefinite leave. My guess is that we'll get a new person in Marystown, at least on a temporary basis. Maybe longer."

"It looks like we're getting more snow," said Tizzard as he pointed outside toward the first flakes. "The forecast said 10 centimetres, but it feels like more than that to me."

"Maybe you can feel it in your old bones," said Windflower, and everybody laughed.

"In any case, let's be ready to go tonight if we need to," said Windflower.

Windflower went back to his office where Betsy had put the memo about MacDonald on his desk. Windflower took a quick look at it, signed it and gave it back to Betsy. "Thank you Missus Molloy, that was perfect."

"You're welcome," said a beaming Betsy as she went back to her office.

A little praise can go a long way. And it makes life much, much easier.

He saw Evanchuk pass by his office on her way to providing the motor escort for the funeral cars, and went to get Tizzard to go to the church.

Chapter Twenty-Nine

Windflower and Tizzard took up their position at the bottom of the steps of the Grand Bank United Church. It was nearly half-full and it was only 9:30. The Grand Bank United Church had actually been formed in the early 1800's when it was named headquarters for the Fortune Bay Methodist Mission. Since those days it had gone through many changes just like the United Church itself, which gathered together many of the diverse elements of Christian Protestants into its fold.

The current building was relatively new, but in need of some upkeep and a paint job. Windflower also wished they fix the beautiful, large clock near the steeple. It was permanently stuck at 10 minutes to 1 o'clock, and since Windflower drove by it every day, he'd love to see the correct time.

The funeral was about to begin because the dignitaries started arriving. Included, of course, were all the sitting Council members, including Francis Tibbo, who was shaking hands and trolling for votes. Some of the last arrivals were government officials and the local Members of the Newfoundland House of Assembly who came with the Federal Members of Parliament, in a rare show of community spirit for the two opposing political forces in town. Windflower didn't see Sheila but assumed she was already inside. She would not want to make this day about anything but the late Mayor.

Soon afterward, the funeral procession arrived led by Constable Evanchuk with her sirens muted and her red lights flashing. The late Mayor's casket was in the long black hearse and behind it was another black limousine with the six pallbearers: two of his sons, two of his fellow lodge members from the Masons, and two of his neighbours. It appeared even the now-departed Mayor wanted the day to be a non-political event.

Behind the two official funeral cars was a long procession of family and close friends, led by Margaret Sinnott, the late Mayor's widow, and his three daughters. The family got out of their cars and stood and watched as the casket was carried into the church, saluted on its way by Windflower and Tizzard. They stood at attention as the procession passed and the snow flew around them. When Windflower looked over at Tizzard, he thought he saw a silent tear roll down his cheek.

In the words of the presiding minister, the funeral was to be a celebration. Holding true to Bill Sinnott and his family's wishes, the only tears to be shed this morning should be tears of joy. So even as family members and community leaders and politicians eulogized the late Mayor, they all had a funny story to tell as well. There was music and singing including a choir singing the deceased's favourite Newfoundland song, Let Me Fish Off Cape St. Mary's. They may have been tears of joy, but there were very few dry eyes in the church after that.

The funeral drew to a close and the casket was led out by the pallbearers and loaded back into the hearse for the interment ceremony at the United Cemetery.

Tizzard and Windflower were once again waiting at attention when the family passed, but this time Windflower reached over to shake Mrs. Sinnott's hand and to express his and the RCMP's condolences on the loss of her husband.

Afterwards, Evanchuk led the procession to the cemetery while most of the mourners went over to the Masons Hall for the post-funeral reception. By now the snow had picked up steam and was partnered with a stiff breeze. This was going to be a storm, alright. It was not even a question of when; it was a question of how much snow they were going to get.

Windflower had a chance to briefly say hi to Sheila as she passed him on the steps of the church. She asked him about his plans for later and he simply pointed to the sky. She understood immediately. She would head to the Masons Hall and spend most of the afternoon there after she picked up a couple of pies she had made. They agreed to talk later in the day.

Windflower went back to the office and let Frost, exhausted from his all-nighter, go home and get some rest. When Tizzard came back, Windflower sent him home too. As usual Tizzard didn't want to go, but Windflower knew they would need him later that evening.

Windflower called the weather centre and got the bad news he'd been expecting.

"There's going to be at least 25 to 30 centimetres of snow this afternoon and overnight, and the usual chance of blowing and drifting snow decreasing visibility to less than 5 percent," said the weather technician.

"Thanks," said Windflower as he hung up the phone.

Soon afterwards Betsy came into his office. "Marystown has called to say they're closing Highway 210 from Swift Current to Marystown."

"I'm not surprised," said Windflower. "I think I'll go and check out the conditions around town for myself."

He picked up his hat and gloves and went to his Jeep for a short tour around the community. There were still quite a few cars at the Masons Hall, and when he went by the Mug-Up the lights were on, yet the place looked deserted. He dropped in to order some food for the overnight shift.

"Afternoon, Marie. Getting stormy out there."

"It is, my luv. What can I do for youse today? You wanna order food for tonight?"

"That would be great, Marie."

"Okay, it'll take me 'bout an hour."

Windflower left Marie to get the food organized and did a quick run around the district. He drove east as far as the Garnish turnoff and he passed the snowplow along the way. He slowed and lowered his window to talk to the driver.

"It's bad, b'y," said the driver, who Windflower recognized as the same one who worked the night of the Ridgeway accident. "I've made a cut, but it's fillin' in faster than I can push 'er out of the way."

"I think we'll shut her down when I get back," said Windflower. Even his four-wheel drive Jeep had trouble getting up some of the steep inclines, especially around Grand Beach.

When he got back to the detachment he called in the road closure for the night. He sent Evanchuk off to put up the barriers on the way to Marystown. "Take my car," he said. "It's getting pretty slick out there. Be careful."

Evanchuk nodded and took his Jeep, while Windflower headed back out in her car and did the same outside Fortune, setting up the barriers and the Road Closed signs. On his way back to the detachment he dropped by the Mug-Up to pick up his take-out order. Herb Stoodley was there this time, busy packing up Windflower's order: four cod au gratin, a large chef's salad and a box of Mug-Up cupcakes, half chocolate and half vanilla.

"That's great, Herb. I'll have to hide those cupcakes away from Tizzard. He could eat that whole box in one go."

"I know how he feels. There are not many things I can't keep away from, but these cupcakes are one of them. I think it's the icing in the middle that's got me hooked."

"Are you closing up soon?" asked Windflower.

"I'm waiting for Moira to come back from the wake and then we'll go home. The place was just clearing out when I left. People are trying to get home before it gets too bad."

"It's already bad. We're closing the roads right now. If people are smart, they'll hunker down till this one blows over. Anyway, thanks Herb. We'll talk to you later."

Windflower went back to the RCMP office, sent Betsy home and put away the food for later making sure to hide the cupcake box at the back of the fridge. He was just settling into his office when the phone rang. It was Ron Quigley from St. John's.

"Are you guys having another snow day down there?" Quigley asked.

"Did you city guys get a break from this one?" Windflower said in return.

"Nah, I'm just pulling your leg. We're shut down tight here, too. I figured I might just as well hang out here for a few hours instead of trying to battle the storm and all those crazy drivers trying to get home. You doin' the night watch?"

"Yeah," said Windflower. "We shut down the highway and are setting up our storm centre again."

"Hey, I hear Ford's in the soup," said Quigley.

"I saw him in Marystown," said Windflower. "He was in bad shape. I think he's going to be off for awhile. He went back drinking and that didn't go so well. But now he's trying to get some help."

"That's good," said Quigley. "I like Bill. He's a good guy. I hope he gets his act together."

"Me too," said Windflower. "So why'd you call, other than checking on our weather?"

"When Carl Langmead told me they had Shawn Parsons I did some checking on our end. Parsons may be right about the Halifax crew being involved. I talked to Guy Simard in Halifax. He said the Russian gang continued to operate even after they put Big Iggy in jail, and they think they're running opiates and other drugs right through all the Atlantic provinces," said Quigley.

"That **is** interesting. How is Simard by the way? I thought he retired."

"He keeps trying to but they keep asking him to stay on. Anyway, I wanted to check in with you and see what you know," said Quigley.

"We're a long ways from figuring it all out but some of the pieces are starting to come together. First of all, Laura Emberley, the pharmacist, is certainly more involved than we thought. But until we find her, that'll be hard to nail down. We also have Shawn Parsons' prints all over the Fallon murder scene, and both people who died were drugged or poisoned," said Windflower.

"I'll do some more checking on Parsons from here. Simard didn't mention him, but maybe that's because he wasn't in Nova Scotia. I thought the guy who died, Ridgeway, was the person you were looking at."

"He was an addict, and maybe more. But according to some sources, he was being blackmailed to carry out the bidding for others, maybe Laura Emberley as it turns out. We found some tapes and notes at his house that we're going through right now. Could you also get Simard and the Halifax guys to check Ridgeway and Emberley?" asked Windflower.

"Sure thing. Anyway, I'll let you get back to your fun in the snow. Let's talk again after the weekend."

"Thanks, Ron," said Windflower. "Be safe."

CHAPTER FORTY

Windflower had a couple of quiet hours by himself at the detachment. There was little activity and anything that did move was storm-related in one way or another. There was a constant stream of updates on the weather and accidents and calls for assistance all across the region, but the only one in the Grand Bank area was an ambulance that wanted an escort to bring a patient back to the clinic. Windflower went along with the ambulance in his Jeep.

It was tough sledding most of the way out to the house, but they made it. The patient was a woman who thought she was going into labour, but it turned out to be a false alarm. The paramedics took her into the clinic anyway because her frantic husband insisted. Windflower wondered what it was about snowstorms and pregnancies. It seemed almost every storm there was at least one event involving a pregnant lady.

When he got back Tizzard was already there.

"I thought you were taking a break," said Windflower.

"I did. But someone had to be here to greet our guest in the back."

When Windflower walked back with Tizzard, he was surprised to see MacDonald at the hot plate in the lunchroom, stirring a big pot of something that smelled awfully good.

"What are you doing here?" Windflower asked.

"I have to report in every day. And I knew you guys would be staying all night so I made a batch of chili."

"Well, thank you very much," said Windflower. "The chili smells pretty good."

"MacDonald makes the best chili in town," said Tizzard.

"You're still suspended and everything," said Windflower.

"I know," said MacDonald. "But I was going crazy just sitting around and I thought the crew might enjoy something besides the sandwiches you usually get."

Tizzard shrugged his shoulders and got three bowls from the cupboard. "She even brought rolls," he said as he handed the bowls over to MacDonald for filling. "I'm going to interview her right after we eat."

This time it was Windflower that shrugged as they sat at the lunchroom table to eat their chili. As they were eating their first bowl, Evanchuk came in from her route and joined them. Windflower had another half bowl and then left them to go check on Lady and see Sheila. Evanchuk was already setting herself up with the tapes and the notebook in the storm control area and Tizzard was meeting with MacDonald in the back. They were quite an efficient bunch, despite the storm.

When he reached his house, he had to leave his vehicle on the road. There was no way to get into his driveway, and if he got in, he wasn't sure he could get back out again. The snow was being fiercely driven by the wind and it had now piled up nearly a metre in places. There was only about 15 centimetres on the ground around there, but high winds produce high snow drifts.

Lady was her exuberant self and pranced around Windflower as he filled her water and food bowls. It was obvious she had high hopes for a walk, but when

Windflower opened the back door to let her out, she quickly realized that wasn't in the cards. She pushed her way through the newly fallen snow to do her business, and then quickly came back in with a full white coating of the stuff, which she proceeded to share with the kitchen floor. He could do little but laugh at her antics and clean up her mess. He gave Lady two Milk Bone treats to keep her happy and promised to visit her later.

He dropped by Sheila's on his way back to work, and lucky for him she had just arrived. She had left her car at the Masons Hall and walked, which to Windflower seemed to be a pretty sensible move. Then again, when was Sheila not completely sensible? He had a cup of tea with Sheila, who was planning to spend the night again over at the Stoodley's house. She gave him a kiss and a left over pie from the wake and he turned around to head back to work. Then he did one more U-turn and went to his own house instead. He thought he might as well bring Lady over to the office with him. It would be a long night for her otherwise, and they could all use the company.

As Windflower and Lady entered the RCMP detachment, MacDonald was all bundled up and leaving. He waved goodbye to her muffled form and went to the lunchroom to find Tizzard.

"Anything new?" he asked.

"Just that the storm is expected to last until about noon tomorrow," said Tizzard. "I called Frost and told him to wait and come in for midnight. We'll need to pace ourselves through this one."

"That's very good thinking, Corporal. Pacing and moderation. That's a first for you I think," said Windflower.

Tizzard ignored his boss' barb and kept talking. "I interviewed MacDonald," he said.

"What did you find out?"

"If we take her at her word, she appears pretty innocent in all of this. No doubt a bit naïve and certainly poor judgement, but nothing illegal from what I can see. Even not filing the break-in report is probably more on the administrative side than anything else," said Tizzard.

"I agree. From what she told me, I think she made a bad choice for a romantic engagement, but it's hard to see where she could be charged with anything. But I want you to write up a draft report as soon as you can, without sugar-coating it in any way, and let me have a look at it. We don't want to be accused of covering up for one of our own."

"She may be able to help us with our case later on. Most of the information she can provide is second-hand or hearsay, but she did see Shawn Parsons in Grand Bank on the day of Ridgeway's accident."

"How did she know it was Parsons?" asked Windflower.

"She was talking about people she saw hanging around and I showed her Shawn Parsons' mug shot. She made a positive ID."

"That's good. That means we have both the prints and a witness linking him closer to the crime scene. Good work, Corporal," said Windflower.

Tizzard walked away to see how Evanchuk was making out with the tapes, looking particularly pleased with himself. Windflower went back to his own office and started to go through more of his paperwork. Lady didn't have any paperwork to do, so she just curled up underneath his desk and had a nap.

The next couple of hours were quiet, with only one call for help from the clinic. They had an emergency call from somebody who thought her husband was having a heart attack after trying to shovel off their walkway. The call came from Fortune so Windflower got the snowplow operator to meet Evanchuk and Tizzard at the clinic. He got them to plow a path to Fortune for them, and then re-plow a similar track to help them get back.

It turned out the man's problem was only a bad case of indigestion, and everyone, especially his wife, was relieved it was only that.

Tizzard and Evanchuk drove back to the detachment.

"All in a day's work," Tizzard said to Windflower, who had heated up their cod au gratin for dinner while they were gone. He also put out the unopened box of cupcakes and the pie Sheila had given him.

All three of the RCMP officers heartily enjoyed their supper and Tizzard was particularly pleased when Windflower opened the cardboard box from the Mug-Up. He had finished two and was reaching for a third when Windflower snatched the box from his hands and put it back in the fridge for later.

"We might need a snack later," he said, as Tizzard grudgingly watched his favourite treat disappear back into the fridge.

Tizzard and Evanchuk went back to surveying the tapes and the notebook while Windflower took up his position at the storm desk. The latest forecast for rising temperatures was both good and bad: it was good because it meant the precipitation would shift from snow to rain, and bad because the transition brought the possibility of freezing rain.

Freezing rain could be a major problem because not only would it make driving conditions extremely hazardous, it could also cause buildup on wires and electrical transformers. When that happened—and it often did with freezing rain—there was a chance the power would go out. And there was also the danger of live wires being exposed. Windflower had already seen the effects of one ice storm and didn't want to go through that again.

The last ice storm led to a massive build-up of ice on the main hydroelectric lines that fed power to the Burin Peninsula. The build-up had brought down wires and caused transformers to burst into flames all over the place. People had been stranded and without power for three days while hydro crews worked frantically to get the power back on. After that, most businesses and many individuals bought diesel generators to keep the heat on.

Windflower passed the word on to his fellow officers. Together they started not only keeping track of the snow, but also the temperature as well.

CHAPTER FORTY-ONE

A round midnight Frost showed up covered in snow from head to toe and holding a large pot out in front of him. "Here," he said, pushing the pot towards Tizzard. "I brought some soup."

Along with the remaining cupcakes and a strong pot of black tea, Frost's chicken soup became a welcome midnight meal. It seemed to raise the spirits of the officers who had been there all night and were now actively engaged in watching to see if an ice storm was developing.

The chicken soup also reminded Windflower how tired he was, and when Tizzard suggested he take first shift on the bunk in the cell out back, he offered little resistance.

He made Tizzard promise to call him in 3 hours, and just to be sure he set the small alarm on his watch as well.

A bit after 3 his watch alarm woke both him and Lady, who was sleeping solidly beside him. The rat-a-tat of the freezing rain hitting the window outside had started rousing him anyway. Tizzard was coming in just as he was getting up.

"Morning, Sarge. It started a couple of minutes ago. Let's hope the temperature keeps rising so it turns to rain before dawn. If not, we're in trouble."

Windflower nodded and went to the bathroom to clean himself up. When he came out, Lady was looking at him, so he opened the front door and let her scamper out into the dark. She didn't scamper as much as slipped and slid.

Windflower could see there was already a thin sheet of ice covering the outside world.

With a cup of hot coffee, Tizzard waited for Windflower to return, with Evanchuk beside him.

"Evanchuk is next on the nap list, but we want to show you what we've come up with so far from the tapes and the notebook. Is that okay?" asked Tizzard.

"Sure," said Windflower, groggy but sipping his coffee as fast as possible. "Let's go into my office and you can run through it for me."

Tizzard, and particularly Evanchuk, looked happy at this prospect and followed behind Windflower. Tizzard nodded to Evanchuk to go first.

"There are a couple of things we picked up. First of all, there are records of something being shipped out of Grand Bank, and other records of boxes being received. Sometimes the shipments were to and from Halifax. At other times they went back and forth to certain points across the island. There are also abbreviations on each of the shipments that we think indicate what was inside the boxes or shipping containers. We think they were transporting drugs, sir: pharmaceuticals."

"Opiates, Sergeant," said Tizzard, unable to contain himself any longer. "Look, here is one date's shipping notice: Fet/Oxy/Perc. And another one: Tyl3/Fet/Dil." He pushed the notebook towards Windflower. "The shipments to and from Halifax are not titled, so we don't know who they were going to or coming from. But we think the ones in Newfoundland may be other pharmacies. Evanchuk has checked a few of the addresses and one is for a pharmacy in Stephenville Crossing, and another for one in Kelligrews."

"You mean to tell me they were shipping opiates in and out of the Fortune Pharmacy? Why didn't we know anything about it? And why would they be shipping opiates into the pharmacy on a covert basis? Unless they were supplying an illegal network," said Windflower answering his own question.

"That's what it looks like to us," said Tizzard. "As far as why we didn't know, why would we? It looks like very little of what was being distributed was staying here, so we wouldn't see it on the street."

"I guess so," said Windflower, though not entirely convinced. He began processing what they'd just told him.

"There's more," said Evanchuk, reclaiming Windflower's attention.

"The tapes are recordings of phone conversations between who we think are Shawn Parsons and Laura Emberley. It seems Ridgeway was trying to make a case against the pair. He probably hooked up the tape recorder to the telephone in Emberley's office and then went through the tapes later. In any case it's all recorded and easy to follow in his notebook."

Tizzard jumped back in.

"We even have Emberley talking to who we think is Parsons, telling him they have to get rid of Fallon. She called him a pig with a big mouth. And somehow Ridgeway managed to get Emberley on tape threatening he would pay a price if he didn't keep going. Not a smoking gun sir, but starting to look like the makings of a conspiracy."

"Very good work, the both of you," said Windflower. "Now let me have a look at all of this for myself. It'll take my mind off the weather outside. And I think it's your turn to rest, Constable," he said, pointing to Evanchuk.

Evanchuk went off for her break while Tizzard went to the front to talk to Frost and to get the latest weather report. Windflower spent the next two hours going through the tapes and notes for himself.

He got up to stretch and to check the weather outside. Visibility was low because the ice pellets continued raining down on the outside walls and windows of the Grand Bank RCMP detachment. Lady followed him to the door and then nudged past him, yet this time walking close to the building, learning from her previous slip and slide performance. She managed to get her business looked after, and back in safely. Just before Windflower closed the door all the lights in town flashed once, and then twice. And then for a few seconds there was total darkness.

The emergency generator kicked on and some of the lights in the detachment building came back on. He remembered the generator was designed to give them about half their usual power, which was enough to run the emergency lighting, the security system, communications and the furnace. It was also enough lighting for them to get to the flashlights and lanterns in the storage room.

Everybody in the office was now active in making sure their systems were operational. Windflower was putting a large battery-powered lantern on the reception desk when he saw a flash outside. He opened the door again and could see the transformer on the pole a hundred feet from him sputter and burst into flame. It threw bright streaks of yellow and blue before it finally died. If it was happening here, it is almost certainly happening in other places in the area.

Windflower also heard a low hum.

"That's the wires," said Tizzard. "We had a big ice storm back in '93 when I was living in Ramea. I remember hearing that noise right before the wires came down. We were in a small isolated community and it took them 3 weeks to get our power back on."

Windflower sighed.

"Let's get the snowmobiles out of the garage. They may be our main form of transportation till this breaks. We'll need to do a quick tour of both here and Fortune. We have to make sure there haven't been any fires. You can be sure some security alarms have already been set off. Check in with the clinic to make sure everything is okay over there."

Tizzard didn't need any other encouragement to get the snowmobiles organized. Within 15 minutes, he and Frost were revving up their machines in front of the building.

"Be careful," shouted Windflower over the noise of the snowmobiles. "Report in every half hour. I'll be on my cell phone."

The two RCMP officers waved as they drove off, their lights fading into the night. They seemed pretty happy with their assignment. At least somebody got to have a little fun.

There wasn't much fun to be had inside the RCMP detachment. Windflower and Evanchuk dealt with a steady diet of phone calls requesting information or support or to just reassure a lonely shut-in they wouldn't starve, at least in the next few hours. But there were a number of encouraging signs, not the least being that it finally got light.

The first good sign was the temperature had risen above the freezing point. Now the participation was just rain, though very cold and still very heavy. This meant the damage could start to be contained. Secondly, when it got light, you could see the absolutely stunning scene the ice storm had created. Every tree, every shrub, every house and every vehicle was decorated with inches of thick, sparkling ice that gleamed in the daylight. "A dangerous and sometimes deadly beauty," was how Windflower had heard it described one time before.

The daylight also meant the snow clearing crews could get back on the roads within town. Inside the detachment they could hear the snowplows crunch their way through the ice-covered roadways.

Tizzard and Frost were back from their emergency tour and before they set out again to begin the process of re-opening the highway, Windflower phoned Herb Stoodley.

"Herb, hope I didn't get you up," he said when Herb answered.

"No worries. I was just on my way over to the Mug-Up to check the place out. We won't have any electricity, but I have propane tanks for the stove and I'll need to plug the fridges into the generator."

"I've got a big favour to ask. I knew you had propane for cooking. Do you think you could cook us up some breakfast? We've been here all night and likely will have to stay until noon, at least. If that's possible, it would be greatly appreciated."

"Let me see if everything is okay first. And if it is, I'd be happy to do it. I'll let you know in about 15 minutes," said Stoodley. Twenty minutes later he called back.

"I'm ready for you whenever you want to come over. We won't be open for business, but we will be open for the RCMP."

"Thanks, Herb. I'll send Tizzard and Frost over first," said Windflower.

When he told Tizzard to go over to the Mug-Up with Frost, Tizzard looked at him and asked if there was a problem.

"Only if you're not hungry," said Windflower with a smile. "And hurry back so Evanchuk and I can get some, too."

By 9 o'clock all of the RCMP officers were stuffed, the weather was much milder and even the rain was easing. Leaving Tizzard in the office against his wishes, the other three set out with the highway crews. They first needed to check the road conditions once the plows made a first cut, and then they'd proceed to get the highways open and operational. By now, too, the hydro crews were starting the process of getting the electricity system back up and running, piece by piece.

Luckily, there was not a lot of structural damage and the wires and poles did not collapse, at least in their part of the world. This meant the crews had to restart the blacked-out sections, and then begin the process of replacing transformers and other equipment damaged overnight. Nonetheless, there would still be pockets of neighbourhoods in Grand Bank that would be without power for the next day or so. But they were making good progress on getting things back to normal.

So too were Windflower and the officers in the Grand Bank RCMP. Tizzard volunteered to stay and work a double but Windflower ordered him and Evanchuk off until 6 that day. He and Frost could handle whatever happened between now and then.

Windflower didn't actually remember much of what happened that day. It was all a blur of activity, most of it mindless. Betsy dealt with most of the in-coming calls, and their power came back on around 3 that afternoon. They spent the last few hours cleaning up the mess they had made and putting away equipment.

A very tired and sore Windflower finally called it a day when Tizzard showed up just before 6:00. He remembered putting Lady in the back, lying in the bath for a few minutes, and then nothing else until his regular alarm went off at 6:30 Saturday morning.

CHAPTER FORTY-TWO

Windflower didn't know where he was or what time it was when he awoke. It was still dark and quiet so he almost fell right back to sleep. When Lady heard him stirring, she nuzzled his face in the universal signal that combined "I love you completely" and "I absolutely gotta go!!" Windflower got up and pulled his hoodie over his head and stepped into his boots to let her out into the back yard. He went back inside and was hoping she was quick. When she didn't come back right away he went back outside and called her.

She still didn't come but could see her shadow moving around near the back fence. He stepped gingerly towards her, trying to keep his weight balanced so he wouldn't crash through the piled up snow. He nearly succeeded but when he got to the fence, he fell through and was soon buried up to his waist. Lady came to try and help him but all she really accomplished was to sink him a little deeper. He pushed her away and then he noticed what she had been hovering over. It was a small rabbit, and it was shaking, partly from the cold, partly from fear.

Windflower pulled himself out of the now-melting snow, and then he shooed Lady away and picked up the rabbit. The rabbit seemed to shiver even more than before. Windflower carried it into the house and while he was trying to figure out what to do with it, he put it in the sink and pulled a large piece of lettuce off a head in the fridge and gave it to the rabbit. After it had nibbled a bit and stopped shaking, Windflower put the rabbit in the tub in the bathroom.

He and Lady then headed out for a walk.

The snowbanks had gone down considerably over the last number of hours and although there was still a crust on top from the freezing rain, the warm weather was melting the snow underneath. Windflower and Lady enjoyed their brisk walk through the centre of town and back up towards the clinic and the road to Fortune. It was early and quiet and peaceful, which was just what Windflower needed after the excitement of the past twenty-four hours.

By the time he got home, the rabbit was warm and safe and sleeping on the floor mat inside the bathroom. He turned on his wood-pellet burning fireplace and greatly enjoyed his first cup of coffee. He was well into his second when his stomach reminded him that apart from a muffin Tizzard had brought in, he hadn't eaten anything since yesterday morning's breakfast at the Mug-Up. At least that was a problem he knew how to fix. Three eggs scrambled, a huge bowl of fruit and two thick pieces of homemade bread smothered in Purity partridgeberry and apple jam made a perfect combination. He even shared a large piece of toast with Lady, who was more than pleased with her treat.

Eventually, he went in and let the rabbit out of the bathroom. While the rabbit carefully considered its possible freedom, Windflower curled up on his couch with his Michael Crummey book. Moses Sweetland was the lone holdout on a lucrative offer to leave his life-long home, and the rest of the community was turning on him because the decision had to be unanimous. He was stubborn and almost unlikeable, but Windflower felt sorry for him because of the difficult choice he had to make. Windflower was completely enrapt in the story when he heard a knock on his door.

He looked out to see his neighbour Edwina Bursey and her little daughter Sarah from down the road. "Good morning," said Windflower, expecting to be asked to buy Girl Guide cookies or chocolate bars for the latest fundraising effort at school. Instead the little girl spoke up.

"I lost my rabbit. Did you see it? It's small and round and white and fluffy."

"Sorry to disturb you," said Edwina. "But somehow Peter, her pet rabbit, got out of the house this morning, and we're hoping to find him before something really bad happens."

"We have to find Peter before the cats get him," piped in Sarah, her candor outweighing her innocence.

"Well, I have good news for you and bad news for the cats. What did you say he looked like again?"

"Small and round and white and fluffy," repeated Sarah.

"I think I might have him. Come in and see if it's Peter."

The little girl didn't need any more invitation and soon held her pretty little rabbit tightly in her arms. Lady was awfully excited too and insisted on running round and round the pair until Windflower gently but firmly grabbed her by the collar. "Everybody is a little excited today," he explained to Edwina. "We don't get many visitors."

"I'm just happy to have the rabbit back. Where did you find him?"

"Lady found him out back this morning. I'm glad you came. I was wondering what I was going to do with another pet."

"Well, you've made our day. Thank you very much. Come on Sarah, let's take Peter home. Thank Sergeant Windflower for finding him."

"And Lady," said Windflower. "She's the one who actually found him."

Sarah gave Lady a big hug and afterward ran to hug Windflower as well.

He waved them goodbye as they walked back to their house. "Good job, Lady. That probably deserves a biscuit." He gave Lady her Milk Bone reward and went back to his good book and comfortable fire. As he was getting dressed around 10:30, the phone rang. He was hoping that it was Sheila, but instead it was another familiar voice.

"Good morning, Winston," said his Uncle Frank.

"Uncle Frank, how are you? And how is Auntie Marie?"

"I am well and she is doing much better. She asked me to call and thank you for calling the police. But I'm bored as anything in this hospital. Plus it's 40 below outside and you can freeze your—"

"So what do the doctors say about Auntie Marie? Will she have any lasting paralysis? Can she talk yet?"

"They say that she will probably get most of her movement back over time, and yes, she can talk again. She slurs some words but I can understand her. She's already on me again about quitting smoking. And she wants to know how you are and when you are getting married."

Windflower laughed. "Tell her not yet. But maybe someday soon. At this point, a dog is enough to look after. This morning I almost got a pet rabbit, too."

"That's a nice dog you've got. And you know that in our tradition a rabbit can be a warning or it can also be a symbol of fear. Rabbit's lesson to us is not allow our fears to stop us from living. Are you afraid of anything?"

"Not that I'm aware of," said Windflower, sounding surprised.

"Just remember, Winston, if you find that you can't reach something you really want, it will be fear that is holding you back. Pay attention to the signs. They are all around you."

"Thank you, Uncle, I will. And give my love to Auntie Marie."

"Bye, Winston. Say hello to the b'ys for me, will ya?"

Windflower smiled at that last remark and went back to dressing himself. Once he was done, he called Sheila to check in. There was no answer at her house or at the Stoodleys, so Windflower decided to go over to the RCMP detachment to see Tizzard.

When he arrived, Tizzard was eating. This time he had what looked like the remnants of a piece of lemon meringue pie. "I hope you saved me some," said Windflower.

"There's a piece left in the fridge," said Tizzard. "I'm waiting for Frost to come and then I'm going over for por' cakes. Do you want to join me?"

"Didn't you just eat?"

"That was only a snack. I need a real meal."

When Frost pulled up in front, both men pulled on their jackets and walked over to the Mug-Up. The café was warm and crowded and noisy. They found a table on the far side and put in their order for por' cakes and pea soup.

There was a crowd of local fishermen sitting at the big table in the window near the door and while some of them nodded to the RCMP officers, many of them turned away.

"What's going on with that?" Windflower asked his young Corporal.

"I think something's up. They were all gathered at the fish plant wharf when I made the round this morning. They looked pretty agitated. I'm not sure what's going on, but I feel trouble brewing. They obviously don't want us to know what they were doing, at least not yet."

Windflower nodded. "Let's put it on the board to watch for suspicious activity around the waterfront for the next couple of days. The sooner we know what's going on, the sooner we can make a plan to deal with it."

Tizzard also nodded, and before he could say anything else their food arrived. There was little conversation after that as they dug into their pea soup and delicious por' cakes. They were finishing up when Sheila walked into the café. She went to the counter to say hello to the kitchen staff and Moira Stoodley, and then came over to sit with Windflower and Tizzard.

"Good morning, Ma'am," said Tizzard. "I was just leaving. I'm finally getting a day off and I want to make the most of it."

"Enjoy," Sheila said as he left, sitting across from Windflower. "Do you get a day off too? It seems like forever since we had a date night."

"I happen to be free this evening. Did you have something in mind?"

"Oh, I have things in mind," Sheila said with a laugh. "But I was thinking about dinner at the B & B. We haven't gone there since the summer."

"That sounds good. Why don't you make a reservation for the early sitting? That way we'll have more time for ourselves later," he said with a twinkle in his eye.

"That sounds great. Good-looking, and a thinker too. My ideal man," she said with another laugh.

Windflower stayed and kept Sheila company while she had her share of the por' cakes and pea soup. Then he walked back to the detachment where Frost looked like he had everything in complete control. Now that everything was looked after, Windflower drove back home and took Lady for a short walk around the neighbourhood. When he got back he tried to read, but before he knew it, both he and his dog were fast asleep.

CHAPTER FORTY-THREE

H e woke while it was still light and ran another hot bath, this time just to relax. He was stepping into the tub when his cell phone rang. It was Ron Quigley from St. John's.

"How's she goin' b'y?" asked Quigley with a booming laugh.

"She's going good b'y. What are up you up today? Just beatin' the path?"

"That's a good one. Although it's more a townie or corner boy saying than a bayman one. You better be careful they don't start thinking you're a townie, b'y."

"No danger of that," said Windflower, laughing. "So what's up?"

"Thought you'd want to know we picked up Laura Emberley this morning at the airport. Heading to Halifax, she was. She's not too bright. She was in disguise but used her real name and ID. When the ID didn't match her look, the Air Canada check-in person alerted the RCMP officer on duty. We are holding her at HQ until we figure out the next move," said Quigley.

"That's good news," said Windflower. "Why don't you bring her to Marystown? We're starting to put together the picture over here and I'd love the chance to talk to her. We're thinking there was some kind of operation that was shipping prescription drugs in and out of Fortune."

"That's interesting," said Quigley. "We had a similar operation running out of Sydney last year. They were supplying all of Nova Scotia and New Brunswick through one pharmacy that had a network of two or three doctors writing fake scripts and a few unscrupulous pharmacists who were filling them. We only found out about it after a courier box broke open at the airport and the drugs spilled all over the floor. When our people went back to the pharmacy to check it out, the guy panicked and ratted out the whole deal."

"So maybe they just moved the operation around. So can you get her to Marystown?"

"I can drive her myself tomorrow," said Quigley. "As long as you're buying supper, I'll be there."

"For sure," said Windflower. "See you tomorrow Ron."

That phone call added immensely to the enjoyment of his bath and after he was clean and shaved and dressed in his nice pinstriped suit, he felt pretty good about himself and his life. And he had dinner and the evening with his girl to look forward to.

He drove to Sheila's and called out to her when he arrived.

"I'm almost ready," she called back. "Sit down and relax for a minute." Windflower sat in the comfortable parlour until Sheila came downstairs. When he saw her he was more than pleased. Sheila wore new black pants that were tight enough to show all her curves when she turned around. She had a brilliant white silk blouse with enough cleavage to hold Windflower's attention and a solitary string of pearls around her neck. She was also wearing the earrings Windflower bought at Swarovski's in Montreal last year.

"Do I pass the test?" she asked Windflower playfully.

"You are an A plus; gorgeous. Come along, my queen, your chariot awaits."

Sheila pulled her sealskin coat over her shoulders and got into the vehicle with Windflower. Moments later, they were walking arm-in-arm into the old B & B. The inn had been sold again, this time to a couple from the Montreal area, who had added their own touches to the unique setting. This meant there were more French dishes on the menu than before, and the food was always very, very good.

Sheila and Windflower managed to get a small room just for themselves near the back. It had once been a maid's bedroom but was now a comfortable and very private dining area. Windflower looked a little puzzled at this special treatment but followed dutifully behind Sheila.

"I thought we should have a private place, in case we want to talk," she said.

"Okay," said Windflower, still a little unsure what was going on. His spirits picked up when one of the owners popped into the room and poured them each a glass of champagne. Windflower and Sheila thanked their host, touched their glasses together and sipped.

The owner left them with a copy of the menu du jour and Windflower hungrily perused his dinner choices. He decided on the seafood soup and the roasted halibut while Sheila chose the soup and the steak frites. When Windflower heard Sheila's choice, he almost changed his mind. But he really wanted the halibut.

They ordered a glass of wine and started talking about their week until their salad arrived. It was a mixture of greens with cooked green beans, shaved fennel and fresh basil. The dressing was simple, crisp and delicious, made of oil, lemon juice, sharp black pepper and sea salt. The pair continued talking about their week, about the storm and Sheila's political discussions. The soup interrupted them, but it was another welcome intrusion.

It was piping hot and had the fragrance of saffron and garlic and the tang of Tabasco sauce in every spoonful. There were peas and carrots and potatoes and onions, along with thick pieces of cod and halibut swimming in the thick broth. They washed down the soup with a glass of white wine and Windflower sopped up the last of the soup with a piece of the homemade baguette.

The main courses were outstanding as well, and while Windflower jealously eyed Sheila's steak frites, his roasted halibut was superb. The fish was meaty yet tender and it was covered in a spinach and watercress mixture which was both light and tasty. It came with an assortment of vegetables that looked like they had been roasted alongside the halibut. There were carrot coins, broccoli and cauliflower, along with several fingerling potatoes.

As usual, Windflower mostly listened throughout dinner as Sheila talked about her ideas for what she would like to do as Mayor. "I guess you've decided then," said Windflower.

"I have," said Sheila. "I am going to run for Mayor of Grand Bank. But I wanted you to know first. I will make it official after the Council meeting on Tuesday."

"Congratulations," said Windflower. "I am very proud of you. You will make a great Mayor."

"Thank you, Winston," said Sheila. "That's the first of my decisions I wanted you to know about."

"What other decisions have you made?" asked Windflower.

Just then their coffee and dessert arrived. Windflower was very surprised when the dessert was not the crème brûlée as advertised, but peanut butter cheesecake. He almost joyously laughed aloud. Then he saw something sticking out of the top of the cheesecake. It looked like a gold wedding band. When he looked over at Sheila she had one on top of hers as well.

"This is my other decision," said Sheila. "I have decided I want to get married. To you. Winston Windflower will you marry me?" she asked.

Windflower sat there with his mouth wide open. Even if he knew what to say, he wasn't sure his lips and tongue would move. Sheila reached over across the table and touched his lips with her fingers. "I do not want your answer tonight. I want you to think about it and let me know your answer when you are ready. I have made my decision. Now the choice is yours. I really love you Sergeant Windflower, and if you will take me home, I can show you how much I love you."

Windflower didn't need any more encouragement. He got up, paid the bill and they were home minutes later. They canoodled on the couch, but quickly moved upstairs. It was a wonderful and absolutely magical evening and as Windflower fell asleep, he thought about what had just happened at dinner. Even though he felt overwhelming love for Sheila, he also felt apprehensive. Almost as if his heart were being tugged in two different directions.

He was too tired to completely process all of these feelings but he knew he would have to. And sooner rather than later.

Windflower awoke early and while he didn't want to leave the warm comfort of Sheila's bed, his other lady was waiting for him. He put on a pot of coffee before he left and then went to see Lady. She was very happy to see him and anxious to go out. He let her out in the back and after a few minutes he could hear her at the door, so he let her back in. He filled her bowls and promised a longer walk later. Lady looked surprised, maybe even disappointed when he got up to leave. But he had other commitments.

He had a cup of coffee in Sheila's kitchen just as the sun was rising and it certainly had the beginnings of a beautiful December day. He turned on CBC and listened to the morning news and then a segment of Weekend Arts Magazine. When he thought he heard Sheila in the bathroom upstairs, he re-filled his cup and got a fresh cup of coffee to bring up to her.

"Thank you, Sergeant. And thank you for last night."

"I can assure you the pleasure was all mine, Sheila m'dear. I can't believe it but I'm starved. I was thinking some fruit and an omelet and maybe some of that low-fat turkey bacon. I'm having supper with Ron Quigley in Marystown, but I'm not sure what or when I'll eat between now and then."

"It's good to plan ahead. Your suggestions for breakfast sound fabulous. I'll take all of the above."

Windflower went into the kitchen, happy with his food plan and very happy with the woman in his life. So why was he hesitating on giving her an answer to her proposal? That was something he could think about on the drive to Marystown. For now, he had to get cracking on breakfast.

CHAPTER FORTY-FOUR

alf an hour later Windflower was walking into Sheila's bedroom with a breakfast tray and a carafe of fresh coffee. Sheila was sitting in bed propped up with pillows and magazines strewn all around. Windflower handed her a plate with half a cheese omelet, toast and a bowl of chopped up fruit. He poured them each a cup of coffee, pushed the magazines aside to make room, and sat down beside her. Sheila continued to read while eating but Windflower focused completely on his meal.

"You look as if every meal might be your last," said Sheila.

"Well, you never know," said Windflower, his mouth half stuffed with a piece of toast.

"Were you surprised at dinner last night?" she asked.

"It was a pleasant surprise, but yes I was surprised. You move faster than me."

"It just made sense to me and I figured why wait? I know it's a little unconventional for the woman to ask, but we're both grown adults."

"I don't have a problem with that. I had thought about the possibility, but maybe farther into the future."

"I understand, take your time. I'm hoping we'll have a long life together."

Windflower smiled and went back to eating his breakfast. When the meal was over, Windflower offered to clean up and Sheila readily agreed. He spent a few quiet moments in the kitchen doing just that and then went back upstairs to say good-bye.

"Be careful on the highway. The weather is clear now, but you know how fast it can turn."

"I will," said Windflower, knowing her caution to be well founded. "I'll give you a call when I'm coming back from Marystown." They had a long and close embrace, and then he left to go see his other female companion.

Lady seemed to be waiting for him when he got back because she bounded out as soon as he opened the door. He grabbed her leash and off they went. They took the long route down by the beach, which was of course completely deserted. It was still starkly beautiful, even in the midst of the dead of winter. The waves rolled across the bleak landscape and the wind pushed everything back to the shore.

Windflower and Lady walked back through the middle of town, and then down towards the wharf. When he got around the corner, he could hear something was up at the fish plant wharf. There was a large crowd of people near the protest signs yelling at the freighter holding the fish plant's scrap metal, which looked like it was ready to leave port. Yet, it couldn't because out in the harbour a string of vessels from longliners to dorys strung across the entrance like Christmas lights.

It took him a few seconds to tune into what was happening. Then he remembered the talk of a flotilla. That's what they meant, a floating picket line. As he stood transfixed, Evanchuk pulled up in her cruiser beside him. She got out of the car and walked over to Windflower.

"What's going on?" she asked.

"They're preventing the ship from leaving," said Windflower.

"What should we do?" Evanchuk asked.

"For now, we just watch," said Windflower. "I have a feeling this one is beyond our capacity to resolve."

He left Evanchuk to monitor the situation and took Lady back to his house. He got a text message from Quigley that he was on his way to Marystown so Windflower got ready to go as well. He was going to leave Lady on her own for the day but then reconsidered and decided to take her with him. She would be good company for the drive.

On his way out of town, he stopped by the wharf where it looked like most of the town was out to see the floating protest. It was a pretty spectacular sight. At a time of year when the port would be almost deserted, it was chock-a-block full of people and boats of all shapes and varieties. The people cheered loudly every time one of their flotilla moved an inch on the water or when a new boat arrived. The boats were all blowing their horns and everyone seemed to have a Newfoundland flag flying from their mast. It looked more like a carnival than a protest.

Tizzard was standing beside Evanchuk when Windflower got back. Windflower nodded good morning and asked what was going on.

"We're just watching," said Tizzard. "It's pretty impressive."

Windflower nodded again. "Let's monitor the situation from here and make sure there are no disturbances. Have you called the marine unit?"

"We've notified them," said Tizzard. "But unless the people out there are willing to move, I'm not sure what one RCMP patrol boat is going to do. We may need the Coast Guard to make that happen."

"Have you seen the fish plant manager yet?" asked Windflower.

"Not yet," said Tizzard. "But I expect he's on his way. Do you want me to call you when he shows up?"

"Sure," said Windflower. "Did you hear we got Laura Emberley? I'm on my way to Marystown to interview her with Quigley."

"I saw the report. Good luck with that."

Windflower waved goodbye to Evanchuk and Tizzard and headed off to Marystown. As he gazed back at the harbour he had to admit the protest might well be illegal, but it was also pretty impressive.

The morning was sunny and bright and the road was clear and dry. It was a perfect morning for a drive. Lady settled in comfortably in the back seat and Windflower turned on the radio again to listen to the end of Sunday Morning on the CBC. The landscape was starkly white and peaceful as he drove along. After a little while, Windflower settled into his tranquil thinking place and remembered the big choice that lay in front of him.

He loved Sheila, absolutely and completely, and it was clear she loved him. So what was holding him back? When he thought hard about it, he realized it must be fear. He thought about what his Uncle Frank had said about fear when he was talking about the rabbit. Windflower was afraid of getting married, but what was he actually afraid of? Was it the commitment? Maybe. Was it the sense of permanency? That might be it too. He liked his nomadic life, or at least he thought he did. Was he simply afraid of change?

The more he thought about it the less comfortable he felt, but didn't someone say that in order to be really happy you had to get out of your comfort zone? Windflower certainly felt like that right now, but the good news was that he just passed the sign for Marystown, 10 km ahead. As he pulled into town, Windflower decided to stop at the trail at Jane's Pond for a walk with Lady before his meeting.

The trail around the pond was kept open all year but the better trails up through the woods were packed with snow. Lady didn't seem to mind as she sniffed her way all around the boardwalk. Windflower had to keep her on the leash for most of the way but when they got to the back of the trail away from the road, he set her free to explore. She enjoyed this and was pretty happy all the way back to the car.

Windflower drove through the community and pulled up to the front door of the Marystown RCMP detachment.

He checked in with the duty officer and was told that Sergeant Quigley was waiting for him in the small interview room downstairs. He headed down.

"Good day, Winston. How are you this fine sunny day?"

"I'm well. You're in a good mood. How about our visitor?"

"She's not as pleasant. Not really in a talkative mood. The only talking she did was to yell about her lawyer. I said her lawyer could come and see her anytime in Marystown."

"I assume he or she is in St. John's," said Windflower.

"Unfortunately for Ms. Emberley, yes. But it will give her a day to cool off and think about her situation, and us a chance to talk to her before she lawyers up."

"Good move. I'm thinking we might want to do a little good cop, bad cop on her to see if we can't shake her up," said Windflower.

"I'm assuming I'm the bad guy, again," said Quigley in mock horror.

"But you're so good at it. Why don't you have her brought in?"

Quigley went out to the hall and asked the female guard on duty to bring Laura Emberley to the interview room. A few minutes later, a disheveled and disturbed prisoner was sitting across from the two RCMP officers.

"You can't hold me unless you charge me and I want my lawyer," she shouted across the table.

"First of all, you are a key witness in an on-going murder investigation and you are certainly a flight risk. Your lawyer will eventually get here, but I'd be surprised if you're getting out of protective custody anytime soon," said Windflower.

"Protective custody, that's a joke," said Emberley. "Anyway, I've already told you everything I know. I'm not going to say anymore so you can frame me with it. Take me back to my cell. I'll wait for my lawyer."

"This might be your last and only chance," said Windflower. "Shawn Parsons is naming you as the ringleader. And it won't be long before he starts talking about the murders too."

"I don't know who you're talking about," said Emberley.

"Listen up, lady," said Quigley. "One of you is going down for murder and I would just as soon believe it was you. Windflower tells me he's got tapes of you and Parsons, and you know Parsons will flip over on you."

Emberley tried to contain her surprise, but couldn't hide it.

Windflower saw it and followed up quickly. "Michael Ridgeway kept records of the shipments from Fortune. And he made tapes of the conversations between you and Shawn Parsons. We're now following up in Halifax. Once we get that info we'll have both of you. The question is: who is going to get nailed for the murder charge?"

Emberley was still hesitating, as if she was mulling her options.

Quigley spoke again.

"I think we're wasting our time. Let's just lock her up."

Emberley looked at Windflower as if to say something, but stopped. Quigley took her by the arm and led her outside.

When he came back in he smiled at Windflower. "We've planted the seed. Let's go get a cup of coffee while we let her think about it."

The two men walked over to the Tim Hortons, stopping along the way so that Windflower could show off Lady to his friend.

"She's a beauty," said Quigley. "Now that you've got the dog, it won't be too long before you get the wife and kids and the white picket fence."

Windflower laughed, but he couldn't deny that might be his path, so he said nothing in response except offer to buy the coffee.

CHAPTER FORTY-FIVE

Quigley and Windflower spent a pleasant hour nursing their coffees and getting caught up on each other's activities. One surprising thing that Quigley said was that he put his name forward for the job in Marystown. "Only on a temporary basis, of course. But I heard they were looking for volunteers and I thought, why not?"

"I think you'd be good at it. But you better stop picking on the baymen. They'll run a townie like you out of town pretty fast if you start acting up."

Quigley laughed. "Yeah, I'll have to tell the locals I'm from Ontario or something. Anywhere but from Sin John's."

They finished their coffees and walked back to the RCMP office. It was still sunny but the temperature was dropping fast. "It's gonna be cold tonight," said Quigley as he pulled his collar up around his neck.

"I just hope we don't get any of that black ice on the way home," said Windflower.

When they got to the detachment, they agreed that Windflower would go in alone to see Laura Emberley. "Try the soft approach," said Quigley. "See if she bites."

Windflower was led to the holding cells by the female guard and stood outside Emberley's cell.

"I thought I'd give you one more chance. Maybe I can help you if you help us."

"What can you do for me?" she asked as she stood to face Windflower.

"First of all, let me ask you one question. Were you involved in the deaths of either of these men in Grand Bank?"

"That wasn't me. But I'm not telling you anything else unless I know what you can do first."

"That depends on what you can tell us about the death of Frankie Fallon, and maybe even Michael Ridgeway, and about the drug operation. You are going down for the drugs, there's no question about that. We've got enough to charge you right now. But someone is also going to be charged with murder, and unless you want to be that person, you better start talking. I can tell you Shawn Parsons is already squealing like a pig in St. John's."

"Shawn Parsons is a low-life. But I'm still not sure what helping you guys will do for me."

"No guarantees," said Windflower. "But if your story holds up, I'll talk to the Crown Attorney. At a minimum, you may not get charged for murder. And he will take what you say into consideration when it comes time for sentencing."

"That's not much. I think I'm better off waiting for my lawyer."

With that she sat down on her bunk and folded her hands in her lap.

Windflower went back to where Quigley was sitting in the interview room and shook his head. "No dice. She's going to hang on for her lawyer, so I guess we better start moving on some preliminary charges. She did say, however, that it wasn't her on the murders. And she didn't react when I suggested Michael Ridgeway was murdered too."

"At least we have that much. We can talk to Langmead in St. John's tomorrow and see what's he's come up with from Parsons. I was going to stay in Marystown for a few days anyway so I can work with the Crown to come up with some charges. Plus, I still need to chat with Simard about what's going on in Halifax."

"Sounds like you might as well move here. I'm going to write up some notes on what we've learned so far. That'll help with the charges. And after I finish up there, why don't we go for dinner? It's early but I wouldn't mind getting on the road a bit sooner if that's okay," said Windflower.

"No problem with me. I can eat anytime. Let's go over to the motel. I think they have a Sunday dinner special tonight."

The restaurant did indeed have a dinner special: thick slices of roast beef, mashed potatoes with gravy, and the standard frozen peas and carrots with puffy Yorkshire pudding. Both men heartily enjoyed their supper, and a piece of blueberry pie with ice cream for dessert. They made plans to talk in the morning and Windflower went back to his car to see Lady and call Sheila to let her know he was on his way home.

He picked up a hot tea at the coffee shop on the way out of town and soon he and Lady were cruising along the highway on the way to Grand Bank. It was quiet on the road and while Windflower was driving slowly and carefully, he could feel his vehicle poorly grip the road surface. He reassured himself that as long as he didn't stop, he would be fine.

And he almost was. When he was coming down one of the steep hills past Grand Beach, he thought he saw something flicker on the side of the road just before the road to the Lanse Au Loup T, which turned out to be only the reflection from a hubcap another vehicle lost along the way. Nonetheless, as soon as Windflower touched the brakes he knew he was in trouble.

His Jeep started to slide, and there was nothing he could do to stop it. He knew better than try and apply more brake because that would only result in the back end of the car swinging around. He tried to steer his way out of trouble but it was too late. The momentum of the slide pushed his vehicle to the side of the highway and before he knew what was happening he was sliding into the ditch.

The ditch was like the one the late Mayor had warned about, with a steep eight foot drop. He was stuck. His vehicle had lodged itself up against a pole on one side and a snowbank on the other. Windflower might have been able to climb out the back window to safety but the impact had bent his door in, pinning his legs. The seat belt holder had also been crushed and was holding him in. He was stuck, though not really hurt. Not only that, but because he was trapped well below the highway he was invisible to anyone traveling along the road, unless they were searching for him. And that was not very likely on a cold and dark night out in the middle of nowhere.

The good news was that his Jeep was still running and there was plenty of gas. No need to panic. Sooner or later, somebody would come around. Lady didn't seem too concerned, so why should he be? Windflower tried to reach for his phone but it was in the charger in his glove compartment. At least he was safe and dry and warm.

After a while Windflower started to feel drowsy. He didn't know exactly how much time had passed. It felt like he was being pulled underwater in a dream, and also thought he heard a phone ringing from a distance.

Finally, he heard a dog barking, barking, barking. Why doesn't that dog just shut up so I can go to sleep? All he wanted to do was go to sleep. Then, somehow, he realized the dog was Lady. He wasn't sure why she was barking but when he finally managed to open his eyes, he knew why. He managed to get one hand free enough to roll down the window of his Jeep. He didn't know how long it had been running, but Lady had managed to wake him up before it was too late for both of them.

Without her, he would have drifted off to sleep and been poisoned by the carbon monoxide from the car. Windflower had a splitting headache and felt a bit dizzy but was otherwise okay. Now as long as someone found them before his gas ran out they might just make it.

After another short while Windflower's radio crackled to life and it sounded like Frost trying to call him. He tried shouting at the radio but of course that wouldn't work unless he pressed the send button, which he couldn't reach either. He would just have to wait.

Finally, after another unknown period of time passed, he heard another car and then shouts. He shouted back and Lady barked louder than he'd ever heard. The next thing he knew, someone was outside digging out the snow from the passenger side. Then the door opened and saw Tizzard, with Frost close behind. They managed to cut off his seat belt and pull him out of the car. They were talking to him but Windflower was fading at this point and the best he could do was put up his hand to show he was okay.

The other two Mounties carried him to the waiting car and one of them, he couldn't remember who, drove him to the clinic in Grand Bank where people were waiting for him at the front door. They whisked him onto a gurney and the next thing he knew he was in a hospital bed with Sheila standing over him. He had a massive headache.

"Hi Sheila," he said weakly.

"Winston, I'm so glad you're okay. You had a pretty close call with the accident and then almost killing yourself afterwards. It's a miracle you're alive."

"Lady saved my life," said Windflower. "I fell asleep and she woke me up. Other than this nasty headache I feel okay though. Can I go home?"

"You are one crazy man. The doctors said you have to stay here overnight for observation. But apparently there's nothing else wrong with you. They obviously didn't examine your brain, though," she said with a laugh.

Windflower tried to laugh too, but that hurt his head too much. "Will you look after Lady tonight?" He must have been given a strong sedative because he was asleep before he heard the answer.

When he woke up it was morning and this time it was Tizzard sitting next to him in the hospital room.

CHAPTER FORTY-SIX

"What time's breakfast around here?" he asked a very surprised Corporal Tizzard. As he was speaking, the duty doctor Doctor Redfern, came into the room. Tizzard got up to leave but the doctor waved him back down.

"I can see you're feeling a little better, Sergeant," said the doctor.

"Yeah, I'm feeling pretty good. Whatever you guys gave me last night knocked me out cold. I had a great sleep."

"We gave you some valium to help you relax. The carbon monoxide you inhaled did the rest. Any dizziness or nausea this morning?"

"Nope," said Windflower. "I've got a tinge of a headache but nothing like last night."

"That will go away too," said the doctor. "You're good to go."

"Thanks, Doc."

Tizzard walked out to the reception desk to wait until Windflower dressed himself. When Windflower was ready, he pulled Tizzard away from the nurses at their station, letting Tizzard drive them over to the Mug-Up for breakfast.

Tizzard had the full gear for breakfast: eggs, bacon, toast and a touton with molasses. Windflower decided to go light, and only had coffee and a breakfast sandwich. He did however, grab a piece of Tizzard's touton. He couldn't resist fried bread dough topped with molasses. There was a steady stream of well-wishers visiting the table and Windflower got tired of telling the story about driving his Jeep into the ditch. The locals loved it however, and were also already spreading the word about Lady, the wonder-dog who saved his life. Windflower just let it all go and allowed them to have their fun.

Windflower got Tizzard to drop him off at Sheila's along the way. Lady was also there, very happy to see him. He got a great reception from both.

"I'm so glad you're okay," she said.

"Thanks to Lady, here," said Windflower.

"I hope you take a couple of days to relax now," said Sheila. "What did the doctor say?"

"He said I'm good to go," said Windflower. "I'll take the morning off and then check in at the shop. But I won't hang around long. I was hoping we could get together later for supper."

"That sounds good," said Sheila. "I'll go by Warrens and see what they've got for meat. I have a meeting with my campaign people to go over a few things before tomorrow's announcement."

"Okay," said Windflower, reaching over to hug her, "I'll be by later."

Windflower walked home with Lady and the cool, fresh air helped clear his head. It even cleared up his headache. Lady was pretty happy too and she seemed to bark at every dog along the way to shout the good news that her Master was okay. The other dogs seemed happy too, since all of them barked back.

He got Lady some fresh food and water and a couple of Milk Bones to officially thank her for saving his life. While he was waiting for his bath to fill, he went outside to say his prayers. After he smudged, he offered thanks for not being more seriously injured in the accident and to Creator for sending him Lady. While he was praying he also gave thanks for all the people and the other creatures that were helping him on his journey.

Finally he prayed for guidance to make the right decision about him and Sheila. The answer he got was a little surprising. He remembered his Uncle Frank telling him one time Creator was always with us on our journey, but he often didn't speak directly to us. That's why other people were with us, to give us more direct answers to our questions. Windflower thought about who that might be today, and since his uncle wasn't there with him, who could he ask? Then it came to him: Herb Stoodley.

Very grateful to have found this path to follow, he closed up his smudge kit and went in to have his bath. After he was clean and dressed, he left Lady and walked down to the Mug-Up to see if he couldn't get some lunch and a little advice to go along with it. The lunch part was easy. He ordered a turkey and dressing sandwich and a cup of hot black tea. Herb Stoodley, however, was busy helping out in the kitchen. He couldn't talk now but invited Windflower to drop by his house later.

The invitation eased his anxiety and the sandwich did wonders for his stomach. He paid his bill and walked up to the RCMP office.

Betsy was very glad to see him and before he could sidestep her, she hugged him tightly. "I'm so glad nothing too bad happened to you," were her first words. Her second were, "I thought you'd be home in bed."

"I'm fine," said Windflower, extricating himself from his admin's grasp. "Is there anybody looking for me?"

"Here are your messages, sir. Can I get you a cup of coffee?"

"No thanks, Betsy. I'm good." Windflower finally got away and closed the door to his office. He ran through the message slips. There was one from Quigley, another from Langmead in St. John's, another from Guy Simard in Halifax and the final one from Wallace Winters, the Crown Attorney in Marystown.

Windflower decided to call Quigley first.

"I heard you had a close encounter with the ditch on the way home," said Quigley.

"Bad news travels fast," said Windflower.

"No secrets in a small town. I was calling to let you know that Winters, the CA, will be giving you a shout."

"Yeah, I got a message from him. What's he want?"

"I gave him a quick overview on Emberley but he wants to talk to you," said Quigley. "He's got to go in front of the judge tomorrow morning. Her lawyer has arrived from St. John's and he's trying to get her out. Winters has named her as a material witness and opposed her release because she's a flight risk, but he wants more ammo in case he needs it for the judge."

"No problem," said Windflower. "I'll give him a call later on. I also got a call from Guy Simard. Do you know what that's about?"

"I asked him to call you too. He's dug up some stuff on Laura Emberley and since you're the prime on this, I wanted you to get it directly. Something about her being suspended from being a pharmacist years ago. In any case, he'll fill you in."

"Great, thanks Ron. Talk soon," said Windflower.

He was about to call some of the other people on his list when Tizzard knocked and poked his head into Windflower's office.

"Got a minute?" he asked. "Thought you'd want an update on our floating protest."

"Come on in, Corporal. I'd love to hear about it."

"The fish plant manager is not very happy. He's been screaming in my ear since he found out about the protest. Demanding we do something about it. You know, the usual stuff."

"And what are we doing about it?" asked Windflower.

"The RCMP cruiser got here last night and it's patrolling the waters outside the harbour, making sure everybody is safe. I got the Captain to make an announcement asking the local boats to disperse. But so far they seem to be ignoring that order. Until the Coast Guard gets here or the weather gets worse, they look like they're going to stay out there. I guess we could start charging them."

"We could. And start a riot," said Windflower. "My sense is that this thing is going to blow over on its own. In the meantime let's keep the peace and 'What fates impose, that men must needs abide; It boots not to resist both wind and tide'."

Tizzard gave him a puzzled look.

"We wait for the weather to change," explained Windflower.

"Oh, okay," said Tizzard, shaking his head as he walked away.

Windflower's next call was to Guy Simard in Halifax.

"Winston, mon gars, how's tings?" said Staff Sergeant Guy Simard. "I hear you had a bit of a smash-up."

He and Windflower went back years, to the days when they worked together at the Halifax airport. Simard took a liking to the shy young man from Alberta and decided to take him under his wing. Windflower learned many things from his mentor, but what he valued most was his generosity and friendship.

"Hit a patch of black ice," said Windflower. "But nothing hurt except my pride. How about you, I thought you were retiring?"

"I can't seem to get out," said Simard with a laugh. "I guess I'm the one with the corporate memory on the crooks."

Windflower laughed too. "So tell me what you know about Laura Emberley."

"I don't recall it, but we have a file on Emberley at the office here. Apparently she lost her license about 10 years ago for falsifying records at a pharmacy in Truro. There wasn't enough for a criminal investigation, but the board yanked her license. She didn't show up again on our radar until last year."

"What was that about?" asked Windflower.

"She was at a drug store in Port Hawkesbury. We suspected the Russians were using that store for one of their operations, but Emberley was gone before we could move in. After she left, we found someone else we knew had been working there as well. Michael Ridgeway," said Simard.

"Ridgeway?" said Windflower with surprise.

"Yeah, he got out first and then, when the heat got hotter, she skipped too. We're not completely sure, but we think the pair did this a few times in different locations across the Maritimes. We're still checking, though. I can let you know what we find out."

"Great. Thanks, Guy. We'll talk again soon."

"That would be good, Winston. Did you marry that pretty woman you're hanging around with yet?"

"Not yet," said Windflower.

"Don't wait too long," said Simard. "I wish I'd met my gal years ago. I've never been happier since we got hitched."

"Thanks again, Guy," said Windflower as he let the older Mountie go.

Maybe Ridgeway was just another crook with a drug habit after all, not the passive victim he pretended to be. In any case, things were not looking good for Emberley. She now had the combined forces of the RCMP all across Atlantic Canada trying to retrace her steps. She had been pretty smart to last in the game this long, but now the noose was starting to tighten around her neck. Windflower wouldn't mind at all giving it a few twists of his own.

Before he could make his next call, Betsy beeped him to let him know Detective Langmead from the RNC was on Line 2. He punched the number and said hello to his friend from St. John's.

Chapter Forty-Seven

"Good morning Carl," said Windflower. "And before you ask about the accident, I'm fine."

"What accident?" asked Langmead.

"Sorry, Carl," said Windflower. "I put my car in the ditch last night and it seems like the whole world knows about it."

"Well, I can certainly spread the word in St. John's, if you'd like," said Langmead.

"No thanks," said Windflower with a laugh. "So how can I help you?"

"I hear you've got Laura Emberley in Marystown. Since we've got Parsons here, I thought it would be good to touch base. Parsons is yabbering on as usual, and we haven't charged him with any more than breaching his conditions at this point. He's certainly connected to the drug operation. But he's such a pathological liar it's hard to believe a word he says."

"I'm glad you called," said Windflower. "There have been a lot of developments on our end. It's pretty clear that Emberley and Parsons were connected in the operation. And we've got a witness putting Parsons in this area on the day of Michael Ridgeway's accident. They both might have been involved in Ridgeway's death as well as Frankie Fallon's. It's hard to say who was in charge yet, but my guess is that it was Laura Emberley. Parsons doesn't have the brains but she certainly does. We've also found some records and tapes relating to the drugs that were shipping in and out of Fortune. It looks like part of a bigger operation headquartered in Halifax, covering most of the east coast."

"Wow, you guys work fast," said Langmead.

"We had a bit of luck with the tapes," said Windflower. "And our people in Halifax have been on top of this file for a while. I'm giving the Crown a briefing on this later today. Emberley is due in court tomorrow morning and we want to keep her in jail until we can find out some more information. Why don't I get the Crown to call you and he can pick your brains as well?"

"Sure," said Langmead. "Parsons is certainly not going anywhere, and if we can help hold Emberley that'd be good too."

"Great. I'm dealing with Wallace Winters in Marystown. I'll give him your number. Once we get Emberley stabilized inside, it might be a good idea to get together and exchange notes."

"Sounds good, Winston. Let's stay in touch."

Windflower tried to reach the Crown Attorney's office but only succeeded in leaving a message. Not a big problem, because that would give him a few minutes to see about getting a vehicle. He walked out to the front to see Betsy.

"I'm assuming my Jeep is in the shop," he said.

"Yes, sir. We don't even have an estimate of when they'll look at it at the garage in Marystown. That's where they towed it."

"My guess is that it'll be a while. In the meantime I'm going to need another vehicle. Could you call Louise Cranford in Marystown and see if they can fix me up with something for the short term? And let me know as soon as Wallace Winters calls. I need to talk to him today before I go home."

"Yes, sir," said Betsy.

Windflower took a few minutes to put together a few notes for his talk with Winters. That was a good idea because whenever Winters called, Windflower felt like he was the one under investigation.

Lucky for Windflower, Winters called shortly afterwards. They greeted each other, and then got down to business.

"We have plenty to go in front of the judge with tomorrow," said Winters. "I'm going to try a few preliminary charges for Emberley and we'll go from there."

"What will you charge her with?" asked Windflower.

"We'll start with trafficking restricted substances and conspiracy to murder. I'll talk to her as soon as I can but I'm not optimistic we'll get anything from her. I also need to come over fairly soon to have a look at the evidence and do some interviews though, because the judge will likely ask for a full set of charges within the next week."

"No problem," said Windflower. "We can get all the stuff ready for you. Who will you need to interview?"

"I've already talked to Quigley and I've got a call in to Langmead in St. John's. I still have to call Simard in Halifax but that can wait. I think I'll need to talk to Doctor Sanjay, and the female Constable. And your Corporal, Tizzard, as well. That should do it."

"Okay," said Windflower. "Let me know when you're coming and I'll set it up."

After the Crown Attorney had hung up, Windflower closed up his computer and left the office for the day. Betsy looked pleased he was leaving early and wished him a good evening. That was the plan, but first, a little chat with Uncle Herb.

Windflower walked the short distance to Stoodley's house up near the B & B and went around the back where Herb Stoodley had his art studio. When Windflower passed by the window in back, he could see that Stoodley was hard at work.

"Come on in," called Stoodley when he heard the door open. "Hi Winston, let me just finish a few more strokes and then I'll get a pot of tea going."

"No rush. I love watching someone paint. I know it's a lot of work but it looks so relaxing."

"It's not work if you enjoy it," said Stoodley, putting away his paints and his brushes into jars to clean later. "And I would say I loves it b'y. Let me get the tea going."

Stoodley walked into the kitchen and filled and set the kettle on the stove, and Windflower followed. Then, while it was boiling, he found a tray of cookies in the fridge and put them on the table between them. Windflower was on his second brownie when Stoodley passed him a cup of hot steaming tea.

"So how's your political life going?" Windflower asked the older man.

"I am but a temporary servant of the people. I'm only trying to keep the peace until the new Mayor can be elected. Speaking of which, I'm hearing Sheila will be throwing her hat into the ring."

"She'll be making the announcement tomorrow," said Windflower.

"How do you feel about it?"

"It's not up to me. But unofficially I support Sheila 110 percent."

"Good man," said Stoodley. "It must make things interesting at home, though."

"We had to work through this one. But I did want to talk to you about the home front. Sheila wants to get married."

"What do you think?" asked Stoodley.

"She asked me the other night when we were out at dinner. I guess I feel uncomfortable that she did the asking and if I was really honest, I would say I'm kinda afraid," said Windflower.

"Of what?"

"That's the thing, I'm not really sure what I'm afraid of."

"In my experience if I can't name what I'm afraid of, it's probably because it isn't real," said Stoodley. "Fears are often about the future; that we will lose something we have or not get something we want. The truth is that if we don't face our fears, they might come to fruition. You might actually lose the thing you want the most."

"That's very good. It helps me think about it in a different light."

"Well, one of the advantages of being old is that you've already made most of your mistakes," said Stoodley. "Let me tell you a secret. When I was a little younger than you, there was a girl I was crazy about. She wanted to settle down and get married and have kids. I wanted to, but I thought I was too young, and wanted to build my career first."

"So what happened?" asked Windflower.

"I let her slip away," said Stoodley. "I regretted that decision for thirty years. But two years after her husband died I went and asked her to marry me. Moira said yes, and the last 10 years have been the happiest time of my life. Don't make the same mistake I did."

Windflower smiled at his friend. "Thank you for your advice. And the cookies."

"You're welcome. You're a good man, Winston. Just be yourself. And remember, 'If men could be contented to be what they are, there were no fear in marriage'."

Windflower shook Herb Stoodley's hand and left to walk over to Sheila's house for dinner.

CHAPTER FORTY-EIGHT

Windflower's first welcome was from the aromas emanating from Sheila's kitchen. Ginger, garlic and frying beef. He though it couldn't get much better, but then he saw Sheila. She had her hair tied in a bandana and gave him a big smile as he entered the room. Apparently it could. He went to her and hugged her closely from behind.

"You're probably just attracted to the beef stir-fry," said Sheila with a laugh.

"I am hungry. But I hope dinner is merely the beginning."

"If you play your cards right, you never know what can happen," she said with another laugh. "But for now, why don't you pour us each a glass of wine?"

Windflower went to the counter and poured two glasses from the bottle of burgundy. "Is this the wine you used in the stir-fry? It looks like a nice bottle of wine."

"It was the last in our supply. But it will add a special flavour to the beef."

"What else did you put in there?" asked Windflower as Sheila removed the beef from the frying pan and then added some onion and freshly chopped broccoli.

"The usual. A little garlic, well maybe a lot of garlic, and some ginger and soy. Plus my secret ingredients. A girl has to have some secrets, you know."

Windflower smiled and sipped his wine. "There are many things I will never know or understand about women. Secret recipes are the least of my problems."

"As it should be," said Sheila as she placed the beef and liquid back into the frying pan. "One more minute and this will be done. Why don't you serve us up some rice?"

Windflower did as he was told and Sheila poured the beef and sauce and vegetables over the mounds of rice. They sat at the table and, as usual, Windflower said little except murmur his approval until he had finished plate number one. Only when he was finishing up his second helping did his voice come back into working order.

"Thank you, Sheila. I'd forgotten how much I enjoyed your stir-fry. It is definitely in my top ten list."

"There are an awful lot of dishes on that list," Sheila said.

"Speaking of dishes, I will gladly do them, as partial payment for a great meal," he said.

"Offer accepted," said Sheila as she went to put on the kettle for tea. She also chopped up some fruit and added a dollop of fresh cream each for their dessert.

They were sitting in the kitchen eating their fruit when Windflower spoke again.

"So I've been thinking about your proposal," said Windflower.

"Oh?"

"I have. I've learned not to let fear hold me back, keep me from getting what I want."

"And that would be?" asked Sheila.

"You, and our life together. I would like to get married."

"Oh, Winston, I am so happy," said Sheila as she wrapped her arms around him. "We belong together, you know."

"I know. Now if you will excuse me for half an hour, I have to go see the other lady love in my life."

"Permission granted, Sergeant."

Windflower walked home quickly in the chilly night and he could feel the breeze from the ocean whipping around his ears. He burrowed down into his coat and pulled the lapels up around his ears.

When he got home, he got his RCMP regulation fur hat out of the closet along with Lady's leash. Lady was soon out the door and doing her business. They did a mini-route around the block, and then went back inside. He refreshed her supplies and said goodnight.

Ten minutes later he was already warming up with Sheila and a hot cup of tea. "It's going to be a cold one," he said. "And the wind is picking up, too."

"That'll probably mean the end of the protest. This was always intended to be a short-term demonstration, something that allowed people one more chance to mourn."

When Windflower looked puzzled she added, "There's no way to sustain a floating protest in these waters in the wintertime. But some people wanted to mark the beginning of the end."

"Is it really the end?" asked Windflower.

"It's the end of an era, but it's not the end of Grand Bank, at least if I have anything to do with it. Grand Bank has been through many transformations in the last one hundred and fifty years, and while this one will be tough, I believe we can do it. There are so many possibilities for our community that can preserve our culture and history, yet still allow for economic development."

"Tell me more, Madame Mayor."

"Well, we can build on what we already have. The fabrication plant employs almost 200 people and if we can attract two or three more small or medium sized enterprises, we'll be okay on that front. And we can liven up the Fisherman's Museum and make it a living library for the history of Grand Bank."

"You know, I've always wanted to hear some of the stories of the schooners and the old Captains," said Windflower.

"Exactly. We could have a presentation on some of them and get their families to bring old photographs so we could get a sense of what things were like in the olden days. Plus I want to bring the Realist Artists of Newfoundland and Labrador over to Grand Bank to see if they'd consider a project like the one they did in Burin."

"I saw that exhibition in Burin. It was amazing the way they recreated the houses and buildings from the past. It made you want to go back in time and visit them."

"Herb Stoodley has agreed to lead that initiative, and Moira and the Heritage committee will be putting together a plan to talk about restoring the waterfront. That's key if we want to build up our share of the tourism market," said Sheila.

"Wow, you have a lot of great ideas," said Windflower.

"They're only partially mine. These ideas already have a champion in the community. All I want to do is help them find the resources to make them a reality. And of course, only if I am elected."

"With that platform, how can you lose?" asked Windflower.

"Some people are very committed to the status quo, even if that means our town slowly dies out. But I believe there are more people who want to create a sustainable community, and that's why I'm running for Mayor," said Sheila.

"Bravo," said Windflower. "You are one smart woman, Sheila Hillier. And a heck of a politician too."

"Thank you, Sergeant Windflower. Now, why don't you have your bath first? I have to dig out my fashion magazines to start looking for a dress."

Windflower laughed and went upstairs for a bath, then went to sleep afterwards.

In the morning Windflower kissed a sleeping Sheila and walked back home through the still-dark town. The wind had picked up another notch and he could feel moisture in the air. Neither of which was a good sign in these parts. Together they could easily create a disaster.

He opened the door and found Lady sleeping on the floor in her bedroom.

"Come on, girl," he called out to rouse her, and she sleepily walked with Windflower out the back door. He smudged while she did her thing. He was grateful for good friends and family, for having a dog in his life again, and for the love of a good woman. He offered up his prayers for all those who were struggling and suffering today, and prayed for compassion to treat everyone he met on his journey with kindness since he couldn't yet bring himself to forgive all the bad things in the world

Windflower made a pot of coffee and cut up some fruit for his breakfast. After his shower, he put the fruit and some granola in a bowl and mixed in a small container of yogurt.

He drank one cup of coffee and then took Lady, who was waiting patiently, out for her morning walk. It was cold and they walked quickly through the empty roads. Empty at least until they got to the wharf.

It was not yet light and there were dozens of vehicles lining the road to the fish plant wharf. Windflower abruptly turned around and walked up to the RCMP building. There was no one there. Whoever was on duty must be out on the highway. He unlocked the door and let himself and Lady in out of the cold. A few minutes later Evanchuk showed up from the last highway tour of her shift and looked surprised to see Windflower sitting in the reception area.

"Good morning, Sergeant."

"Good morning. Did you see all the vehicles down at the wharf?"

"Yes, sir. They were just starting to arrive when I went out, and they're still coming."

"Something is going on down there. Can you stay a bit longer this morning? We're going to need some traffic control to start with."

"Sure," said Evanchuk. "Let me get a fresh mug of coffee and I'll head down there right now. Wanna cup?"

"Sure," said Windflower, thinking this might be a big coffee day in Grand Bank.

Evanchuk left and Windflower had a couple of minutes of quiet time before Tizzard burst into the office.

"Hey, Boss. What are you doing here?"

"Waiting for you to show up. Have you been by the wharf this morning?"

"Not yet. Is something going on?"

"There's definitely something happening down there this morning. Evanchuk is down there trying to keep things quiet, but she'll need some help. Give me your keys and I'll run Lady home and then we'll both go down to check it out."

Tizzard somewhat reluctantly handed over the keys to his Jeep and Windflower laughed. "I'm not going to steal your vehicle, Corporal. Betsy is already working on getting me a new one."

With that, Windflower drove Lady home. He was back at the detachment soon after and picked up Tizzard to go to the wharf.

Chapter Forty-Nine

The scene at the fish plant wharf resembled a full-out carnival. The media had arrived and were setting up as close as they could to the water. Two giant speakers had been set up in the back of one of the pickups. It seemed like most of the town was already there, so Evanchuk had her hands full. She had given up trying to keep people from parking on the side of the road and was focused on keeping the drive-by gawkers moving along. She looked very relieved to see Windflower and Tizzard, the latter of whom came to help her direct traffic, while Windflower walked closer to the scene of the action.

He greeted two men setting up a microphone near the speakers and waved to the people from the media. Since everyone was fully engaged in their tasks they basically ignored him, so he wandered around looking for a friendly face. He found Herb Stoodley in a gaggle of people and motioned him aside.

"Morning, Herb. What's going on?"

"They're closing up the protest. With the wind picking up it's not safe out there for most of the smaller boats. They're going to come into the harbour to get out of the storm. This is their welcoming party," he said, pointing to the crowd on the wharf.

"Thanks, Herb."

Windflower walked back up to the road to check in with Tizzard and Evanchuk.

"They're stopping the protest and I guess there will be some form of ceremony to officially end it," said Windflower.

"That makes sense," said Tizzard. "The forecast is calling for high winds growing throughout the day and some snow as well. Not enough to cause big problems, but enough with the wind to make it pretty dangerous on the water."

"Let's just keep traffic moving and wait for whatever happens next," said Windflower.

They didn't have to wait long for that next development.

One by one the boats that were lined up across the harbour started breaking away and headed for shore. Each of them was flying a Newfoundland flag and blowing their horns, which was responded to by the cars and trucks lining the waterfront. The sounds echoed back and forth in the shelter of the harbour. Windflower and his fellow officers stopped to watch in amazement.

When all of the boats were within the confines of the Grand Bank Harbour, someone played a taped version of 'The Ode to Newfoundland' and every person on land and shore joined in the singing. There were speeches by politicians, including the federal MP who blamed the provincial government, and one by the local provincial MHA who blamed the federal government. The final speech was by a local fisherman who Windflower recognized as Fonse Tessier from Grand Bank.

Tessier didn't speak long but he spoke of the history surrounding the fishery in this part of the world and how many times they had been told it was a thing of the past, only to see it reclaim its place as part of the town's on-going economy. "Ya can knock us down, b'ys, but ya can't keep us down." With Tessier's speech the protest was over, and while the smaller boats found a place to tie up along the wharfside, the long liners and larger vessels left port to return home. Windflower thought it was a sad moment, but at the same time he felt the pride the people of Grand Bank had in their little community.

He saw Sheila for a moment as she was coming up from the crowd at the wharf. He waved at her and smiled. He sent his silent hopes that the Council meeting would go well for her. Windflower let Evanchuk go home while he stayed with Tizzard to help people and cars get safely away from the protest area.

After about an hour, they both left to go back to the office. When they arrived, Betsy greeted Windflower with good news. "We've got a new vehicle for you," she said. "Someone is bringing it over from Marystown after lunch."

"That is great news, Betsy. Both I and Corporal Tizzard are relieved."

Tizzard didn't say anything, but he was smiling as he went back to make a snack and a pot of tea. Windflower worked away in his office for another hour until Tizzard came to get him.

"Lunch?" he asked.

"Absolutely," said Windflower and they got into Tizzard's car and drove to the Mug-Up.

The café was surprisingly quiet, probably because most people had already been in for a visit after the protest. Herb Stoodley, still dressed in his suit and tie, came over to take their order.

"I like the new uniforms," said Windflower.

"Oh, that's from the Council meeting. Thankfully, there won't be too many of those for me. They decided to call the election for one month from now. Sheila made her announcement right after the meeting. It was good timing. All of the media that was here from the protest stayed around. So look forward to seeing her on the news tonight."

Tizzard was going to make a joke but wisely decided not to when he saw the look in Windflower's eyes. Instead he said, "I'll have the turkey soup and a grilled cheese sandwich."

"Same for me," said Windflower.

Their food came quickly and was gone just as fast.

They said goodbye to Herb, and left. They were getting into Tizzard's Jeep when a large black vehicle rumbled by them. They didn't think anything of that until they got back to the detachment and saw the vehicle in their parking lot.

Inside, Betsy had a worried look in her eyes. Ron Quigley was sitting across from her with a big grin on his face.

"What do you think of your new ride?" asked Quigley.

Windflower went back outside to take another look at the black vehicle parked in front. Quigley followed him out.

"She's called Black Betty," he said.

Black Betty was a Chevrolet Yukon, and the numerous dents, scrapes and other markings revealed how she was not even close to new.

"What year is it?" Windflower asked.

"It's a 2008. It's a bit old and clunky but it's ideal for driving in this type of weather."

When Windflower still looked a little incredulous, Quigley added, "I thought it might be safer for you if you decided to run into another ditch."

By this point Tizzard could no longer contain himself and both he and Betsy started to laugh. Windflower wanted to get mad, but just couldn't. He tried to smile but all that came out was a grimace.

"It's only a loaner. I've put the order in for a new vehicle for you, but that will take a while. This will at least give you wheels until then. And despite its looks, it's actually quite reliable."

"Thanks," said Windflower, relieved his discomfort would not be permanent.

"Can we go to your office? I need to talk to you about a few things," said Quigley.

Windflower led Quigley back into his office, glaring at Tizzard along the way. Tizzard wisely opted to stay silent while his boss passed by.

"I brought the vehicle over myself because I wanted to tell you in person I am the interim Inspector for this area," said Quigley.

"Congratulations, Ron, or I should say Inspector Quigley," said Windflower.

"We've known each other too long to be formal. I don't want that to change. And this situation might be very short-lived. They asked me to take over while they continue their search for a full-time replacement. Bill Ford won't be coming back, not as Inspector anyway, and they are not yet sure of their long-term direction. So they asked me to take it on for three months while they figured it out, and I said yes."

"Well, I think it's good news. And you'll do a good job. Whatever you want from me, you got it."

"Thanks, Winston. I know you and I are going to be okay. I'm more worried about the higher-ups. They tend to eat their young pretty quickly, and I will be the youngest one on the block."

"I assume you want an update on what's going on around here," said Windflower. "Why don't we start by introducing the staff to their new Inspector?"

Windflower led Quigley out to meet the troops and afterward Tizzard joined them to go through the current files in Grand Bank. Betsy interrupted them because Windflower had a call from the Crown Attorney.

"Good afternoon, Mr. Winters."

"Afternoon, Sergeant. The judge has agreed to hold Laura Emberley in custody, but wants us to move quickly to lay the formal charges. That means I will have to come over there sooner than I thought to do the interviews. Would tomorrow work?"

"Sure, I'll get my admin to set it up for you," said Windflower.

"Great, I'll be there just before lunch," said the Crown Attorney.

Windflower stopped at Betsy's desk to relay the information about Winters' visit and to ask her to get a meeting room at the Justice Building for the Crown Attorney. He also asked her to call Doctor Sanjay and MacDonald, and then let Tizzard know to be on call for an interview.

"Winters is coming over tomorrow," said Windflower. "The judge has agreed to hold Emberley but the Crown wants him to speed up the process. You and I are on tap," he said pointing to Tizzard.

"I might as well stay over too," said Quigley. "I need to talk to Winters and I can get a ride back when he's going home."

"Great," said Windflower. "You can bunk at my place if you want. We'll have to shift Lady out of her room but she'll like the company. I can probably scrounge up something for supper too."

"Much appreciated. I hear you're quite good in the kitchen. Looking forward to it."

Tizzard went off to check on Frost who was just coming in for the night shift. On his way out Quigley threw the keys of the Yukon to Windflower. "She's your baby now," said Quigley.

"Thanks," said Windflower, still not quite convinced he should be over-grateful, but happy to have wheels again.

The Yukon was actually a lot better on the inside than it looked from outside. It was comfortable and ran very smoothly. Windflower had to admit it was actually quite a safe vehicle and that he really would be much safer if he slid into another ditch. Not like that was going to happen though.

It was getting dark when they got home, and although it was too early for supper it wasn't too early for a cold beer. Windflower got them both an India Beer from the fridge and heated a batch of microwave popcorn to tide them over. He took Lady for a late afternoon walk while Quigley was relaxing on the couch. When he got back Quigley's beer was gone and he was fast asleep on the couch. Lady took her position on the floor beneath him as extra security while Windflower rummaged through the fridge to find something for supper.

Chapter Fifty

Windflower pulled out a couple of salmon steaks from the freezer and while he would love to throw them onto the barbeque, it was too cold outside. Not only was it windy and freezing, but the snow was becoming quite thick and swirling. He turned the heat up a notch and silently prayed there wouldn't be too much of the white stuff; at least not tonight.

While the salmon was thawing, he called Sheila to check in. She was home but had visitors as well. He was welcome to join them, but he told her about his own visitor.

"What did Ron say about our engagement?" she asked.

"He's having a nap right now. I'll tell him when we're having supper," said Windflower.

"Oh. You better start telling people before they find out from other sources," she said.

"What do you mean?" asked Windflower.

"Well, it's not really a secret and I have told a few people, including Sandra who will likely tell Ethel."

"You might as well put it in the Southern Gazette, then," said Windflower.

Ethel was known around Grand Bank as the gossip lady and if she didn't have any gossip on you, she just made some up. To have this real and juicy info on Sheila and Windflower would bring great joy to Ethel. Everybody in town would know by the end of the week; sooner if Ethel could get around to all of them.

Windflower grimaced for the second time that day. Luckily, no one was around to witness this one, except for Lady who was looking up at him strangely. He told Sheila if everything worked out he'd come over later, and then he said goodbye and hung up. Windflower gave Lady a couple of Milk Bones to buy her silence, and pulled out his stack of Canadian Living recipes to look for a nice sauce for the salmon.

He found one called Smothered Salmon Steaks, and it looked perfect for a mid-winter meal. He hadn't tried it before but when he checked, he had most of the ingredients including the requisite chicken broth and the spices. He greased the bottom of a baking dish with olive oil and then added the onions with a heavy sprinkle of thyme on top. Then he poured in the chicken broth and a little lemon juice, stirring the whole mixture together. He microwaved the salmon for just over a minute to take the freeze out of the fish and then put the thawed fish in the dish. The final touches were salt and pepper, and zest from a lemon which Windflower had in the fridge.

He covered everything in tin foil and put it into the oven to bake. While the salmon was cooking he put two large potatoes in the microwave and chopped up some broccoli and carrots that he would steam at the last minute. He was taking the salmon out of the oven and warming a frozen apple pie when he heard Quigley stir in the living room.

"What is that delicious smell?" asked Quigley as he walked into the kitchen.

"If you sit down I'll serve it up, and you can taste it for yourself," said Windflower.

"Winston, this is fabulous," said Quigley. "Where did you learn to cook like this? You haven't got your woman hiding in the closet around here, have you?"

Windflower laughed as he sat down to enjoy his meal as well. "No, Sheila's not here. But you should be prepared to see her around much more in the future."

"You're not getting married?" asked Quigley, his mouth full of salmon and potato.

"I am," said Windflower. "We haven't set a date yet, but sometime in the new year. And I would like you to consider being my best man."

"I can't say I'm shocked. And I would be honoured to be your best man. Congratulations." He raised his beer bottle to Windflower's in an informal toast.

When they finished dinner, Quigley was equally as impressed when Windflower pulled the apple pie out of the oven and cut them each a big piece and topped it with vanilla ice cream. "Man, do you eat like this all the time? I'm living on take-out and frozen dinners."

"Get yourself a girl who likes to cook and read all those magazines with the recipes in them," said Windflower. "That's my secret."

"Mmm..."

Quigley had already moved onto his apple pie à la mode.

After dinner the men watched a hockey game on TV and Quigley begged off to go to bed early. "Long day," he said.

Windflower called Sheila but she still had guests and by the sounds of it, more than a few. Such was the political life. They said goodnight and made plans to have an early lunch or late breakfast in the morning. Windflower took

Lady for her final walk and although it was still bitterly cold, the snow had stopped, and the moon was peeking out from behind the clouds. He and his dog had a brisk walk through town before heading back to the warmth of his little house. He was in bed minutes later and while he made an attempt at reading, he awoke in the morning with his book lying on the top of Lady next to his bed.

The morning was coolish when Windflower opened the back door to let Lady out. He followed along and did his morning prayers and meditation. The sky was clear and he could clearly see the various constellations which occupied the sky in this part of the world. It was a wondrous sight and easy to find things to be grateful for this morning, starting with a very happy Lady who awoke in this mood every day. Windflower thought it was something to which everyone could aspire.

He put on the coffee and quickly showered and shaved. Before breakfast he took Lady out for a quick tour of town. They walked down near the wharf and Windflower could see the freighter at the fish plant mooring was all lit up and looked ready to leave. It would probably set out for sea as soon as the sun came up. There would be little protest this morning. Even the sea gulls were quiet as they recognized there was nothing of interest happening anymore.

When they got back, Quigley was up and in the kitchen drinking coffee. Not only that, but he had bacon frying in the pan and was stirring up some scrambled eggs. "I hope you don't mind I got breakfast started," he said.

"No problems here. I can finish up if you want to have a shower."

Fifteen minutes later, the two Mounties were enjoying their bacon and eggs, along with homemade toast and the last of Windflower's blueberry jam. After they cleaned up, Windflower drove them back to the detachment in his new/old vehicle and was once again surprised at how comfortable it felt.

At the office Windflower dug into the paperwork that had been neglected for a couple of days while Quigley checked his e-mail and messages. He came into Windflower's office a few minutes later with two cups of freshly brewed coffee and some information.

"I got a message from Wallace Winters. He said he talked to Langmead in St. John's last night and they are getting ready to charge Parsons with trafficking and the murder of Frankie Fallon," said Quigley.

"What about Laura Emberley?" asked Windflower.

"Winters says he's going to charge her with the same murder," said Quigley.

"That's interesting. Charge them both individually to see if one of them tries to rat out the other. Not bad."

"Not bad at all, as long as everything holds up when he does his interviews," said Quigley.

The two men were nursing their coffee when Tizzard arrived.

"Good morning Inspector. And congratulations, Boss," he said, holding out his hand.

"Thank you, Corporal. Don't tell me. Ethel?"

Tizzard laughed and went to the back to get his coffee.

CHAPTER FIFTY-ONE

The rest of the morning passed quickly. Around 11, Wallace Winters arrived from Marystown. Betsy had arranged a meeting room at the Justice Building but since Windflower wasn't scheduled for his interview until later, he left to meet Sheila at the café for an early lunch.

Windflower arrived first and sat at his usual corner table, and a steady stream of well-wishers approached him to offer their congratulations on his impending nuptials. When Sheila came in, the same crew came over to congratulate the bride-to-be as well. And to wish her success in the election.

"Good morning, Sergeant," said Sheila as she reached in to give him a squeeze and a peck on the cheek.

"Good morning, Missus Hillier. How was your evening?"

"It was good, but late. There's a lot to do for this election in a short period of time."

"I bet there is," said Windflower as Marie came by to take their order, but not before congratulating both Windflower and Sheila. "You make a lovely couple," said the waitress.

Windflower smiled and ordered the cod au gratin while Sheila ordered the all-day breakfast.

"I was thinking we should have a little party to celebrate our engagement," said Sheila.

"Just invite Ethel and she can tell everyone how it went. Tizzard was congratulating me before 8 o'clock this morning.

"Good news travels fast too. What did Ron Quigley have to say about it?"

"He was pleased for both of us. I asked him to be the best man and he agreed."

"That's great news. I'm going to ask Moira to stand for me, as soon as I get a chance."

"Speaking of Ron, he's been appointed interim Inspector," said Windflower.

"That's good news too. Is that his black monster parked in front of your office?"

"Unfortunately, that's my temporary vehicle replacement Ron brought over from Marystown. At least I hope it's temporary."

"It will be good if you happen to run into the ditch again," said Sheila mischievously.

Windflower thought of a smart aleck response, but before he could get it out their lunch arrived. That ended their conversation until all the food was gone. Windflower left shortly afterwards while Sheila stopped to talk to a few potential supporters and to speak with Moira Stoodley about her wedding plans.

When Windflower got back to the detachment it was almost time for his interview with Wallace Winters so he drove over to the Justice Building. When he arrived, he asked the reception for the meeting room. As he was going in Tizzard was coming out. "How'd it go?" he asked.

"I felt like I was on trial. I hope he's as good in the courtroom."

"I hear he is," said Windflower as he left Tizzard and walked into the interview room. For the next hour Windflower knew what Tizzard meant. It was a brutal interrogation, but Windflower understood its purpose was to make sure there were no holes in the Crown's arguments by the time the case got to court. Wallace Winters clearly believed in the Holiday Inn approach to his casework: No surprises.

After the hour, Windflower invited the Crown Attorney to come have coffee with him at the Mug-Up. Herb Stoodley was finishing up his work and he and Winters had a grand chat about the good old days when Stoodley was on the job. After he left, Windflower got the chance to probe the CA about his plans for the case against Laura Emberley.

"I've got enough to charge both her and Shawn Parsons with the murder of Frankie Fallon. The fingerprints show they were both at the scene and had the opportunity. The means look pretty clear and I can make the case for greed as a motive. For both of them."

"What about Michael Ridgeway's death?" asked Windflower.

"Well, that one is a bit more difficult. It looks like he was poisoned before his crash, but it's hard to make the direct link between all of the pieces and either Parsons or Emberley. A good defense lawyer could easily poke holes in my arguments and make a pretty good case for the accidental death of a known drug user. I like my chances better with the Fallon murder."

"That makes sense," said Windflower. "Now what?"

"I'm going back to Marystown to draft up the charges and then we see if either of them decides to blink," said Winters.

"Or tries to pin the blame on the other one," said Windflower.

"Parsons has already started to do that. But he doesn't really have much to trade. According to the RNC he keeps talking about the network in Halifax, but your guy up there, Simard, says he's got nothing new. Apparently, they've got the big guys in jail and without Laura Emberley, they have no other pharmacist to keep their drug transfer system going."

"I think we'd all sleep better if Parsons didn't get any breaks," said Windflower. "He's like a cockroach you just can't kill."

"At this point it doesn't look like we'll be doing him any favours, but we'll have to wait and see what Laura Emberley, and particularly her lawyer, thinks about their chances. If we're going to get a deal with her it will likely happen quickly." Winters began picking up his papers and putting them into his briefcase. "Anyway, I gotta go pick up Quigley and head back. I'd like to get on the road before it gets dark."

"Good plan," said Windflower. "If there's anything else you need from us, just let me know."

Windflower left Winters and drove back to the office. The rest of the afternoon ran smoothly. He was glad for the chance to catch his breath. The past week or so had been crazy, but it looked like things were finally slowing down. Sheila called to invite him for supper; an offer he was happy to accept. She also suggested they have a quiet night in, maybe watch a movie. That sounded great too.

He left work as Evanchuk was coming in for the evening. He wished her a good night and headed home.

Lady got a quick walk around the block and a promise of more later. Windflower had a hot shower and changed into his jeans and RCMP hoodie.

He jumped in his vehicle and drove over to Sheila's where she had already laid out supper and was scanning the movie network for a possible choice of their evening's entertainment. Their meal was simple but delicious, with cold cuts and salads left over from last night's mini-campaign meeting, and a selection of cupcakes, squares and cookies for dessert.

After supper Windflower cleaned up while Sheila found their movie. It was All About Eve, starring one of their favourite actresses, Bette Davis. In this movie, Davis starred as Margo Channing, an aging Broadway star whose life and career are threatened by an ambitious young fan. It was a fabulous old-time movie and both of them enjoyed their relaxing time together.

Windflower left after the movie to take Lady for her late night walk. He was back and snuggled up against Sheila on the couch as fast as he could. The rest of the night was as enjoyable as the movie and if Windflower could have rated it, he would have given it two thumbs up.

In the morning Windflower awoke early and was out again with Lady before the sun rose. The wind had dropped dramatically overnight and the temperature had risen in return. By December standards it was relatively balmy. But he also knew such a quick change in the weather was not always a good thing. His premonition proved to be correct because on their way back home Windflower felt a few tiny flakes brush his cheek. By the time he had finished breakfast and was on his way to work it was snowing thick, fat, fluffy flakes.

Chapter Fifty-Two

Windflower was not the first into the detachment. When he arrived Tizzard was sipping coffee and eating a croissant from a package already half empty.

"Having a light breakfast, Corporal?" Windflower asked.

"They're good," said Tizzard with his mouth full of pastry, offering Windflower one from his package.

"No thanks," said Windflower. "What are you doing here so early?"

"I thought I'd come in and catch up on some paperwork," said Tizzard. When Windflower looked mildly surprised, he added, "I do have a lot of paperwork, you know."

Windflower smiled. "It's good to see you on top of it, Corporal."

"Plus, I think we're going to get a fair dump of snow," said Tizzard. "I haven't seen the forecast yet, but it sure feels like it outside. I figured it might be a long night ahead so I'd come in early and then maybe take off for a few hours this afternoon."

"Good thinking. I might do the same. You may be right about the snow. The good news is the wind has died down. Snow will slow you down, but the wind is the killer."

Tizzard nodded again with his mouth full of croissant. He looked about to say something when Betsy arrived.

"Good morning, Betsy," said Windflower. "And how are you this snowy morning?"

"I'm grand. Isn't it beautiful outside? I love when it's warm and snowing. It makes me feel all Christmassy. I know it's early but I can feel the holiday spirit on days like this. How about you, Sergeant?"

"Oh yes. I can feel the spirit this morning. I just hope we don't have to rely on sleighs to get home tonight."

Betsy laughed and went to her desk in front. Tizzard continued his journey through the pack of croissants, and Windflower went into his office to check his e-mails. There was nothing pressing, so he took the time to go through some of the magazines and periodicals he liked.

He was leafing through Law Enforcement Today when Betsy buzzed him on the intercom. "Inspector Quigley on line 1," she said.

"Good morning Inspector. How can I help you today?"

"That's the attitude I want to hear from the troops. Snowing over there this morning?"

"Yeah, she's coming down pretty good. I'm assuming you're not calling for the weather report, although if that's what you want…"

"Nope," said Quigley. "I'm calling about Constable MacDonald. I had a look at your report, and also talked to Winters about her case in generalities. His take was that unless there is a clear breach of the law, it's an internal matter. That means you and I get to decide what happens next to her. If she's still willing to resign, I think we let her go with a note on her file."

"I agree. She may have been naïve and acted inappropriately, but it's hard to see what advantage there'd be in prosecuting her, or even imposing additional discipline. If we put that note on her file, her punishment will be she can never be on the Force again. I think that's enough."

"Okay, you draft the letter as the ranking officer and send it over to me. Then I'll get the paperwork started. If Winters needs her to testify later, he can pull her back," said Quigley.

"Thanks, Ron."

"Good luck with the snow. At least you've got Black Betty this time in case any ditch rises up to try and trap you."

Windflower thought of several witty replies but not before his new Inspector was gone. He called Betsy back and got her to bring him Constable MacDonald's file. He spent the next half hour drafting up the letter for her file. He made a copy of the draft and showed it to Tizzard. After all, he was supposed to be her immediate supervisor.

"I guess that's the best we can do, isn't it?" asked Tizzard when he came back with the letter.

"I think it is, Corporal."

Windflower went back to Betsy and got her to put the draft into the correct format for Inspector Quigley. Tizzard hung around for a few more minutes and then went home so he could later return fresh. Just before lunch, Windflower was thinking about doing the same.

That was when Frost came in from a tour of the roads, shaking his head.

"It looks pretty, but it's getting hard to get through in places," he told Windflower. "The plows are out in force, but if the snow keeps falling at this rate, they won't be able to keep up. We're lucky there's no wind, though there's still drifting out on the barrens."

"Be careful out there," said Windflower as he too realized it might be another long night on storm watch. "I'm going to take a break this afternoon so I'll be ready for tonight."

He left the detachment and drove by Sheila's, hoping to catch her at home for a few minutes, but her car was gone from the driveway. He made a mental note to call her later to check in, and continued home to see his other favourite female.

Lady was, as usual, happy to see him, and even happier to get out and run in the snow. She made sure to taste the different varieties in at least a dozen different locations along the way, and when she got back home she was totally covered in snow. She looked very happy to have her Master home for an extended period during the daytime. She was settling in for their joint afternoon nap when the phone rang.

At first Windflower thought nobody was on the other end because the voice was so faint. But finally he made out "little rabbit," and knew it was his Auntie Marie.

"Auntie, I am so happy to hear from you. I hope you are feeling better. I was very worried about you."

"Yes, I'm feeling much better," said his aunt in a voice that was little more than a whisper. "My voice is returning and so is my strength. I am still in Edmonton, but hopefully I will be going home soon."

"That is very good news, Auntie. Is Uncle Frank still with you?"

"Yes, Frank is here. He has been a big help and I am glad he came home to be with me. But how are you my little rabbit? I had a dream you had fallen into a hole and couldn't get out."

"I did have an accident, but luckily I was not hurt. I also have some good news to share, Auntie. Sheila and I are going to get married."

"Ah. That is what the other dream I had was about. I saw you with a bunch of little children chasing after you. Frank had the same dream."

Windflower laughed. "First we get married and then maybe, just maybe we have children. One step at a time, Auntie. Now I'll let you rest. I hope you continue to recover. I'll say a prayer for you."

"Thank you, nephew. I'll call again when I get home to Pink Lake."

After he hung up from his aunt, he gave Lady a fresh bowl of water and two dog biscuits and he had some soup. Then they both had a long and refreshing nap.

It was still snowing when Windflower woke up from his nap. If anything, it was coming down harder than before. When he let Lady out, he guessed almost a foot of new stuff was on the ground. It looked like a winter wonderland in his backyard, but he knew this volume of snow could be deadly out on the highway. He fixed Lady up with fresh supplies and drove slowly back to work.

He passed by Sheila's, hoping to say hi, but again saw no car in her driveway. He hoped that meant she had holed up somewhere out of the weather. When he arrived at the office, Tizzard was back and already turning them into snowstorm central.

"I'm thinking we should close the highway," he said to Windflower.

"You can make the call," said Windflower. "I'll do the long route towards Marystown when you're ready."

"Thanks, I'll get Frost to go with you," said Tizzard as he went to make his phone calls to Marystown HQ and the highways people.

When he returned, Evanchuk was coming back in. "It's not good out there," she said. "There are cars stuck all over town."

"Why don't you look after Fortune?" said Tizzard. "The Sergeant's going to close off the other end with Frost."

Frost got into Windflower's vehicle and they maneuvered their way around several cars stuck in the streets of Grand Bank. It was slow going even for Windflower's big SUV, but luckily they pulled onto the highway in front of a plow. Windflower turned on his flashing lights and indicated to the driver to pass them. Once they had a snowplow to lead the way things were still slow, but much smoother. He was grateful to have his big rig tonight. His Jeep was good, but Black Betty was a tank out here in the heavy snowfall.

Out on the open highway the drifting snow was creating a problem. Even with the plow guiding them it was a difficult drive, especially on some of the steep hills. But they made it to their turnoff just outside Marystown without incident and while the snowplow waited for their return trip, they put up the barriers and the flashing lights to close the highway.

Their return was even slower than on the way out, but they did make it back safely. Windflower flashed his lights to thank the snowplow operator as they made the turn back into Grand Bank.

A cup of hot chocolate later, he and Frost were toasty warm as they waited for the inevitable calls for assistance the storm would bring.

Chapter Fifty-Three

The early evening was quiet, but once the calls started, it seemed like they didn't stop. And neither did the snow. The RCMP officers were busy all night and into the early morning, especially after the power went out in a few areas around town when the electrical wires became overburdened with the snow. However, there were no real emergencies because the weather was mild, and no real cause for panic either. That didn't mean some people, especially the older folks, didn't get upset, but Windflower and his crew were able to calm and reassure everyone that if the storm continued, they would be brought supplies and assistance.

Tizzard had gotten to the Mug-Up before it closed, so they had lots of sandwiches and a large tray of desserts to tide them through. Windflower was happy when Sheila called to let him know she was staying overnight with her friend, Madge Malloy, out near Grand Beach. Windflower went home after midnight to check on Lady and bring her back to the office for the night. She was great company and everyone enjoyed having her around. Evanchuk came in around the same time and Frost got to go home for a break. Finally, just before dawn the snow slowed, and then stopped completely.

Windflower forced Tizzard to go home as soon as it got light, and he held the fort with Evanchuk as the town came back to life after the storm. There would be tons of cleanup, but they could hear the snowplows making their forays back onto the streets of Grand Bank, followed closely by a pair of tow trucks to move any errant vehicles out of their way.

Once the first pass was completed, Windflower followed the lead snowplow out to the highway and back up to Creston to re-open the road. Once he reached there, he called the highways people to give them a status update and reversed course to return to Grand Bank.

He was tired but not as exhausted as he had anticipated: the power of an afternoon nap. He was about ready to call it a day, or at least a morning, when Sheila called.

"Hi Winston, how are you? Did you stay up all night?"

"We did. But I'm fine now. I was just about to close up shop."

"That's good," said Sheila. "We heard the plow go by, so we know the road is open again. We were wondering if you wanted some breakfast."

"Thank you, Ma'am. Tell Madge to put the coffee on. There's one hungry Mountie on his way. I'm starved," said Windflower.

Sheila laughed. "We'll get breakfast going. See you soon."

Windflower smiled and roused Lady from her early morning nap under his desk. "C'mon, girl. It's breakfast time."

As Windflower drove out of town, the hydro crews were just coming in. He waved good morning to them as they went to restore the power in the blacked out areas. He also noticed it was even milder than last night, which was good because it meant this latest dump of snow might be gone fairly quickly. He could also see that the large fog bank that often lurked outside the harbour was creeping in near shore. The fog would also help get rid of the snow, almost eating it from the inside out.

He arrived at Madge Molloy's and parked his vehicle on the side of the road with his emergency lights flashing. There was no way to get into the driveway. The snow and the drifting had covered both Madge and Sheila's cars completely and would take a while to dig out. He plodded through the snow, and as soon as he opened the front door he smelled bacon and toast. He reminded himself to save a piece of toast for Lady, who unfortunately had to stay in the car.

Sheila greeted Windflower warmly, which was nice. But all further thoughts of that kind were deferred once Windflower saw the breakfast spread Madge had laid on for them. There were scrambled eggs, bacon, bologna, fried potatoes and homemade toast, with an array of jams, jellies and preserves. Madge Molloy was the jam expert in Grand Bank and she proudly displayed a sample for Windflower's enjoyment.

And he did enjoy himself. He ate some of everything and then more of everything. He even remembered to add a little conversation in between bites which entertained Madge and kept Sheila happy. At the end, he tucked a piece of toast into a paper napkin for Lady and pronounced himself 'well and truly sufficed'.

"That means he's full," interpreted Sheila.

"Yes, Ma'am," said Windflower. "Thank you so much, Madge. That was great. Now what can I do to help?"

"Nuttin," said Madge. "I can clean up 'ere while I'm waiting for Tommy to come by with the plow. He'll get 'er cleaned up quick."

"I'll take a ride back with you, if you don't mind," said Sheila. "I'll come by later and pick up my car, if that's all right Madge."

"Yes b'y," said Madge. "You'se run along. I'll be fine 'ere."

Sheila gave her friend a big hug and Windflower went to shake her hand, but Madge was having nothing of that. "Come 'ere b'y. You'se almost family now, b'y," she added as she gave him a big momma bear hug.

On the drive back to Grand Bank, Sheila held Windflower's hand. When they got to Sheila's house she smiled and said, "I wonder if you'd like to come in for a few minutes. The house is probably cool after being left alone all night and you could help me warm up."

So that's what the affectionate touch was about. "I just have to take Lady out for a minute and I'll be right in to help you out," he said.

True to his word he was back in a flash and Sheila and Windflower had a wonderful morning warming each other up. Afterwards Windflower curled up beside Sheila and had a late morning nap. When he awoke it was almost two o'clock and Sheila was sitting downstairs in her robe.

"Thank you for this morning," said Windflower as he walked towards her.

"Thank you," said Sheila.

They gave each other a long and lingering kiss.

"I love you, Sheila," he said.

"I love you too, Winston Windflower. But now I've got to get going to meet my campaign team. We're picking colours for my signs," said Sheila.

"That's pretty exciting. I guess I should go home and get cleaned up. It's been so crazy I don't know what day it is."

"Thursday," said Sheila. "I'm busy later this evening, but I was thinking we should have a few people over this weekend to celebrate our engagement. How about Saturday night?"

"That sounds good. I'll invite Tizzard and Doc Sanjay," said Windflower.

"Okay. Let's talk later." Sheila drew close to Windflower and hugged him tightly. "You be careful out there," she added.

"I will. I got Black Betty now to keep me safe on the highway. In case any ditches rise up to try and snatch me."

"Bye, Winston," called Sheila.

Windflower showered and shaved at Sheila's, and then gave Lady the piece of toast from his pocket. She was more than pleased.

When he got back to the detachment, Tizzard was leaving.

"I'm going over to check on the hydro guys. We're still getting a few calls about some houses without power. I'll see if we can find out how much longer it will be."

"I hope they restore them before dark," said Windflower.

"Me too," said Tizzard.

"Are you free Saturday night? Sheila's having a few people over and you're invited. Maybe you can bring that cute girl from Fortune?"

"She and I are history. I'm too young to settle down with just one girl. But I might be able to find a date for Saturday night."

"I bet you can," said Windflower as he waved Tizzard on and went into the detachment.

Betsy was pleased to see him and handed him his messages. The one on top was from Carl Langmead in St. John's:

Winston, thanks for calling back. I wanted to check in and see what was going on with the Emberley case. I tried to reach Winters, but he was in court. I can tell you Shawn Parsons is pretty upset about everything.

He called Langmead back in St. John's.

"Winters was planning on charging both of them with the murder of Frankie Fallon and see what shook out. I made no secret of how I would prefer Parsons to be the one who takes the fall," said Windflower.

"Me too. He keeps screaming about a deal, but he's got nothing to bargain with. Let me know if you hear anything else."

"Will do," said Windflower.

Windflower started going through the rest of his messages and noticed a note from Tizzard: Sorry, Boss, but you're on tonight. Hope that's okay. It was signed E.T. and had a happy face at the bottom. Windflower had forgotten about that. Oh well, at least it looked like a clear night. He packed up his office and went back home for a break before his night shift.

The day was mild so water was everywhere. It was pooling at the end of every driveway and running freely down every hill in town. He and Lady had to tread carefully as they took their early evening walk, though still managed to get their boots and paws completely drenched. Windflower dried Lady as best as he could, and had a long hot shower to warm himself up again. He made a couple of sandwiches for a late-night meal, and took his dog along as company for the overnight shift.

When he got back to the detachment, everyone else had gone home for the night. That was okay with Windflower and Lady too. After she made her full inspection of the offices and rooms at the back, she came in and assumed her position under Windflower's desk. It was a quiet evening with little else happening except the drip, drip, dripping of the melting snow outside.

Windflower called Sheila but she was too busy to talk because she had people over for a chat, no doubt with date squares present. This might turn out to be the cookie campaign. He'd vote for that. They talked briefly and said goodnight. Both sounded disappointed not to be together, but this was the life they'd chosen.

The only phone call from the outside came around 10:30 when Ron Quigley called from Marystown.

CHAPTER FIFTY-FOUR

"I heard you were on the midnight shift," said Quigley. "Don't you have any pull over there?"

"I like doing the overnighter once in a while," said Windflower. "Makes me feel like a real cop."

"I hear ya. Anyway, I wanted to let you know that Laura Emberley is freaking out. Her lawyer has called me three times already today. I think they want to talk."

"What did Winters say?" asked Windflower.

"He said to let them stew overnight and that he'd talk to them tomorrow," said Quigley.

"That's good news, isn't it? But what can he offer Emberley? Regardless, she's going down for trafficking," said Windflower.

"Which could be 10 years," said Quigley. "A murder charge could bring 20 to life, if you get a conviction. This way you can guarantee at least one of them goes down for murder."

"Let's hope it's Shawn Parsons," said Windflower. "Langmead phoned me earlier. They really want to be rid of that guy. Me too, for that matter."

"We'll have to see what Winters can come up with."

"I guess so," said Windflower. "Thanks, Ron. Oh, by the way Sheila's having a bit of a 'do' on Saturday night if you're around."

"Thanks for the offer, but I think I'll be in Marystown."

"Okay, Ron. Talk soon."

After talking to Quigley, Lady and Windflower did their first highway tour. Nothing unusual to report, just lots of water on the highway.

They went back to the quiet detachment and Windflower had his late night snack. Lady watched and waited patiently while he ate his sandwich and was rewarded with a few scraps at the end. The rest of the night was just as quiet. Windflower passed the time finishing off his neglected stack of police magazines. He took a walk around town with Lady around 4 and then did his final highway rounds just before 6.

By the time Frost showed up, Windflower was barely able to keep his eyes open. He said good morning and goodnight to his colleague and trudged home with Lady.

Soon after, both man and dog were solidly asleep. When he awoke it was nearly noon and while he could have lain there all day, Windflower pushed himself out of bed and went outside to check the weather.

There wasn't much to see. In fact you couldn't really see anything. "It's pretty tick out der today, b'y," he said to a mildly interested Lady who was keener on getting outside to test it for herself. He opened the door and she bounded out. It was very mild and as he had noted before, very, very foggy. Windflower did a quick smudge and an even quicker prayer before going back in with Lady to have a snack and clean up.

Half an hour later he was on his way into the RCMP detachment. Betsy was busy on the phone though greeted him with a wave from her perch at the front. He looked in his message slot, but it was empty. When he went into his office, there was nothing in his in-basket. Those were the benefits of working an overnighter. He called Sheila and got an update on her evening. He hoped to get together later, but she had an event to attend. Instead they would try and have coffee later.

While he was sitting there wondering what to do next, Betsy buzzed him. "Constable MacDonald is here to see you, sir."

"Send her in," said Windflower.

"Good afternoon, Sergeant. I just wanted to thank you for your help," said MacDonald.

"I didn't do anything," said Windflower.

"Yeah, you did. This could have turned out a lot worse for me. I know I really screwed up and while I'm disappointed in myself, I'm more upset I disappointed people like you."

"No worries. Like I said before, we all make mistakes. Learn from this one and you'll be fine. You're still plenty young enough to have a good career. Just not in the RCMP."

"I'm thinking about going into social work. I like listening and I might be able to help some people."

"You'd be great at that. Good luck." He stood and shook her hand.

"Thank you Sergeant," said MacDonald as she shook his hand back and left the office.

Soon after, Tizzard came in and Windflower told him about his visitor.

"Yeah, she called me," said Tizzard. "It is a bit sad, but I think she'll make a great social worker."

"We're all social workers at heart. She's just going to make it official."

"Maybe it was her fate," said Tizzard.

"'What fates impose, that men must needs abide; It boots not to resist both wind and tide'," said Windflower.

Tizzard looked at him with that puzzled look. "I still don't get it."

Windflower laughed. "C'mon, Corporal, you can buy me a cup of coffee," he added.

The two drove to the Mug-Up, sloshing their way through the streets of Grand Bank. The café was quiet and when they had ordered their coffee and turkey with dressing sandwiches, Herb Stoodley joined them for a chat. They had a pleasant late lunch and were leaving the Mug-Up when Doctor Sanjay was walking in.

"Hey, Doc," said the policemen almost in unison.

"How's she going, b'ys?" answered a smiling Sanjay. "I am not usually at the café but Repa asked me to pick up a dozen cupcakes. She is going to some event tonight with our new Mayor."

"That means you and I are in the same boat," said Windflower. "I cannot offer you the festive hospitality you offered me, but I do have a chessboard and some Kingfisher beer if you'd like to drop by this evening."

"That would be great. I gladly accept. I can come over around 6:30 if that's good for you."

"Perfect. See you tonight."

Windflower and Tizzard said goodbye to Doctor Sanjay and returned to the office. When he arrived Betsy gave him a message to call Wallace Winters in Marystown.

"Thank you for calling," said Winters. "I have some news to report on Laura Emberley. I met with her lawyer this morning and they want a deal. She says that Shawn Parsons killed Frankie Fallon, and she is prepared to testify against him."

Mike Martin

"That's good news," said Windflower. "What's the deal?"

"Emberley pleads guilty to all the drug charges and as an accessory to murder. She's willing to testify she gave Parsons the drugs and saw him slip the drugs into Fallon's drink. The most important thing is she will say she saw Parsons hit Frankie Fallon over the head with a shovel and then stab him. An eye witness. In return for her plea I am making a recommendation of 18 years for her and of course we'll throw the book at Parsons."

"Parsons and his lawyers won't be pleased," said Windflower. "But you will make a lot of law enforcement officers pretty happy with you. Can you make all of this stick in court?"

"I think so. I'll make sure we get the judge we need and while they would like more, they know the routine. We're getting what we can at the least cost to the system. We do the best we can, Sergeant."

After Winters hung up, Windflower went to tell Tizzard the good news. Tizzard was pleased and when Windflower phoned Carl Langmead in St. John's, he too was overjoyed. Windflower spent the last few hours of the afternoon feeling pretty pleased with himself as well.

He was home soon after work, cleaning up his place and getting a few snacks and the chessboard ready for Doctor Sanjay's visit.

Promptly at 6:30, Vijay Sanjay knocked on Windflower's back door and came in. Lady thought he was an intruder and gave him a loud and startling welcome. Once she figured out he wasn't, the two were fast friends. Sanjay had brought a couple of dog biscuits as a welcome gift for Lady because he'd heard Windflower had a new dog.

"Looks like you made a friend for life," said Windflower as he officially welcomed the doctor to his house.

"I brought a gift for you, and me too," said Sanjay. "I stole a small plate of samosas from Repa's basket before she left. I thought the chess might make us hungry."

"That's very kind of you. Let me offer you a beer," and he went to the fridge to get them each a Kingfisher beer.

"Ah, Kingfisher," said Sanjay. "It is the most famous Indian beer in the world. A pale lager that is mild enough to quench the thirst of fire-breathing curries, and the American public. To your health," he said, raising the bottle to his lips.

"And to yours," said Windflower. "Come to the living room. I have the chessboard all ready to go."

The men enjoyed many games of chess yet Windflower was victorious in only one. They also devoured the samosas along with a few spicy sausages and some other cold cuts and cheese Windflower had put out for them, as well as a few more beers. At the end of the evening, Lady and Windflower walked Doctor Sanjay to his house across the brook. He invited the doctor to the party at Sheila's, but was told Repa had already gotten the word. Sanjay said he was looking forward to it.

When they got back, Windflower gave Lady a piece of leftover sausage as a treat and called Sheila. Her house sounded busy in the background, and she was in good spirits. They agreed to go for por' cakes in the morning, and then said goodnight. Windflower read a few chapters of his book and was fast asleep before midnight. He was looking forward to a long and relaxing sleep and succeeded in that goal because when he awoke it was light. Despite the fog, it was bright enough for him to know it was way past his usual wake-up time.

He let Lady out and did his morning rituals followed by a long, hot bath. Afterwards he took Lady down by the beach where the fog and mist had cleared enough of a path to reach the ocean. They walked along the slippery beach rocks until Lady was reluctant to continue. Windflower acknowledged her predicament and led the way back home.

He had a light breakfast of fruit and yogurt because he wanted to save an appetite for por' cakes later. He spent the morning tidying up from the night before, and reading his book. It felt like a well-deserved day off after the chaos of the last two weeks. Just before noon, he drove over to Sheila's and together they went to the café for lunch.

The Mug-Up was full, but Sheila managed to get them squeezed in at the end of the long table in the tea room. It was Mayor Sinnott's old table, which might be appropriate.

They had their meal and Sheila did an informal round of the café to say hello and to informally seek support. She had a notebook and took down the names of anyone who offered to volunteer or wanted to order one of her new purple signs when they were ready. After lunch, Sheila walked the short distance to her campaign office that was in one of the abandoned buildings on the wharf. It was a busy and visible location. Sheila also wanted to send a message that if she was elected, she would make sure the dilapidated buildings on the waterfront still had an important and useful role.

Windflower gave her a big hug and went back home where he and Lady had a very enjoyable and sleep-filled afternoon. He awoke from his nap and took Lady for an extended late afternoon walk. It was pea-soup fog again that evening and he literally could not see across the road. Lady didn't seem to mind, and was happily following her nose towards many interesting and usually dirty things that had appeared out of the melting snowbanks.

Windflower settled Lady in with plenty of food and water and walked over to Sheila's for the party. When he arrived it was already in full swing. In addition to Herb and Moira Stoodley and the Sanjays, there was a roomful of people Windflower recognized as some of the political and business elite of Grand Bank. Sheila explained to him they weren't going to be there all night, but rather just for drinks and snacks. Later there would be a full dinner with only their select guests.

Windflower got a beer from the kitchen where Madge Malloy was taking a fairly large turkey out of the oven. He offered to help but Madge said she was fine on her own. "I just 'bout got everyting going good now. Supper should be ready 'bout 7."

That was fine with Windflower. When he snooped into the pots on the stove Madge shooed him away, but not before he figured out supper was going to be a Jiggs Dinner, with a turkey to boot. Jiggs Dinner was a traditional meal commonly prepared and eaten on Sundays in many regions around the province. It got its name from a long-running comic strip years ago called Bringing up Father whose main character was Jiggs. And Jiggs loved his corned beef and cabbage.

The Newfoundland version featured salt beef or riblets boiled together with potatoes, carrots, turnips and cabbage. There were also two kinds of boiled puddings, pease pudding and figgy duff. Pease pudding had split yellow peas and generous amounts of salt and pepper tied up in a cloth bag and boiled along with the vegetables. Figgy duff was a dessert pudding you actually ate along with the meal, gravy and all.

Windflower had learned from Quigley, the local expert on desserts, that figgy duff had nothing to do with figs. These so-called figs were actually raisins, which many people across the island used to refer to as figs. It was a traditional Irish or English pudding with butter, flour, sugar, molasses and of course, raisins. He was also glad there was a turkey. The turkey was optional at a Jiggs Dinner, but welcome, and Windflower certainly welcomed all of the above.

He spent a few minutes talking to the people he knew, mostly small talk about the amount of snow they'd had so far this winter, and the hopes the rest of the year would be less snow-filled and mild.

A great hope they all agreed, but the consensus was against that possibility. One by one the early guests excused themselves and drifted off, saying goodnight to Sheila, promising their support and quietly, their money.

Tizzard arrived as the last of them were departing, and his date was a bit of a surprise to Windflower. It was Constable Evanchuk, although in her civilian clothes she looked little like a police officer, and much like a petite model.

"It's not a date," Tizzard whispered to Windflower when Evanchuk went off to say hello to the Stoodley's. "I asked Carrie if she wanted to come. I hope you don't mind."

"No problem at all. I'm glad she's here."

Madge announced supper was ready, which was laid out buffet style in the kitchen. Windflower was on his way out of the kitchen with his first over-flowing plate when Ron Quigley walked in.

"Ron, I didn't think you'd make it."

"I didn't either, but Marystown is generally slow on Saturday night. I heard all the action is over here."

"Grab a plate, we have plenty of food," said Sheila.

After a second plate of salt meat and vegetables along with another slice of figgy duff, Windflower was absolutely stuffed. He was pretty happy too. As he looked around the table he realized again how lucky he was. He had a beautiful and loving woman, good friends he could rely on, and great people to work with. As he was thinking how grateful he was, Herb Stoodley rose from his seat and raised his glass.

"To Sheila and Winston. May they always be as happy as they are today. To quote the bard: 'If music be the food of love, play on.' To the happy couple."

After they drank their toast, everyone looked to Windflower. He paused and went to Sheila. He kissed her and raised her up so she could stand with him and hold his hand.

"Thank you all. Sheila: 'Doubt that the stars are fire, Doubt that the sun doth move his aides, Doubt truth to be a liar, But never doubt I love you.'" With that he raised his glass and said, "To Sheila—"

Again they all raised their glasses and toasted Sheila.

"And to you, my friends, 'I count myself in nothing else so happy. As in a soul remembering my good friends.' Thank you all."

The party broke up soon afterwards and Windflower and Sheila said goodnight to all of them at the door. When everyone else had left, he noticed Ron Quigley was hanging behind.

"A little bit of police work," he said to Sheila. "I hope you don't mind."

"I understand. I'm getting married to a policeman. Good night, Ron. I'm going to help Madge clean up in the kitchen."

"What's up?" Windflower asked Quigley.

"I just wanted to tell you Winters called me to let me know he's laying another charge against Shawn Parsons. He's going to be charged with the murder of Michael Ridgeway. Laura Emberley told Winters she gave Parsons the nicotine and that she saw him put it in Ridgeway's drink out at Molliers."

"That way both of them would be gone and we'd think Ridgeway killed Fallon before the accident," said Windflower. "That's pretty smart thinking for a dummy like Parsons."

"I'm not convinced it was entirely his idea, but we'll get what we can. You know, the courts may not be working any more, but as long 'as everyone is videotaping everyone else, justice will be done'," said Quigley.

"That's pretty smart thinking," said Windflower. "Not Shakespeare, but not bad."

"Marge Simpson," said Quigley with a laugh. "Anyway, I gotta go. We'll talk."

"Goodnight, Ron," said Windflower. "Drive safely."

After the dishes were done and Tommy came to pick up Madge, Windflower took off back home for a quick walk with Lady. When he returned, Sheila was sitting on the couch, looking exhausted but very, very happy.

"Let's go to bed," she said.

"Now that is certainly the best offer I've had all day," said Windflower.

The End

About the Author

Mike Martin was born in Newfoundland on the East Coast of Canada and now lives and works in Ottawa, Ontario. He is a longtime freelance writer and his articles and essays have appeared in newspapers, magazines and online across Canada as well as in the United States and New Zealand . He is the author of "Change the Things You Can: Dealing with Difficult People and has written a number of short stories that have published in various publications including Canadian Stories and Downhome magazine.

The Walker on the Cape was his first full fiction book and the premiere of the Sgt. Windflower Mystery Series. The Body on the T was the second book and Beneath the Surface was the third installment in this series. A Twist of Fortune is the fourth book in the series.

He is a member of Ottawa Independent Writers, Capital Crime Writers, the Crime Writers of Canada and the Newfoundland Writers' Guild.